T0066946

Just to
Get
Away

S.K. LANGIN

Order this book online at www.trafford.com
or email orders@trafford.com

Most Trafford titles are also available at major online book retailers.

© Copyright 2014 S.K. Langin.
All rights reserved. No part of this publication may be reproduced,
stored in a retrieval system, or transmitted, in any form or by
any means, electronic, mechanical, photocopying, recording, or
otherwise, without the written prior permission of the author.

Printed in the United States of America.

ISBN: 978-1-4907-4153-6 (sc)
ISBN: 978-1-4907-4154-3 (e)

Because of the dynamic nature of the Internet, any web addresses or
links contained in this book may have changed since publication and
may no longer be valid. The views expressed in this work are solely those
of the author and do not necessarily reflect the views of the publisher,
and the publisher hereby disclaims any responsibility for them.

Any people depicted in stock imagery provided by Thinkstock are models,
and such images are being used for illustrative purposes only.
Certain stock imagery © Thinkstock.

Trafford rev. 07/09/2014

 www.trafford.com

North America & international
toll-free: 1 888 232 4444 (USA & Canada)
fax: 812 355 4082

CHAPTER ONE

Leaning tiredly back against the hot leather seat of the ancient, dust-covered truck; Randi Colon brushed a slender, tanned hand across her heated forehead. Sitting quietly, she let her rather dispirited glance sweep over the simmering, rolling landscape of the Australian outback.

Landscape much like that of New Mexico, she reflected with a slight twist to her lips. Those had been good, friendly times; the days she had worked on the large guest ranch. Good friends that were like family. Now here she was in the great outback. How long had she dreamed of visiting this land of young challenges? Years and years. But she had never really believed she would do it.

A dry laugh caught in her throat. There had been a lot of things happen that she had never dreamed of. Like falling in love or what she had thought was love. Getting engaged and giving up so much to please the man she loved. Then, the wedding day and no groom or maid of honor. Only a very short, painful note. How could they have waited so long to tell her? All the lies.

Randi still could not remember everything that had followed the shattering of all her dreams---she had finished packing and booked a flight to California. As far away as she could get from her mid-western Iowa hometown. Not back to New Mexico and her friends. They would want to know what had happen and she just could not explain or accept their concerns.

While on the flight to California she had read an article concerning employment in Australia. Without giving herself time to really think about all it would entail, she had booked transportation and started the long, lonely journey.

Now here she was in the middle of nowhere. . . .

What if Mister J.R. Lewis did not approve of her as a secretary-cum-do-all? What on earth would she do then? She could not go back now. Turning her head slightly; she threw a swift glance at the silent, rather dried-up old man driving the truck. The elderly gentleman had hardly spoke two words since they had left the small, desolate landing strip about ten to fifteen miles back.

She had flown in with the post and supplies on the mail plane ------ apparently, Boss Lewis was away and had not known of her intended arrival. Oh well, that would give her time to rest and clean up before meeting the master of Getaway. Would his wife be at the station house? Or would she have gone with her husband?

Grinning slightly, she hoped that they would not turn out to be as elderly as her driver.

Tiredness swept over her once again and she closed her eyes against the white-hot glare of the sun. Her face, a small, lightly tanned oval with large, dark-fringed gray-green eyes with a light dusting of pale freckles across the small nose. Thick, long strawberry-red hair fell past her slim hips and pooled on the old leather seat.

Randi Colon was small in stature and boyishly slender, standing at almost five foot. She would easily be mistaken for a high school student. But she was not a teenager, but would soon be twenty-five years old. The youthful looks was misleading and she hoped it would not have a bad impact on the job she had applied for.

Frowning slightly, she realized she had changed from a fun-loving, out-going friendly woman into a rather serious one. Cautious and unsure. And why? It was the simple fact that after having waited so long to find the one person she could love, she had been so terribly wrong. So very stupid. A damn fool.

Never again, her heart cried, never again. She had given up so much, friends she had cared about and her livelihood, and all for nothing. Nothing more than a skimpy note telling her that Rod, her beloved Rod, had not truly loved her. Had in fact loved her best friend, Lynn, the intended maid of honor. How could they have lied to her and pretended? Waited so long, until the very last minute!

Shadowed green eyes burned behind pale lids as she forced her lips together with suppressed anger and hurt pride. No tears – never tears. She had yet to cry; or to sleep, really sleep. Her body was exhausted, yet she failed to find the solitude of restful sleep.

Feeling the truck slow down to almost a crawl, her eyes opened and she looked out of the dusty, cracked windshield. The scene before her was outstanding after the dry country they had been traveling through. The low ranch buildings with a wide, screened verandah encircling the whole of it was nestled in the shade of Jacaranda and tall, silvery trees and lush, thick green grass. Very lovely, very.

As the ancient truck shuddered to a jerky halt before the low, white gate; a dark-skinned Aborigine woman of tall stature appeared at the porch step. Stiffly Randi reached out a hand and pushed open the truck door. Sweeping back the heavy fall of hair, Randi looked up to meet the dark, liquid-brown eyes of the dusky-skinned woman who was standing at the porch. When the woman's eyes rested on the glinting red fire of Randi's hair and slender figure, they opened wide in surprise.

With her arms making agitated movements and excited words tripping over each other, the Aborigine was finding it difficult to make Randi understand her. Seeing that the girl was frowning in puzzlement, the unusual woman stopped and then smiled. Slowing her speech down, she said, "Boss Man will be big surprised. He not look for 'you'."

Oh dear, thought Randi, that must mean she would be some sort of shock. The Agency must not have been able to get in contact with J.R. Lewis.

Still muttering to herself; the Aborigine, who appeared to be the housekeeper, motioned Randi to follow her into the house. Randi bent and picked up her two small suitcases and followed.

Regardless of the heat outside, the inside proved to be bathed in blessed coolness. The interior was shadowed and with the tasteful furnishings, blended together to create a restful, gracious atmosphere. The walls were done in rich, deep-grained wood paneling and soft, muted colors complemented the rooms beautifully.

As they walked down a long hardwood hallway, Randi noted that all the doors were left open so that a gentle breeze drifted throughout the home. Upon reaching a partially open door, the woman motioned Randi on through. Stepping inside, the red head noticed the cool greens and cream colors that predominated the small, but airy room. Standing next to the screen door that lead to the enclosed porch, was a single bed with a pale-green and muted cream spread covering its length. Her first glance at the room was nothing more than pleasing, to the eye as well as to the senses. Now if only Mister Lewis liked his first look at her half as well.

The housekeeper smiled her wide, beautiful smile and asked, "You like alright, Missy? If you too hot at night – sleep – out on verandah, yes?" And she pointed a slender finger towards the door and the screened verandah beyond.

"Everything is fine, really. My name is Randi. What's your name?" questioned the redhead with a friendly smile.

"Tico, Miss. Boss Man, he be plenty surprised when him see you. He never think you come." Then she shook her dark head and started for the door. Just before reaching it she once again stopped and looked back at the girl. "Shower is down the verandah and the bathroom is farther down the hall. Boss Man be back later – so do what you like, Missy."

Randi watched as the tall graceful figure disappeared from view, then with a deep sigh she stretched out on the narrow, yet comfortable bed. Going over what the Aborigine woman had said, Randi concluded that the rancher had not had much luck acquiring the help he needed. Well, in that case maybe she would be acceptable.

Straightening into a sitting position, she brushed back the heavy fall of rich red hair from her warm face. A shower would sure feel good – and a change of clothing. Swiftly she unpacked and put her clothes away. Then laying out a pair of faded denim blue jeans and a light-weight, pale-green shirt; she padded her way down to the shower tank.

Cool, lukewarm water cascaded over her warm, slightly-golden body; making her skin tingle with a refreshed feeling. Wrapping a large towel around her slender figure, she went along the screened verandah to her newly acquired room. Just before reaching the connecting door, she stopped and listened. Horses. And then with an extra spring in her step, Randi moved on inside.

Swiftly she dressed and pulled on western riding boots. Just the thought of being in the saddle once again caused a happy, yet gentle smile to touch her lips. Swinging effortlessly down the verandah, she came to a place where she found an assortment of hats. Picking out a wide-brimmed one with a chin strap that fit, she unconsciously twisted the long hair up and stuffed it under the hat.

Striding down off the porch steps, she headed for what she believed to be the corrals. Nearing the fences and buildings, she rolled the shirt sleeves up over her elbows and then with a grin and an experienced eye leaned against the fence, letting her green-gray glance slide over the corralled horses.

About the time she had decided on a small, sharp-looking roan gelding; five stockmen appeared. Two were older and the other three, quite young. All five were Aborigine. Randi had heard that they made great stockmen. And looking at these men's lean, wiry bodies and rather handsome dark faces, she could well believe it.

Straightening up to her full five foot height, Randi approached one of the older ones who appeared to be the leader. Had she but known that she looked no more than a mere boy at first glance, she would have been more likely to understand their startled reaction. But as soon as they came closer and the sharp eyes took in the very definite features of a young woman, they were stunned almost speechless.

"I would like to ride. Would that be possible?" questioned Randi hesitantly.

The older stockman nodded his slightly greying head, coming out of his surprise first. "Shore, Missy."

"Good. I'd like that little roan over there, please." And she pointed to the gathered horses.

"But, that's not one of the safer mounts, Missy." Cautioned the stockman.

Randi placed hands on slim hips and with an unconscious toss of her head, stated calmly in a quiet voice, "I'm an experienced rider and besides, I'll take full responsibility."

The Aborigine shrugged his shoulders and with a helpless glance at the others, went to get the horse. One of the younger ones separated himself from the rest and went to retrieve saddle and gear.

Randi watched as they rigged the horse up and a small, slow smile touched her lips. She was glad that she rode the Australian way. Even on the guest ranch she had always rode in just that way, with a rather long stirrup. Tim Richards, the head wrangler, had told her that she rode like an Aussie. Now, she found, she was thankful.

More than anything else, she found she missed the life at the guest ranch. She had liked the hot, sunny climate and friendly people. And especially her job as trail guide and wrangler. The only female one at that.

Glancing up once again, she saw that they were finished, so walked forward and prepared to mount. With a graceful, lithe movement she swung up into the saddle and as the little horse moved skittishly, she quickly and easily reined him in. The mount did a little sidestep and danced with energy, but Randi just grinned and settled herself deeper in the saddle.

The stockmen grinned too. Yes, the little lady knew what she was about. She would be just fine on the roan.

As she was about to turn the horse away, the older stockman stepped closer and reached up with a light-weight jacket in his dark, nimble fingers. "Clouds gathering, Missy, you take just in case."

"Sure thing." Smiled Randi as she turned to tie it on behind the saddle. Then before moving on, she asked, "What are your names?"

Again the handsome smile flashed. "I am Tom. That is Choco, Larry, Ben and Cal."

"Call me Randi. I'll see you a little later. Bye." She called as she moved the roan towards the mountains and open spaces beyond.

CHAPTER TWO

Pulling the Australian bush hat farther down on her head, Randi halted the roan gelding. Hooking a slender leg over the top of the saddle, she let her gaze settle first on the darkening clouds that were building close by. Then her green-gray eyes once again found the nearing dust spot.

Someone was riding hell-bent-for-leather. And whoever it was had now caught sight of her for the dust trail suddenly changed direction and was quickly shortening the distance between them. Glancing once again at the sky, Randi hoped whoever it was would hurry or they would end up soaked. Suddenly then the rider was almost upon her.

Whoever it was could sure ride and the horse was large and anything but easy to control. The man was tall and from the brief glimpse she had of his tanned face, very angry. But before she could even open her mouth to speak, the man was – and very loudly.

"What the hell! Didn't you see those clouds? It's going to pour any minute!"

Then looking closer, he let out a disgusted sigh, "They sent me a boy! Why a kid?"

As the words penetrated her dazed mind, she realized she had pulled on the rather large jacket at the first sight of the threatening clouds. And with her hair up, under her hat she would appear to be a boy – but?

"I asked for a man, a young man, I'll warrant, but sure as hell not a boy!" rumbled the deep, fully masculine voice.

A man! Something was wrong! No one had said anything about the position being for a man!

The rancher sat his horse like a ruler. He was handsome and very bronze-colored with silvery-gray eyes that were at the moment hard as flint. Extremely light-blonde hair showed from under his hat. So this was J.R. Lewis!

A slight groan escaped from her tightened lips. Apparently the man heard for he remarked, "Never mind, maybe we can work it out. But, right now I'm hoping that you can ride – 'cause if we don't hurry we'll be in for it. Here it comes!"

Swinging his horse away from the direction of the homestead as the first rain drops started to fall, he yelled above the roar of the accompanying thunder, "See that clump of rocks on the rise? Head for it and fast!"

Turning the little roan, Randi kicked the mount into a full gallop and leaned low over the extended neck. One thing for sure, Randi Colon could ride and the small roan could run. Nevertheless as they slid their mounts to a halt before a cabin that was built right into the side of a rock face, they were soaked through.

Thrusting open the door, Lewis fairly pushed Randi into the cabin.

"Wow! What a soaking!" he said. Then as he swung back to the door, he flung over his shoulder, "Get out of those wet things while I go put the horses in the lean-to. Get a move on!" With a last angry glance, he disappeared into the pouring rain.

Shivering, Randy sank to the cot that was placed against the wall. He thought that she was a boy! He was put-out now, what would he do when he found that the boy was a woman? Yes, what then?

Jay Lewis was soaked to the skin and in a foul state of mind when he shoved his way back into the dimly-lit cabin. Upon entering and seeing the boy slumped dejectedly and still dripping on the cot, his short temper cut loose.

"Boy!" And seeing the slight figure jump, he continued in the same angry tones, "I told you to get out of those wet clothes. So why are you still in them?"

"I . . . I" stammered the slender figure confusedly.

"Stand up. If you want anything done you have to do it yourself."

The forlorn little figure stood up slowly, but as Jay went to remove the soggy jacket; the youth pulled away with a start. "No!" croaked the husky, low voice. "You don't understand."

"You bet I don't. But I won't have you catching pneumonia --- now let me help you out of that jacket . . ."

Once again Randi pulled away. But Jay was angry now and he leaped forward, grabbing the slender shoulders. With a swift jerk, he pulled the wet form toward him. "Enough of this nonsense!"

To the Rancher's surprise after giving the youth another shake, the flat-crowned hat slid to the floor and long, dark-red hair cascaded over his hands that were still holding the narrow shoulders. With a muttered oath, Jay let go and backed away.

"A girl! Oh God! -- what next?"

The girl's face was pale and the eyes enormous as she backed nervously away. Irritation at seeing the rather frightened expression, Jay's voice sounded sharper than he intended. "What are you doing here? And masquerading as a boy?"

With that the girl froze. Her small chin tilted up with sudden anger and the eyes blazed hotly.

"Masquerading as a boy! Wrong! Why in the hell should I?" she demanded furiously.

"What do you call this get-up?" he questioned sharply, stepping closer and touching the large jacket that was still managing to drip.

"Your stockman, Tom, gave it to me just before I left the homestead." She flung back at him.

Randi was breathing hard now and she was angry clear through. How dare he! What did he think she was?

Jay Lewis remained quiet, his light-colored eyes narrowing as they flicked once again over her. His voice was low and silky when he spoke again. "And your hair hidden under the hat?"

"Habit, if you must know." Randi remarked with an edge to her voice. "Anything else, Mister Lewis?"

She could see that he was still angry. His stern, handsome face whitened and became set. Suddenly she was frightened. Not of losing her new job, she had accepted the fact that she had already lost that. But now, now she was afraid of the man.

A man he was too. Tall, lithe, broad-shouldered with bronze, hard; yet handsome features. He was older than she had first thought, somewhere in his early or middle thirties. He was lean with hard, rippling muscles. She could see the movement of them under the wetness of his shirt. Yes, he was man – the all dominant male.

Apparently some of her thoughts must have shown on her face for a slight, sardonic smile touched the grim set of his lips. "Alright, so you weren't pretending to be a boy. But that still doesn't answer my question as to why you are here?"

Randi took a deep exasperated breath before answering with a little bit of her own sarcasm. "Well, it wouldn't be for your company."

A glint crept into the light eyes. "Oh, really? Well, you'd be wasting your time anyway. I don't seduce babies."

Randi's face surfaced with hot color and wisely she chose to ignore his last very pointed statement. "I saw your job offer in a paper and answered it. Was accepted by the agency and they sent me out here."

"Did they meet you?" he questioned dryly.

"Well, no. I talked to the man from the agency on the phone and gave them my references and they took my name and a few minutes later I was on the mail plane for Getaway."

"It's pronounced Get Away." He remarked absently. Then once more looked hard at her. "Why would you apply for a job that specified a man?"

"But, it didn't." Randi snapped. Her small amount of patience giving away.

"What! Well, the agency knew. Why didn't they tell you?" He demanded.

"How in the hell do I know? I've had quite en----"

"What's your name?" interrupted the rancher sharply.

"Why - - it's - - it's Randi Colon." She frowned nervously.

"Randy! That's a boy's name." He remarked.

"R-A-N-D-I. And it happens to be my name." Mumbled Randi. She felt suddenly very tired and realized that she was shivering quite badly.

Jay Lewis noticed this, also, for he took hold of the jacket and gave it a tug. "Get out of this. I'll start a fire and light a lamp."

Randi glanced up at his retreating back. His voice had been indifferent, he just didn't want her coming down sick. Besides she figured he was rather uncomfortable, also, in his cold, wet clothes.

Weariness made her shoulders and arms ache as she struggled out of the heavy, wet jacket that was two sizes too big for her. As it came off, she was dismayed to find that her pale-green shirt was also wet and clinging to her chilled, damp body. Oh, what did it matter anyway?"

The long hours of travel and hardly no sleep were swiftly taking their toll on her. She felt absolutely rotten.

With the fireplace giving off a soft warmth, Jay Lewis turned to a kerosene lamp that was sitting on the table. Striking a match, he carefully held it to the lamp until it was lit, then replaced the glass top. With the light from the lamp the room was now bathed in a golden glow.

Turning he saw the girl was standing, huddling closer to the fire. She was in profile to him and he let his glance study her. Seeing how wet her shirt was, he was about to tell her he'd find some blankets. His gray-colored eyes were still on her and as she moved slightly, he realized that the boyish slenderness was quite misleading. Suddenly he frowned to himself. What the hell was he thinking?

Starring into the flames, Randi felt tears burn behind her lids. Raising her hands, she pressed her fingers to her temples and willed herself not to cry. Not here. Not now. He really would think her a child. Hearing the soft, deep voice close behind her, she nearly jumped out of her skin.

Jay found himself startled as he stared into emotion bright, clear green-gray eyes with long, dark, thick lashes framing them. The fire's glow caught and intensified the copper-sheen of the long red hair that hung clear down past her narrow waist.

"You're right, you'd never pass as a boy." He said dryly.

Randi felt her face burn with color as the rancher's cool, sardonic eyes studied her from head to foot. Her chest was heaving in erratic breaths from the fright he had given her and seeing his gaze take in the fact, in turn made her breathing that much more difficult. What was he thinking?

Jay had noted her confusion and he deliberately let his glance rest on her throat. A throat that was slender, lightly tanned and at the moment a tiny pulse was beating rapidly at its base. Letting his eyes travel farther down, he saw that the open-necked shirt was parting erratically with each nervous, confused breathe. A button had come loose, more than likely when he had struggled with her earlier, and now the thin shirt exposed the shadowed valley between firm young breasts.

Once again he let his gaze travel up to her blushing, small oval face. A very pretty face, he conceded to himself. What had he said to her earlier about not seducing babies? Well, sure as hell, she didn't look like any baby.

Seeing that her eyes were penned on his face, he grinned dryly and asked rather abruptly, "How old are you, Randy?"

"A—a—twenty-four. Almost twenty-five." She stammered, her soft lips trembling slightly.

At first surprise silenced him, then he looked straight into the troubled green eyes. Eyes that looked so young and innocent, hardly that of a teenager, let alone twenty-four. "So you're not a baby by any means." His voice was soft and silky. Dangerous?

Her mouth firmed. "I never said that I was. You said it."

"So I did."

Stepping closer, he let his hand fall heavily to her shoulder. As he did so, he felt her stiffen beneath his grip and then he smiled faintly to himself.

His lean, hard fingers tightened slightly and Randi felt herself go tense with dread.

"You know for not being a baby you sure act like one. I want you out of those wet clothes and wrapped up in that dry blanket. Now." He whispered through stiff lips. With a shift of broad shoulders, he sent her toward the cot and a pile of blankets.

Randi silenced the sigh of relief before she could utter it. She did not want him to guess what she had thought or feared. Oh, no! Then as she reached for the top blanket, another thought struck her. This was only a one room cabin! Where? How was she to change with that large hunk of male still in the room! She was about to voice her objections when the masculine voice sounded determinedly from the other side of the room.

"I'd advise you to get a move on or I might just be obligated to help you." Then he added softly, "and don't make the mistake of thinking that I won't."

"Oh, I wouldn't think that for a minute." Muttered Randi to herself.

Leaning back against the cabin's rough wall, she proceeded to play tug-of-war with the rain-soaked boots. Finally managing to get them off, Randi straightened and picked up one of the large blankets from the cot. Draping it around herself tent-fashion, she began to remove the wet shirt and jeans.

All the while the rancher had kept his back to her and was clanging noisily about the small pot-bellied stove. Quietly Randy hung the clothes close to the fireplace, then padded softly back to the cot. Wrapping the blanket snugly around her, she curled up on the narrow bed with her feet tucked under her. Glancing up at the rancher, she let her eyes rest on his back and broad shoulders.

Strong, firm muscles rippled under the damp, clinging material of his shirt and once again Randi felt the impact of his masculinity. Effecting her nerve ends and jumbling her senses. One look from those hard light eyes and her whole body grew tense and her breathing more difficult. She shrugged; just nervous tension. Nothing more. That had to be the explanation, what else could it be?

Realizing the loud clanging had stopped, she looked up and straight into the icy-gray eyes. Disconcerted to find that he had caught her watching him, warm color flooded over her cheeks clear to the hairline. She became very conscious of the nudity of her chilled body beneath the blanket, as his insolent eyes slid over her. She wished that she could read some expression in the gray eyes, but to her they remained inscrutable.

Stepping closer to the huddled girl, Jay Lewis let his cool glance rest on her left hand that was clutching the blanket ends closely together. "What happen to the ring?" He asked dryly, his eyes lifting to her face in time to catch the pained expression that flickered swiftly over her delicate features.

"How? --- Why do you say that?" she stammered in a husky voice.

"You have a thin strip of lighter skin showing on your ring finger." Came the calm answer.

Her face seemed to tighten and pale as she looked away from him. When she finally managed to speak, her voice was strained and cold. "I was engaged. He changed his mind."

"Better before than after." Interrupted Jay calmly.

He was unprepared for the hot flash of green eyes and cold, cutting voice. "I agree----ooh, I sure do. Bu—but they could have done it before the wedding day!"

"They?" quietly questioned the rancher.

"Yes, 'they'. My best girlfriend and my - - fiancé. They lied to me all those weeks and months." her voice broke on a sob.

It was as if a dam had busted loose. Sobs racked her slender body, tears ran unheeded down the small face. Her hands abandoned their grip on the blanket to cover her face.

Lewis sat down next to the girl and gently, yet firmly, pulled her to him until her head rested against his chest. With his hand under the heavy fall of hair at the nape of her neck, his fingers massaged the soft skin lightly. After a short while the sobs quieted and Jay felt the girl's body start to tremble and so he tightened his arms around her.

Softly he asked, "When did this all happen?"

"Oh, a few days or so." Came the muffled reply.

His fingers halted their movement for a brief moment, then continued slowly. A few days? No wonder the water works. With a frown, Jay wondered what now? What was he supposed to do now? What was he to do with a girl?

Pushing herself away from his chest, Randi tried to pull herself together. Her small, pale face stiffening with anger, anger at herself for the foolish tears.

"I'm sorry about crying all over you like that. I'm quite alright now, thank you."

CHAPTER THREE

Still sitting on the cot beside the redheaded girl; Jay remarked quietly, yet with a hint of the old cynicism back in the silky voice.

"Sort of decided to take this job on impulse? To get away? Run?"

A rather dry, humorless smile touched the girl's lips. Her green-gray eyes, more green than gray, slid slowly over his tanned, handsome face. "Yes, guess you might say that. I had to do something. Why not the outback of Australia?"

"Yes, why not?" muttered Jay dryly.

The lovely eyes had narrowed and the soft, slightly husky voice teased with a faint bite of sarcasm. "But it doesn't appear that I chose right. Since the job is for men only. Are you prejudice, Mister Lewis, or is it that, you just don't like women? You have heard that women can do most any job?"

"Oh, yes I have heard that. And as for not liking the fairer sex, well, I like 'em as much as the next man."

"But only in their proper place and at the proper time? And of course, they are even better if they appear, shall we say, decorative? Oh, yes, and very meek." Interrupted Randi with a quiet calmness she was far from feeling.

"Oh, ho, the lady has claws." Jay grinned. "Only you were wrong about the meekness. I like mine with a little fire. It makes it much more interesting trying to tame her."

Randi thought it better to remain silent, but her face revealed the challenge of his statement. Then as she was about to speak, Jay said with an indifferent shrug. "Now about the job. The one main reason, among others, why it was for a man is because there are no other women on the station. No other white woman."

"But Tico is there." Declared Randi, a faint hope stirring inside.

"Yes, but she is an Aborigine. Convention means absolutely nothing to them. Besides, Tico is only there part-time. She doesn't live-in."

With a very unladylike snort, Randi leaned back against the wall. "So what's so wrong with me staying there? This isn't the Mid-Victorian era – people don't, they wouldn't think . . ."

"No? Well, you are wrong if you believe that. They would and do. The outback is a tough, hard place to live. Many don't make it. The people that do have certain standards, traditions. They depend on each other to survive." Stated Lewis with truthful conviction.

Randi felt her heart plunge to rock bottom, but she would be damned before she would let him know.

"Well, that's too bad, then, isn't it? It didn't appear that you have had very many applicants to your ad." She grinned wickedly. "Just out of curiosity, what are the requirements – other than being male?"

Lewis had caught the wicked little grin on the young woman's face, but chose to ignore it for the present. "It requires a little bit of everything. A sort of secretary. Typing, phone calls, computer work; and able to ride and work cattle. Other odds and ends as they turn up. An all-round worker." Slowly he looked her over once again, deliberately trying to unsettle the girl.

Feeling the blush climb up her neck and over her cheeks, Randi clinched her small white teeth together to keep back the sharp retort that rose to her lips. Those eyes of his, seemed to be able to penetrate right through the enveloping blanket; and the blush didn't help matters.

Summing up her courage, she remarked as haughtily as she could with a blanket wrapped about her. "Well, one thing for sure. I fit every requirement you mentioned. I ride, type, have a passable amount of accounting sense, can answer a phone; and I have worked cattle. The only requirement I can't meet is the sex. Sorry about that."

She knew that she was being provocative, but was past the point of caring. Nothing much else to lose. Besides this hunk of male, this Mister J.R. Lewis thought he was really too much.

Randi had not worked on a working guest ranch for four years without being able to hold her own in banter. She had not only the other trail guides and wranglers, but some smart ass male dudes, too, to contend with.

Jay Lewis watched as the changing expressions moved across her face; wishing he could read what they meant. One thing for sure, her remark about no takers for the position was very accurate. He frowned, if only she weren't a female.

Randi caught the frown and said smoothly, "Yep, it's too bad you're afraid of what your neighbors would think."

Jay caught back a growl, and just managed a stiff smile. The little lady was digging deep. Must have a temper to go with that red hair and green eyes. Well, she just better watch where she dug her claws or she would wish she had.

Choosing to ignore the remark, he rose and walked over toward the stove. Unbuttoning the still clammy-wet shirt as he did so.

"How 'bout some hot tea?" he questioned quietly, his face remaining expressionless.

Randi stretched out her cramping legs and answered rather too meekly, "Sounds fine to me. I can't seem to get warm. Which is unusual for me. But," and with a green glint in her eyes, she added, "you don't seem to be bothered. With such hard, cold feelings you wouldn't realize if you were warm or not."

He turned then and Randi forced the beguiling smile to remain on her lips. With a mug in each hand, Lewis retraced his steps back to the cot until he was looking down at her. His shirt was open all the way down to the top of his jeans, exposing curling gold-tipped hair on a deep-bronzed, well-muscled chest. Her stomach took an upward swing as she met the gray eyes. They were smoldering, but the man seemed to remain completely calm; and that, thought Randi was what was dangerous.

Handing her one of the mugs filled with steaming, hot tea, he sat down once again on the cot beside her.

"How long do these storms usually last?" asked Randi, avoiding his gaze.

He took a sip of the tea before replying with, "Some only a few minutes, others, sometimes for hours."

Glancing toward the small window and seeing only pouring rain, she asked, "How long do you think this will last?"

He, too, glanced out the window. "More than likely last all night."

"All night!" stammered Randi. "You're kidding, right?"

A deep, soft chuckle sounded from the man beside her. "Not kidding. More than likely will last most of the night." Then with the same cool-calmness, he added, "Nothing else to do about it – but wait it out. Besides with your open-mindedness about staying alone in a man's house, and my apparent cold nature, there should be no worries."

That brought her head up. "It's not the same thing, and you know it." She hit out shakily. "What will your good neighbors have to say about this?"

"Quite a bit, I would imagine. But I doubt if they will ever hear of it." Then before she could interrupt, he added, "And even if they should, they'd understand the circumstances."

"I don't understand. How can it be considered alright for an unmarried man to stay the night with a . . . a partially naked woman in a one room cabin, when it's immoral for a woman to get paid for doing a job and stays in a house with plenty of rooms? It doesn't make sense at all." Snapped Randi in a tight, angry voice.

His eyes were once again on her face and Randi tried vainly to mask her expression. His voice when he spoke, was cool and sardonic. "What has happen to us was unavoidable in the circumstances. They'll take that into consideration if they should hear of it at all."

"That's nice of them." Muttered Randi.

"What are you so upset about? I'm the one who lives here. After this, I'll be the one who will be involved, not you." Then giving her a long glance, he remarked mockingly, "Not afraid are you, Miss Colon?"

Green eyes flashed and the finely-molded lips tightened as she faced him. "Of what?" she demanded sharply.

Her insides felt slightly sick with butterflies and her muscles ached with tenseness. Not afraid? Not much. The man beside her stretched lazily, his steel-gray eyes still on her face.

"Oh, a lot of things. The storm, thunder, the night or being alone; or the man."

Randi forced a smile to stiff lips and hoped her voice wouldn't fail her.

"Could be." Was her answer.

"Could be, what?" he pressed her.

"Could be any one of those things, if it wasn't for one small fact." She replied in a cool husky voice.

Her copper-colored hair glinted in the fire's glow and the smoky-green eyes were leveled determinedly on his expressionless face.

"And the one small fact being?" Lewis added.

"Being that I'm not afraid." She answered untruthfully. For she was scared, and not of the storm or the darkness.

Jay Lewis once again let his gray glance run over her. Slowly and deliberately. Finally he spoke. "Well, that's fine, then, isn't it?" His voice was soft and Randi thought she detected a trace of mockery.

Nervously she shifted her body, trying to ease the stiffness of her muscles. As she did so, her leg brushed up against the warmth of his thigh. Hastily she pulled it away as if burned. Flicking a quick look at his face, she saw the dry smile touch his mouth and cursed herself as a fool.

"What does the J.R. stand for?" Her voice was as cool as she could make it and slightly aggressive.

Lifting the mug to his lips, he finished the last of the tea before replying.

"Jay Randal Lewis, your friendly station owner. JR to my friends, or Jay. Whichever suits you."

Green mischief skipped over his tanned features. A curious smile playing about her mobile lips. "Randal, huh?"

"Yes, Randal." At first not comprehending what she was getting at.

"Never called Randy?" she murmured with a soft chuckle.

"I get it. But, no. Never."

Then setting his empty mug on the floor beside the cot, he questioned, "What about you? No middle name?"

Her face turned pink. "Not really. Just depends on how you say it or spell it." She muttered.

"So what is it?" he prompted quietly.

"RandiLee." Then she spelled it for him.

"The I sounds like an A, huh? Very different. Sort of cute." His voice was soft and low.

Randi looked up quickly; and was disconcerted at what she thought she saw in the rain-colored eyes as he watched her.

"When Keel, the man from the agency, asked for your name, what did you tell him?"

"I just gave him my name." came the jerky reply.

"Which name? Randi or RandiLee?" he persisted.

"I told him Randi Colon." She snapped defiantly. Her head raised proudly, the dusky-green eyes burned angrily.

"Just what I suspected."

Her heart thudded and the short temper was threatening to cut loose as she made her stiff lips move. "And just what is that supposed to mean?"

The gray eyes were flint-hard, the handsome mouth twisted into a cynical smile. "Should be fairly simple. You wanted this job so bad to hideaway, that you purposely omitted your whole name. Very clever, little one. Only it didn't quite work out."

Anger made her breathing difficult and humiliation flooded her being. The small oval face paled and the green eyes darkened. "If you think . . ." she started chokingly, but he interrupted.

"If I think?" he demanded dryly. "That little scene you pulled almost had me believing you. Some actress yo---"

"You stupid jerk? You conceited, arrogant . . ." she spat the words out through clinched teeth, then with her hot temper exploding, her hand flashed out, catching him squarely on the side of his face.

All cool indifference faded from the once icy-gray eyes to be replaced with smoldering, uncontrollable anger.

Seeing the change that washed swiftly over the man's features, Randi drew back in panic. The blanket had slipped off one shoulder in her anger and at her sudden movement her empty cup went clattering to the floor with a crash.

The sound seemed to galvanize the blonde man into action. His hand reached out and grabbed a fistful of fiery-red hair at the back of her head. Then savagely he jerked her toward him.

With a gasp from the pain of her hair, Randi shoved desperately at the solid, bare chest. She was no match for the powerful rancher as he bent his head toward hers.

"Little bitch." He breathed through tight lips, then he brutally crushed her mouth with his. With a sudden growl deep in his throat, Jay forced her back against the cot, his lips burning and demanding a response from her.

Randi fought him with every ounce of strength she possessed, but only seemed to intensify him that much more. The more she fought, the more he demanded. She could feel the warmth of his bare skin against hers and as his kisses became more practiced, she found herself responding. The blanket had completely fallen away from her small, gently curved body and she could feel his warm hands as they moved up over her ribcage. His touch sent fires coursing through her veins, making her nerve ends tingle. Desperately she tried to regain control of her drowning senses.

Then just as suddenly as it had started, it stopped. Slowly Jay pushed himself up off of her and ran shaky fingers through his hair, his face pale beneath the tan.

Randi looked up at him from where she lay. Her face white and strained. The eyes dark and haunted. With a choked sob, she turned on her side, her back to him. Staring unseeingly at the wall.

Jay pulled the blanket up over her and quietly rose from the cot. Straightening slowly, he walked over to the table and blew out the lamp, throwing the room into darkness except for the orange flicker from the glowing fireplace.

Once again he turned to look at the small huddled form of the girl. She hadn't moved. With a silent groan he sank into one of the wooden chairs and covered his face with his hands. He had never meant for anything like that to have happen. But it had. If only. If only what? He asked himself disgustedly. If only he hadn't provoked her? If only she hadn't provoked him? It should never have happen.

Maybe he was wrong about her; but he had written the ad himself. What was the answer? Looking once again at the still quiet form, he said, "Randi" hesitantly, "Randi, about what I said, mayb---"

A cold, empty voice cut in. "Think what you like. It doesn't matter. Doesn't make the slightest difference."

Jay turned his head and heaved a hopeless sigh. Staring into the fire, he waited for dawn.

CHAPTER FOUR

Randi woke with a start. Her body ached and at first she did not realize where she was. Then, she remembered. Glancing up carefully, her eyes searched the cabin; but found not a sign of the blonde-haired rancher. Had he left? Would he?

No. Not JR Lewis.

Pulling herself up into a sitting position, she sighted her now dry clothes neatly folded on a chair beside the cot. Struggling into them, she let her thoughts go back over the decisions she had made the night before.

It had taken her a long while to fall asleep, and while doing so she had made her plans. Plans for a very speedy departure. Mister JR Lewis should appreciate that. But she had no intention of asking his permission, or for that matter, of telling him anything at all about her plans. And considering the insidious opinions he had of her, he could go right ahead and think them.

Serve the arrogant fool right. She would more than likely never set eyes on the man again, so what would it matter?

Her next problem was to find another job. One thing that he had said last night was all too true. GetAway would have made a perfect haven for her to have been able to try and forget the hurt, the shattered dreams, or the deceit of those who she had trusted most. But the welcoming haven had been doomed from the very beginning. Fate was having a real hayday with her. Hopefully it had finally run its course to an end. Randi just did not think that she could handle much more.

Before she could do more than straighten the few blankets, the door opened and Lewis stepped inside. His handsome features were set, the cynical smile back on his firm lips. With an effort, Randi dragged her gaze from those lips, to a place just behind the sun-bleached blonde head.

Cool gray eyes slid over her from head to foot, before he said, "Guess you're ready. Let's go."

Randi's eyes met his. Purposely she lowered her long, dark lashes and gave him a rather seductive beguiling look. She even managed a rather sexy smile to go along with the husky-soft voice.

"Sorry, Mister Lewis. You should have woke me if I kept you waiting."

Jaw muscles bunched and the gray eyes turned icy and harder, if that were possible.

Secretly Randi was thinking that he could go ahead and think anything he damned pleased.

Jay's voice was soft, yet strained as he stepped aside. "After you."

With a defiant nod, Randi stepped out of the cabin and walked to the roan gelding. Before she could mount however, JR's hand touched her arm.

"One question, Miss Colon. How were you going to convince me to keep you after I found out you were a woman and not a boy? For you must have realized that I would discover it sooner or later."

Indignation flared in the smoke-green eyes, but Randi checked it swiftly. Leaning slightly back against the horse, more for support to weakening knees, than anything else, she answered just as calmly as she could.

"Actually, it never crossed my mind."

"You must have thought we were pretty hard up for women to let you get away with that?"

Her voice was husky, but from pent-up anger. The impish grin stemmed to add to the provocative effect. "Never can tell. Men usually like most anything they can get."

Even before he could form a reply, Randi twisted and vaulted onto the saddle. The roan was at full gallop as she settled over the graceful neck, leaving the startled man standing where he had been. Tears blurred her vision, but still she kept the roan moving.

The ranch wasn't far, and the morning was still crisp and cool. After a night's rest, the roan was peppy and kept at a fast pace. After one quick glance thrown over her shoulder to see if the rancher was following, she breathed a soft sigh of relief. He was following, but at a much slower pace.

A few minutes later, she was pulling to a halt in front of the stables. As she slid to the ground, Tom and the one called Larry appeared from the inside of the tack shed. Seeing her with the reins still in her small, slim hands, Tom stepped forward and took them from her. As he handed the horse over to Larry, he said, "We'll take care of him, Missy."

"Thank you, Tom." Smiled Randi. Then as she was about to turn toward the house, she asked carefully, "Tom, when does the mail plane land the airstrip again?"

"Tomorrow morning, Missy. Very early. On his way back to the city. Stops to get fuel."

"Oh, I see. One more thing, Tom, is there a jeep or something that I could use once in a while?"

"Oh, yes, Missy. A small jeep and a Landrover are in the shed over there. Also the Boss's pickup."

"Thanks again, Tom." She said, a thoughtful expression on her face. Then she turned once again toward the house. Instead of going in through the front as she had first planned, she went around the side and to the back by way of the verandah until she reached her room.

With a shaky sigh, she sat down on the bed and for a few minutes just stared down at her feet. Slowly pulling her raw, hurt feelings together, she rose wearily to her feet. Then with a sad shake of her head, she stripped off the dirt stained clothes and hurriedly took a shower. That done, she crawled into the soft, cool bed and immediately went to sleep.

Randi woke to the sound of a car horn, and sleepily she brushed the hair back from her face with nervous fingers. Sitting up, she heard first, Tico's voice saying that a Missy Darla was outside; then she heard Lewis's voice and felt herself tremble. Frowning at herself, she missed what he had replied, but figured he was going out to meet the woman. Laying back against the pillow, she turned onto her side and determinedly closed her eyes once more. But sleep wouldn't come this time. Woman, huh? Thought he had said no other white woman was around the station?

Just as she was about to try for some sleep once again, voices from outside drifted in to where she lay. One, a soft drawling voice of a young woman. Definitely that of a white woman.

"Now, JR, you just have to come to our party next month. It just wouldn't be a get-together without you, Darling."

Randi grinned dryly. Darling? No wonder he didn't want another woman on the place. His 'Missy Darla' wouldn't like it.

Thoroughly awake now, she climbed out of bed and walked over to the verandah door. She was in shadow and as she looked out into the garden she caught sight of the two. The woman was tall, ebony-black hair, and possibly in her thirties. Pretty. Elegant. Her clothes were expensive and she carried herself with arrogant dignity.

Slowly Randi turned and went back over to the bed. Glancing up, she caught sight of her reflection in the dresser mirror. She saw a rather small face with large eyes and a mass of red hair. In the evening dusk, her complexion appeared paler than it was and she looked more like a little girl lost than a young woman of almost twenty-five years.

With a dry, humorless smile touching her lips she stared almost defiantly back at her reflection before the tears slowly filled her eyes and blurring her vision so that she couldn't see the image any longer. Sighing she went back to the bed and laid down on the top of the sheets. A few minutes later, she heard the sound of a car engine as the woman drove away. Randi just tiredly closed her eyes.

Jay watched as the bright red convertible left the drive, then he turned back toward the house. Darla Russell had quite a long drive just to invite him to the party. A good month off. Wonder where her brother Carl was?

Upon entering the front door he met Tico coming from the kitchen. "Missy Darla go back to Bangon, Mister Jay?"

Jay nodded absently. His thoughts once again returning to the young woman he tangled with earlier. "Tico, have you seen the red-haired lady?"

"No, Boss, but she in her room. I looked in earlier and she sleeping."

"Oh. Well, guess she's alright then." Muttered JR.

"Yes. Your supper is ready. I will take little Missy hers when you finish." Grinned the dusky-skinned woman.

"Alright."

A good hour later, Jay looked up from his paper covered desk to see Tico nervously standing in the doorway. "Yes, what is the matter, Tico?"

"It's little Missy, she not eat supper. She not eat all day. Not yesterday after she got here."

Jay rose to his feet. "She didn't have anything after old Bill dropped her off here?" Unease tightening his voice.

"Nope. She went ride horse." A smile touched her mouth. "My man, Tom, said she ride good."

"Very. I'll see to it that she eats. Where is she?"

"Her room, Boss."

"Right." Mumbled Jay, his features setting in firm lines and the gray eyes taking on a glint of ice.

Damn little chit. Why did she have to land on his doorstep? She'd eat if he had to shove it down her throat. He wasn't about to have her get sick while she was here. Scheming women. She probably figured she'd have a real fling here for a while, then take off.

Fleetingly a picture of her white, strained face and large eyes after the scene the night before came to mind, but irritably he thrust it aside. More likely a good case of play acting. Once again the provocative scene of that morning came to mind. His expression stiffened.

Stopping beside the closed bedroom door, he could hear no sound from within. Quietly twisting the doorknob Jay shouldered through the doorway, stopping just short of the foot of the bed. The small room was in darkness, the faint light from the hallway spilling gently over the sleeping form of the girl.

Moving to the side of the bed, he bent and switched on the small light on the nightstand. At the sudden flare of light, the girl sat up in startled confusion. Her dark-green eyes clouded with sleep. At seeing him standing there beside her bed, towering over her with steel-gray eyes never leaving her face, she gave a quick indrawn breathe and shrunk back against the pillows.

"What do you want?" she stammered in a whisper.

A strange glint swept into the gray eyes as he looked down at her. "I'd say that was a very leading question. Especially after what you said this morning. Could be taken as an invitation."

Color came and went, leaving Randi's features paler than before. She felt suddenly cold and her slender frame started to tremble. He had to be joking. Didn't he?

Jay watched the play of different emotions wash over her small, expressive face. Then as her dusky-green eyes met his, she once again turned a becoming pink.

Randi tightened her lips in an effort to control the shaking, just managing to say in a hoarse whisper, "That's not what I meant."

"We'll see." Was the tall man's answer as he leaned his muscular body toward her. His light-colored eyes glinted as they swept over her, taking in the tenseness of her face, her whole body. With a quick, decisive movement he leaned even closer and scooped her up into his arms as if she weighed no more than a small child.

A gasp broke from her stiff lips at the surprising action. "What . . . what are you doing?"

A dry chuckle, then, "You're a smart girl. Isn't it obvious?"

Surprise, which had held her motionless, now faded as anger swept over her. Twisting, she tried to get out of his iron-hard grasp; but he just tightened his hold and she was helpless.

His arms were like steel bands encircling her slight form. Randi could feel the warmth from his hard muscled chest through the thin material of her T-shirt. Panic threatened to choke her. Forcing her lips to move, she said, "You wouldn't."

He came to a brief halt before a closed swing-like door and then dropped the gray glance to her face. "I most likely would, if given enough provocation. But not right now." Shoving his booted foot against the door it swung quietly open and he carried her inside.

A kitchen! She was in the kitchen!

Setting her down in a chair, none too gently, he pulled up another chair beside hers and said sharply, "Now, Miss Colon, you are going to eat."

At first Randi just stared at the bronze-tan face. Taking a deep breathe, she started, "But, I'm not . . ."

"Oh, but you are. Whether you like it or not. Because if you don't eat it on your own, I'll feed you."

Looking at the hard, arrogant features, Randi could well believe him. He would, and no doubt, without mercy. Turning to the food that was on the table before her, she had no appetite. In fact her stomach felt as though it had turned over and would do so again at any moment.

But another quick glance at the man's stern, unyielding face and Randi slowly lifted a bite to her mouth. After a few bites more, she felt his eyes on her and remembered that all she had on was an over-large T-shirt that barely covered her hips.

Sitting across from her, Jay was thinking almost the same thing. Except that he could not help noting that the short, light green garment showed her figure and her burnished hair off to their best advantage. Not without considering the smoky-green eyes, which he found fastened on his face.

A muscled jumped in his lean jaw and with an effort he pulled his gray gaze away from her flushed, confused face. Slowly he rose to his feet and when he spoke his voice sounded harsh, even to his own ears.

"Make sure you finish that. We'll have to figure out something tomorrow about what to do with you. It's too bad you didn't think more before deciding to pull this kind of wild stunt. I don't know what you expected to find out here, but I can pretty well guess it wasn't at all what you found."

Taking a deep, exasperating breathe, he added dryly, "Now it's up to me to get you out of here, and to bring some order back. This is a working cattle station, not a resort. No place for young women out looking for a good time."

Without another glance at her, he turned on his heel and swiftly stalked from the room.

Silently she stared at the softly swinging door. Tears filled her eyes and slowly made their way down the pale cheeks to drop off the curve of her chin into the partially finished food. Humiliation vied with anger as her jumbled mind went back over what the rancher had said to her. He must really think that she was some kind of loose, pleasure seeking hussy. Biting her trembling lip, she straightened her slender shoulders and rose to her feet. 'Well, Mister Lewis,' she thought, 'No need for you to worry, I'll be long gone by tomorrow.'

With a last look at the kitchen, she turned and made her way cautiously back to her room.

CHAPTER FIVE

The pale green glow of the bedside clock numerals met Randi's sleep tired eyes. Only four-thirty. How many times in the past two hours had she glanced at that clock only to find that the hands had hardly moved? Throwing a quick glance out the screened verandah door, she gave a disgruntled sigh and decided to get up and dress.

She wanted to be far enough away by the time the household came to life so she would be able to find her way back to the landing strip in the early morning darkness.

Pulling on faded blue jeans, a dark-colored T-shirt, and jamming her feet into soft brown moccasins, she picked up her suitcases and headed through the screened door to the verandah.

Swiftly and on silent feet she made her way down the long verandah to the front side steps. Reaching the ground, she headed for the shed that housed the jeep and other vehicles. A slow smile touched her lips. It was a good thing she had learned to drive a four-wheel drive jeep while on the New Mexico guest ranch, because she would not dream of taking the impressive looking pickup.

The smile turned to a tight grim line as the sudden picture of JR Lewis's face flashed before her mind. What would it look like later that morning when he found both her and his jeep gone? She dreaded even the thought of it.

What was the matter with her? In a couple more hours she would be miles away and would never have to set eyes on the rancher again. Or GetAway. Sighing, she stopped and looked back toward the house and surrounding buildings. Yes, never to see them again.

Turning into the shed, Randi felt a momentary tightening of her throat. Determinately she shook her head and pushed the two small suitcases into the passenger seat of the jeep. Automatically she slid behind the wheel and shoved the clutch in before turning the ignition on. The engine throbbed into life almost immediately, shifted smoothly into reverse; then swiftly backed out of the building. Swinging the wheel in the direction of the remote landing strip, she refused to chance even one glance back at the ranch.

A good time later Randi was sitting in the jeep quietly watching the sun as it slowly rose over the distant horizon. Having arrived a brief few minutes before, it was a nice ending to her long drive to be able to enjoy the ever changing tirade of rainbow colors. Lost in the pinks and golds of the early morning sunrise, the faint sound of a small aircraft was loud and even unpleasant; as if it didn't belong there at all.

Turning her head in the general direction of the slightly increasing throb of the aircraft's engine, she was able to see the flash of the wings as the sun's gold touched them. The same mail plane she had ridden in only two days before. Or almost that long. It seemed much longer than that; so much had happen in so short a time.

The pilot was a tall young man with sandy-colored hair and daring dark eyes. As he stepped down from the plane, his eyes found the slender girl leaning against the GetAway jeep. That sure had been a short visit. He smiled suddenly, JR must be getting brave to bring his girlfriends out to his homestead. Though this girl didn't look the type. JR's type anyway. Too much of the tomboy; and far too small. Oh well, maybe he wanted a change?

To tell the truth, no one had ever heard of Lewis messing around with women. But anyone with his money and looks was bound to have the females almost throwing themselves at him or his money. Darla Russell for one. No one overly cared for the elegant woman, but he had to admit she was really something to look at.

"Hello again, Miss. Short visit?" He drawled with a smile.

Randi did not really care for him; he was the type that liked to pry into everyone's affairs. Also he was rather full of himself. On the flight from Adelaide, he had done nothing else but relate all sorts of information about everyone else's troubles to strangers or to anyone that would listen. Well, she was not about to be the next bit of gossip for him to throw around all over the area. Not from anything she had to say, anyway.

"Oh? It was as long as I had intended. Just a short holiday in the outback. Quite interesting." Randi grinned tightly.

"I see. I'll be ready in about fifteen minutes." Then glancing at the two cases, he asked, "Just these?"

"Just those." Remarked Randi as she turned back to the jeep and slid inside. "I'll wait here."

He carelessly shrugged his shoulders and carried her cases to the plane. Randi lazily watched him move around the plane, checking certain parts; but her mind was on other things. Like what she would do when she reached Adelaide.

A slight, cynical smile flickered over her lips. She had quite a bit of money left. Money she had saved for over three years. Money for her honeymoon. What a joke! Only she found that she was not laughing. She would spend it. Get rid of all the clothes she had bought for the 'Big Event'. Ha! And buy new ones. Yes, she'd spend it all; or almost all, and on herself.

Clothes, like she had always just looked at; but never would have bought. Because of price and yes, daring!

Sitting there in the jeep she knew that what she planned was wild, crazy! But, that was what she found she wanted. JR Lewis had thought her a swinger out for a good time; well, now she would be. Oh, after most of the money ran out she would have to find a job. If she could. But for now, well, for now she was going to live it up and try and forget.

Forget? Forget what or whom?

Rod? Lynn? What they did to her? No, hurt pride and not much more, except her own self confidence. But to forget GetAway? Or its handsome, disturbing owner? Once again the low, lovely buildings of GetAway flashed across her mind. Yes, the station she could have loved. But, forget?

When Randi saw that the pilot was in the act of finishing up, she climbed out of the jeep and moved slowly toward the plane. It was funny, but as she glanced back at the grayish-green vehicle, it was almost as if she was leaving the last of GetAway behind. A deep sense of sadness engulfed her as she walked to the plane. Regret that it had not been different.

Coming up beside the aircraft, she remarked to the tall, sandy-haired pilot. "Ready to go?"

Don Starck turned at the sound of her soft voice. "Right now, Miss Colon, isn't it?"

Gray-green eyes slid indifferently over his tanned-brown face. "You have a good memory, Mister Starck. Shall we go?"

Don helped her up into the cockpit and as he lightly dropped down to the reddish-colored earth, he still was wondering about her apparent coolness. Almost coldness. A sly grin touched his mouth before he climbed into the aircraft.

Maybe things hadn't worked out as well as the girl had hoped; or maybe as well as Lewis had planned? Throwing a quick glance at her delicate profile, he saw only a mask of remoteness.

Randi turned her head and looked down at the now receding ground. As the plane went higher; an image of a strong-featured, bronzed face with piercing gray eyes flashed before her mind. She closed her eyes, but that only made the image more clear. Once again the tightness caught at her throat. Just physical attraction, she acknowledged; yet, she had acknowledged it.

It had taken her that long to just realize it. With a firm shake of her head, she cleared it of the image. Hopefully for a while, anyway.

After the pilot informed her that it was just about twenty minutes until they reached Adelaide, Randi leaned back in the leather seat. Turning her cool, gray-green glance on the sandy-haired pilot, she asked quietly, "Which hotel is one of the most expensive and close to the boutiques?"

Don Starck looked momentarily surprised, but quickly recovered and asked a question of his own. "How long have you been in Adelaide? I thought, well, I thought you were from there."

A stiff smile came fleetingly to her lips. "No. I arrived only a short while before my, uh holiday visit. Now, where would you say is a good hotel?"

He thought for a minute, then smiled, "Yes, the Melbourne House on Sydney Blvd. It's one of the best and is centrally located. Do you plan on staying there?"

A secret, knowing smile touched her lips, but she was clever enough not to let him see it. "I have no real idea. I'll just have to wait and see. Thanks for the advice. I had also heard that the Jacaranda Hilton was one of the best in Adelaide."

"Yes. All the well-to-do people stay there or at the Melbourne House. In fact, I believe Lewis has his penthouse there. At the top, anyway. I've heard it's really something; not exactly a penthouse, but nice none-the-less." Remarked Starck with a quick glance at the silent girl.

If he had hoped for a reaction to his statement, he was swiftly disappointed, because nothing showed on the redhead's face. Her delicate features remained softly masklike.

Too bad that he hadn't looked a fraction sooner; for he would have seen her face go pale and the lovely lips tighten into a grim line. But she had quickly concealed any sign of distress before he could notice.

"We're nearing the airport. Just a few minutes, now. All set?" Don Starck replied quietly.

It was not long before they had landed and with a sigh of relief, Randi left the pilot behind and headed for the taxi stands.

CHAPTER SIX

Leaning quietly against the hood of the jeep, JR watched the silver Piper Cup land a few hundred feet away. It was time for the once a month mail drop and pick up. Seeing Starck jump to the ground, JR unbent his tall, lean frame and walked toward the pilot. "Afternoon, Don. Nice day." He called.

Don looked up and then waited until Lewis reached him. "Yea, not bad at all." Then eyeing the rancher guardedly, he said quietly, "I see you must have recovered your jeep."

"My jeep?" JR asked puzzled.

"Yes. The last time I saw it was when I refueled on the way back to Adelaide last trip. Took that 'nice' looking filly of yours back to the big city. Funny, though, she must have been from Sydney. She said she had only just arrived in Adelaide."

Lewis' face had paled beneath his tan. But his voice was under complete control. "Oh, really? I didn't know."

A nasty sort of snicker broke from Starck. "I must say, JR, you are a fast worker. What happen, wouldn't she play along with your game? Is that why she left so soon?"

A muscle jumped in Jay's lean, tanned jaw. "What are you trying to say, Don?"

Dark eyes met flinty gray. "It should be very simple. The whole district knows about 'your' little redheaded girlfriend. Most indiscreet of you to bring her here."

Jay forcibly controlled the desire to strike the other man. But just managed stiff lips to say, "One never knows. Now, I believe you have some mail for GetAway?"

"Yea, sure. There is a letter there from Rockwood Station. Well, I'll be on my way." Suggested Starck. Then before he climbed back into the plane, he added with a touch of maliciousness, "If you should decide to get rid of her; give me her number. I believe she is staying at the Melbourne House. I'm not sure."

No answer came from the now stony-featured, blonde-haired man; so Starck gave an elaborate shrug of his broad shoulders and entered the aircraft.

Without another glance at the plane, Lewis turned and walked slowly back to the jeep. What a mess, if what Starck had said was true. God, what a mess!

Three weeks ago he had been angry when he had found the girl had gone. But after finding the jeep at the airstrip, he had figured that it had been for the better. But now? Now he wasn't at all sure. Course it could just be that Starck was telling just what he thought and had added the part about the whole district knowing. More than likely that was the truth of the matter.

It was sort of a blow to realize the girl hadn't been from Adelaide; but Sidney was a much larger city. Maybe that was why her accent hadn't been hardly noticeable. Well, she had an accent of sorts, but he couldn't place it. It wasn't the usual Australian accent, yet it was. While she had been there, he hadn't really paid much attention; but after she had disappeared, he had found his thoughts very much on her.

Some rich girl with nothing better to do than go cause trouble in the outback. And for nothing more than a kick! Her friends more than likely had dared her; or maybe part of that story about the boyfriend had been true. Only it probably was altogether different from how she had pictured it to him.

Easing himself into the jeep, he glanced at the letter from Rockwood Station. The Bellington's, Jewel and Tad, had been family friends for more years than he cared to count. They had a son, Chris, who was around sixteen years old. Being born late in their lives, Chris would have been spoiled by most parents, but not with Jewel and Tad.

Slipping a finger under the envelope flap and opening it he shook out the single sheet of paper. Halfway down the page, he stopped and went back over it to the very beginning. His face turning once again hard as he read over the neat handwriting.

> Well, JR, we've heard the rumors and knowing you like we do, know that it couldn't be true. You know what it is like out here if you should become blacklisted by the others. So please try and scotch this thing before it blows all out of proportion.
>
> Love from us all,
> Jewel Bellington
>
> P.S.
> You can guess who started the rumor.

Crumpling the letter into a ball, he grimaced. Yes, he could guess who. Starck. But that did not help matters now. What in the hell could he do?

Frowning he absently flicked through the remaining mail, until his eyes came to rest on a typed envelope. The return address being from the employment agency he had sent the ad into. Ripping it open, he read it through.

Hoped he found the young woman they had sent satisfactory and that she was meeting his requirements?

What the hell?

Also enclosed was a copy of the newspaper ad. Reading it over, he swore under his breath. It wasn't the ad; or at least, it was not quite like he had written it. Almost the same wording, except for the preference of a male.

Randi had been telling the truth about the ad all along. But then why the act that morning before they left the cabin?

He would have to straighten the whole mess out. Best thing he could do would be to fly into Adelaide and find out just what he could. He would have Ted fuel up the twin engine plane, while he made arrangements at the station.

Catching a glimpse of herself in one of the long hotel mirrors, Randi stopped for an instant before continuing on across the lounge. She smiled dryly, she had hardly recognized herself. Not with a dark, honeyed-colored tan; dark-red hair touched with pale sun lightened color at the ends and around the temples. She looked quite a different woman.

White, silky slacks that emphasized the slender length of leg and thigh; and a low-cut brief top showed off her slim, shapely figure. As she crossed the wide lobby, she could feel the glances of the men as their eyes followed her. Her fine lips twitched bemusedly.

The money would soon be completely depleted. One more week of luxury, then she would be one of the working class or at least looking. In a way, she mused to herself, she was glad the money was about gone. She had not liked being a lazy, free and easy swinger. After a few dates with handsome, but decidedly immoral males with huge egos; she had resorted to making up excuses not to go out.

One had told her that playing hard to get didn't work anymore. She had been hard pressed not to have laughed in his sulky face. That was just what she did not want. Never would she marry; not for so called love. It just did not pay to fall blindly in love. It hurt far too much when you discovered that the one you loved had not truly loved you in return. Maybe not at all.

True, she reasoned, she had found that she had not actually loved Rod. More of a case of being in love with love. But it only served to make the actual emotion of love even more unreasonable. She was not willing to take that kind of responsibility, not now. She had become afraid of trusting her own judgment in anything as important as love. To put her trust in someone else's hands was now totally unthinkable.

Giving her long hip-length hair an unconscious toss of independence, she headed toward the bar and dining area. Just before she reached the arched doorway, she had the most unusual feeling. A feeling that someone was watching her movements intently. Not like the looks that the men have been giving her, but with . . .What? This was ridiculous!

With a shaky laugh, she laid the thought aside and quickly entered the dimmed, muted room. It was quiet, with the soft under tone of voices mixed with soft, relaxing music. The colors from the lighted candles setting on the table tops, were reflected in the soft, silky material of her outfit. The slacks and top now a muted rainbow of flickering colors.

The glow from the candles caused the deep-red hair to intensify to a rich deep mahogany. Even as she slid into her chair in a secluded corner, the strange feeling seemed to return with strength.

Determinately she let her eyes scan the menu and as the waiter approached she smiled nervously and ordered her lunch. After he had asked if she would like a drink before her meal, which she accepted, he turned quietly away. She kept her eyes on the waiter's retreating back, watching as he collected her drink and returned.

Raising the glass to her lips, she smiled slowly; then leaning back, she could feel the coolness of the velvet-like material against her almost bare back. It seemed to have a calming effect, for she actually found herself idly glancing around the dining area. Looking for what exactly, she could not really say.

For a brief moment, it was hard to believe that she was sitting in an exclusive hotel dining room in Australia. It could just as well have been back in the States from the actual look of things. The people seated talking, the fashionable clothes they were wearing. The atmosphere. Except?

Except for that extra feeling. That newness, the excitement of still unknown areas and the sort of pioneering feeling that seems to envelope one. A new world. A new beginning. But could a person actually start over? New? Different?

No. She answered herself. No, because what ever had happen before would reflect and guide what one does in the future. It all relates back to one thing: the beginning. The events up till the present.

A bitter twist touched her mouth. A never ending revolving circle. One thing always leading to another, but back again. The main thing to remember, learn from the mistakes. Life is full of choices and it's your choice that makes the difference.

Sitting there staring into her half full glass, she thought back. Past the present, back to her high school days. She had not dated. Why? Simple, who would want to take out a girl; who was shy to begin with, that looked about eleven or twelve? Skinny, with freckles and red hair. And a tomboy.

Now here she was; twenty-five, almost. And could appear about eighteen or sometimes even younger. Oh, she had changed. Became more matured. Only one thing remained the same. Her feelings, emotions. She was lucky in that she had always had a good dose of common sense.

And she was still a tomboy at heart. That was who she was, and she found she rather liked that fact.

Randi had not actually stopped to look at herself since high school. She found when she had today, just how much of a change had taken place. True, she was still small and slight; but there were curves and shape, not just rough angles. Her face had become more? What was the word she looked for?

Now there were cheekbones, a firm small chin, not just a face with freckles covering it or guileless eyes. Now the gray-green eyes held depth, pain and yet . . . . challenge. She could not give up; she would not.

Suddenly then the waiter was there with her meal. Smiling faintly, she thanked him then quietly started in on her lunch. Thinking as she had been, she fought to forget the image that kept creeping into her lonely hours. The strong, tanned features of JR Lewis. For the life of her she could not forget the man. Just the thought of that – kiss – would cause the blood to run warm and surge into the small oval face.

With an unconscious deep sigh, she pushed the remaining portion of her lunch away and motioned for her bill. As she rose from the table, that uneasy feeling seemed to engulf her once again. With a quick, silent glance around, she hurriedly reached the cashier and then moved swiftly through the doors.

With a slight shrug of her shoulders, she ran lightly up the first flight of stairs to her room. Flinging her handbag onto a nearby chair, she headed into the adjoining bedroom and grabbed up her new bikini of different shades of blues and with a splash of pink here and there.

In no time at all she was ready and quickly braiding the long, red-glinted hair; she made her way down to the large sun bathed swimming pool. A good, cool dip in the pool ought to dispel the shadowy feeling she had been having. So with a soft smile of pleasure she slipped into the blue-green water and headed for the far side.

Smooth, even strokes soon had her at the other side. Glancing around she found the pool area almost deserted. Good. She smiled. Now she could relax. Lying on her back, she closed her long-lashed eyes and floated slowly once across the pool. About half way across, she heard the faint plop of the water as someone dived into its depth.

A slight frown touched the lips, but she quickly wiped it from her face. It was not her pool. She knew she was nearing the side of the pool, so turned onto her stomach and reached out to touch the cement side.

Wiping the water from her face, she turned back around and was confronted by cool, rain-gray eyes.

Shock, if nothing else, moved her back against the cement siding of the pool and the sun-bronzed JR Lewis placed his well-muscled arms on each side of her, leaving no escape. "What are you doing here?" She managed to stammer through suddenly stiff lips.

A dry, humorless; yet attractive smile touched the man's lips. "Just dropped in."

CHAPTER SEVEN

Her heart was pounding so fiercely that it almost was sure to be heard by the tall, lean man blocking her way. He was the same. Even to the cynical smile.

"Oh, the man made a funny. You know that's not what I meant."

"Yes, I guess I do at that. How 'bout dinner tonight?" He drawled slowly.

"Are you kidding?" She laughed shakily.

"Nope." JR grinned.

Anger stirred and Randi said sharply, "Well, sorry, but I'm..uh..busy."

The sun-lightened brows rose a fraction. "Really? You didn't stay very long at the station; sort of run off. You weren't thinking of running off again were you?"

Dusky-green eyes flashed. "Of all the nerve. You really are the limit, Mister Lewis."

A dry chuckle. "I keep trying. What's the matter, Randi, you afraid?"

"Of course not. I told you; I'm busy tonight." She lied, her small oval face blushing.

Jay let his cool-gray eyes slide carelessly over her features before saying, "I'm sure you are. That's why you had lunch alone this afternoon. I still say that you are afraid, of me."

That feeling of unease she had. It had been him. But, afraid of him. Yes. But she did not want him to know that.

"I'm not afraid of you."

"Okay, then. Prove it, my girl."

"I'm not 'your girl' either. What time?" Randi mumbled.

A dangerous glint lit the gray eyes. "I'll pick you up at eight. Sharp. Be ready."

Not trusting herself to speak, Randi nodded shortly. Then before she knew what he was up to, she found herself sitting out of the water, his warm, strong hands still at her waist.

"Remember, be ready. I'm a very impatient man." He said softly.

Silently she watched as he lifted himself out of the water and walked leisurely toward the hotel building. Fading sunlight glinted on blonde hair and wet, bronzed shoulders. He was a very disturbing man. At least to her peace of mind. She had not expected to see him again; yet, in a strange way she was excited.

After quite a number of laps across the still empty pool and a few minutes more of just pacing back and forth in her room, Randi found herself still in a damp swimsuit and not quite knowing what to do. A bath, a good long bath. That should help her feel more back to normal again. So dumping a handful of pleasant smelling bath oils into the water, she went to look at her wardrobe.

Glancing over the large assortment of new clothes, she wondered where he would be taking her. Oh well, something that would fit any occasion. Her slender, tanned hand skimmed over the many outfits until it stopped at a multi-colored pastel outfit. It was not a dress, but neither was it a pantsuit. One piece that reached to the floor in soft, clinging folds of material. An elegant, yet simple outfit.

Yes, she thought, that would do just fine. Set him on his ear for sure. So with a mischievous smile, she went into the large bathroom and gratefully sank into the deliciously warm, delicately scented water.

At five minutes to eight, Jay stepped out of the silent elevator and walked softly along the thickly carpeted corridor to Randi's room. His handsome face was set in stubborn, almost hard lines as he stopped in front of her door. Raising a well-tanned, lean hand he knocked softly on the wood panel.

His features, which had been so hard a moment before; quickly became polite.

With a gentle, yet forced smile, he looked into the dusky-green eyes that stared back at him so defiant, yet in a way very beguiling, almost challenging. One cool glance took in the softly clinging material that showed the slender figure of the girl to perfection. The colors were just right for her unusual coloring and brilliant hair. And if anything could be called sexy, thought JR, that outfit definitely was. Not excluding the girl; correction, woman inside it.

"Right on time, I see." He drawled slowly. His voice soft and still very masculine.

Randi looked up at him through thick, dark lashes. Her small chin came up at a decidedly stubborn angle. "Usually." Before she could add anything to that; the tall rancher stepped past her and walked inside.

"Aren't you going to ask me in?"

Softly Randi closed the door, then turned back around to face him. "Why? From the looks of things, you already are."

"So right. Was afraid you would bolt the door at the last minute and say you've changed your mind."

She smiled. Her dusky-green eyes flashed a small warning. "Not after that bit about being afraid of you. My feminine pride would never let that happen. Besides, women would be after me for backing down from the almighty male."

Jay leaned back in the chair he had found and eyed her carefully before saying with a definite smile in his voice. "In that outfit you definitely look like a woman."

Randi could feel the color begin to sweep over her face and tilted her glowing head to look at him closer. "I'm not sure if that was a compliment or just the opposite. But as you failed to tell me where we were going, I had to do the best I could."

"Well, you'll do just fine. Guess we just as well get a move on. Not knowing about you, but I'm hungry." He smiled ever so slowly.

Randi watched that smile and she became much more nervous. What was the man up too? Maybe she would be smarter to back out. Then she caught him looking at her; not on your life would she let him know that she was afraid of him. Never.

"Yes, why not? To tell the truth, I'm starved." She lied.

With a graceful, silent movement he pushed his lean, hard muscled frame up out of the chair; and with a mock bow, smiled slowly. "After you, my lady."

A flutter of panic started in her throat that threatened to choke her. Why did he always have that effect on her senses? It never failed, as soon as they got together sparks flew and she always managed to come out the loser. Not this time, she promised herself as she forced her lips into a smile.

"Right with you, my Lord."

An eyebrow went up, but no comment came from the stern, firm lips of the man. Together they left the apartment, he making sure that her door was pulled closed. Nearing the elevator, Randy turned her bright head and looked up at her companion.

"You still haven't said where we're going?" she asked softly, a hint of impatience in her voice.

With the elevator door swishing open, JR ushered her inside before replying, "Wait and see. I'll guarantee you've never dined there."

"Really?" she frowned slightly. "Hope the food is good."

"The best." Was his soft reply.

CHAPTER EIGHT

Stepping out of the large plate glass doors of the hotel, Randi glanced at the dark, star lit sky. Then she turned her smoky-green gaze to the man at her side. His hand on her arm, Jay remarked, "The silver-gray Jaguar over there near the curb."

Except for the one glance; true, a surprised one, there was no other sign of her inner confusion. "Very nice."

And it was; with lush, soft black interior. Very expensive, and very close. A small, almost cozy trap.

"Thought you might like it." Was his reply.

Was he laughing at her? She sure could not tell by the polite expression on his teak-brown features. After closing her door, he went around and slid into the driver's seat. In a swift, quick movement they were gliding down the wide street.

At first they rode in silence, until Randi thought she would scream. So to break it, she asked, "Do you come to Adelaide often?"

A slow glance swept over her, then he smiled carelessly. "Often enough. Mostly on business of some kind or other."

"Oh." Was the only answer she could come up with. Then on a deep sigh, "How…how did you know where to find me?"

Another encompassing glance, then he answered in his soft drawl, "Our pilot friend. Don Starck. Remember him?"

Just stopping a very unlady-like snort, Randi remarked instead, "Couldn't forget him. Nosiest damn man I ever met."

A gentle chuckle sounded from the tall rancher beside her. "That he is. He sure didn't forget you either."

Her gray-green eyes opened wider, "Oh, you don't care for him either."

"No." Was the single, very precise answer.

"Well, that's one thing we agree on." Smiled Randi hesitantly.

"True enough."

Glancing out at the darkening night, Randi asked quietly, "How much farther is this restaurant?"

"We're almost there. Just a few more minutes."

True to his word, in a very short time, he turned the silver car off the main street and onto the gracefully elegant driveway of a large building with a uniformed man stepping smartly forward to open her car door.

Smiling politely at Randi and then swinging swiftly around to the driver's side, the man remarked to JR. "Good evening, Sir. I'll park it for you."

"Thank you, Henry. Put it in the garage, please." Then turning his handsome head toward Randi, Jay said, "This way."

She remained silent as they entered the plush lobby. And it was a lobby. And if she were any kind of judge; this was a very expensive hotel. Very impressive, also. With his hand on her arm, he directed her toward some elevators off to one side. "We have to go up a few floors."

After stepping inside, the doors swished closed and with barely any feeling at all, the elevator moved upward. But a few floors? It seemed to just keep going and going. It had to be the top floor. What would be all the way up on the top floor? Why hadn't she heard of it before? But before she could voice her questions, the doors opened silently and Lewis moved her out into a hallway.

"What?"

"Right through here." And he pushed open an elegant door. He was directly behind her and without stepping through him, which would be impossible, she had no choice but to go on in.

As soon as they were inside, she heard the soft click of the door as it shut. A muted light was switched on that bathed the hall and connecting room in soft, pleasing light. Plush cream-white carpet was thick underfoot and a set of marble steps went down into the sunken large living room.

Wide, startled eyes turned on JR. "This is some kind of joke, I take it?"

Leaning his tall frame against the door, Jay replied softly, "Not at all."

"But this isn't a restaurant. This is your suite or apartment. Well, isn't it?"

"True." He smiled thinly. "Go on in and sit down."

"Are you kidding?" she flashed.

"No."

"But…" Randi stammered.

"Not to worry, I won't bite. Besides the food is superb. I told you that you have never eaten here." He drawled quietly. "Besides that, I want to talk to you."

"Really? I wonder what you would want to talk to me about?" Her lovely eyes had narrowed slightly and the lips stiffened with stubbornness.

Pushing himself away from the door, JR walked toward her. "Why not relax and enjoy yourself. Come on, I'll show you around while Kim puts the finishing touches to the meal."

An eyebrow shot up. "Kim?"

"Yes, he cleans and on occasion cooks. Beautifully, too, I might add." Lewis answered with a hint of amusement in his voice.

Then with a firm, but gentle grip on her arm he led her down into the living room. As she stepped down her foot sank into the thick pile carpet. The same pale ivory color was on the one wall, with thin curtained sliding doors and windows making up the long side of the room. A patio or balcony could be seen through the pale curtains. The farther wall contained an old fashioned large fireplace with dark wood mantle and trim; staggered shelves were on both sides containing a number of books. A expensive stereo with speakers were set on one of the shelves, while a large flat screen TV filled the rest of the wall.

A couch of velvety-soft material in burnished browns and black was set at an angle so that you could see out the sliding doors and the fireplace wall. Very beautiful, yet somehow simple.

Jay watched her as she looked over the large room, and from the expressive features, he decided she liked what she saw. Again touching her arm, he said, "Down the hall to your left is the bathroom and sleeping area. A little farther is the master suite. Down the other hall is the kitchen and dining area, with a smaller room that is a study."

Randi looked up at his tanned face. "It's really quite amazing. I could love this. You must really enjoy stopping over here?"

Jay nodded slowly. "Yes, I guess I do at that."

After lifting the glass of water to her lips, Randi looked over at the rancher through her thick lashes. His silk shirt was open at the throat and she could see the sun-touched dark-blonde hair curling over his well-muscled chest. The fine material did little to cover the rippling muscles of shoulder and arm. Looking away she felt a tremor streak through her body. She could feel the power of those arms as they had closed around her the night at the cabin. What was even more disturbing was the fact she almost longed to feel them again. She must be suffering from too much wine at dinner. And she almost smiled.

The meal had been superb and though she had hardly been able to taste it, had eaten with a forced appetite. Nerves, stress; probably both. The lean man sitting directly across from her had the ability to cause her nerves to tense and vibrate at his very nearness causing her now to feel thoroughly strung-out. Like a too tightly wound watch.

Not only his nearness, but she had the oddest feeling that they were completely alone and that it had been all previously arranged. Which was totally ridiculous since she had no reason to suspect such a thing and also for the small fact that she had not seen the man, Kim, leave. So it had to be a case of over-tensed imagination.

She had wine with the meal, and she could detect the slightest hint of liquor in the rich fragrant coffee. Which she never drank. But for some reason had decided to do so that evening. True, she had only sipped the coffee, and only drank a small amount of the wine. Breaking into her scattered thoughts came JR's soft voice. Hesitantly she lifted her eyes to meet his. Quickly though, she lowered her lashes as his cool gray glance traveled over her face.

"Yes?" she asked.

"I asked if you would like to go in and sit down?" drawled the rancher with a calmness that Randi wished she could possess.

"That would be fine." She nodded as she rose from her chair and walked toward the couch.

Jay watched her and as he moved to follow, he deftly turned down the lights and asked carefully, "What kind of music?"

Randi had noted the dimming of the lighting, but tried desperately to ignore the panic clamoring in her ribs. "Oh, whatever you would prefer will be fine."

With a small nod of the blonde head, he inserted a CD and as the soft, romantic music flooded the room he walked over and stood quietly in front of her. Almost afraid to look up, she did so very slowly. And as she did, she caught a rather secret smile on the man's firm lips.

"Would you care to dance?" he drawled softly.

"Here? Now?" she stammered. Her smoky-green eyes wide and uncertain.

"Why not?" he shrugged his broad shoulder and took her wrist in his lean fingers. Gently, yet somehow very firmly, pulled her up into his arms. Randi could feel the warmth from his body where it touched hers. And if it had not been for the gentle force of his hand on her back, she felt sure she would have turned and ran.

Feeling the caressing movement of his fingers on her bare back, she stiffened in self-defense. A warmth seemed to spread from where he was touching her and she was becoming a teeny bit afraid.

"What's the matter, Randi, nervous?" he whispered in her ear, his breath warm against her skin. Then the firm lips settled on a spot just behind her ear.

Frightened now, Randi tried pulling away. Effortlessly he tightened his arms about her slender shape, bringing her even closer. "Mr. Lewis. I…" breathed Randi through panic-stiff lips.

He stopped dancing then and stared down into her uncertain green eyes. Again that rather unpleasant smile touched the firm lips. "Little One, you do not call me MR. LEWIS. It's either Jay or JR. For now."

I don't care what I call you. But I think this has gone quite far enough." Snapped Colon with nervous anger.

"What has gone far enough? I've just started." Calmly stated the very male man that was still holding her.

Panic vied with sudden helpless anger as she stared up into his expressionless face. His light eyes had a lazy, almost shuttered look about them. Leaving her more confused than ever. Once again she wondered just what he was playing at? For sure he was after something. Determinately she made her voice as calm as she could manage under the circumstances. "What is that supposed to mean? That bit about just starting?"

Coolly he looked over her features, taking his time and then deliberately letting his glance settle on her slightly trembling lips. "Just what it sounds like."

Anger, or was it fear, shook her slender frame as she started struggling within his hold. "You must be crazy. You've had too much sun."

With a swift move he pulled her up against his hard chest, his fingers tangling in the thick hair at the back of her head. A disturbing, husky laugh sounded in his throat, "Not at all. Maybe a little bit of a spitfire, but no sun." Then with a handful of hair he pulled her head back, exposing the small oval face and slender, creamy throat.

Firm, demanding lips met hers. At first almost exploratory, then after parting the trembling lips he seemed to become almost brutal in his attempt to take the sweetness of her young, tender mouth. Shuddering, Randi felt the first flames of desire lick along her nerve ends, causing her already confused head to spin. As his mouth left hers and traveled down her throat, his tongue and lips caressed the small pulse beating wildly at its base. Warm, strong hands moved sensuously over her gentle curves and she could feel the male hardness of him against her thighs and hip. With almost a moan, she gasped, "Jay, please!"

"Please what?" he asked against her neck.

"Stop." She could feel tears burning behind the tightly closed lids. She had to halt him before her traitorous body gave into his well-practiced demands.

"Why?" he demanded now. But Randi noted the hardness in the silky voice.

"Because." Then as the short temper reached its limit, she almost yelled at him. "Because whatever it is you are playing – I'm not one of the toys."

With that said, he looked at her tense face and then roughly pushed her down onto the sofa, following close beside her with his own body; his hands still maintaining their firm hold. Flames smoldered in the steel-gray eyes as he stared at her. His lips tight with a thin white line about them. That he was angry, Randi had no doubt.

"I'm not playing. I'm very serious. And you are very definitely in this, Little One. Whether you like it or not." He stated quietly.

"Well, I don't…and…and I'm not staying any longer." Declared the redhead with more force than she felt.

A dry chuckle broke from the stern-faced man. "Oh, I think you were liking it." At the high-color staining her cheeks, he continued, "And you won't be leaving."

"That's what you think, Mister…." Snapped Randi as she made to stand.

Strong hands tightened their hold and as she struggled with him, his anger increased. Jerking her small frame toward him; she was slid over his lap and onto the cushion of the couch, his own body forcing her down.

Fiery sparks flashed in the dark-green eyes as she made to swing an open hand at the hard, handsome face above her own. But Lewis caught it easily before it could connect. Taking it and her other arm, he pulled them both together above her head, pinning them in his one strong hand. A stiff smile touched his lips. "You weren't thinking of trying to slap me again were you, Randi? Remember the last time you did that?"

Swift color flooded her face and silently she glared at him.

His bold gray glance traveled over her tense features, lingering on the slightly parted lips and then moved slowly, tantalizingly on down over her body. Then as he felt her stiffen and once again try to pull free, he brought his eyes once more to her face. His free hand reached out and gently his thumb traced the line of her lip and then along the delicate jaw. As her fine lips tightened into a thin line, he moved his fingers down over her neck and then farther down along the shadowy valley between the small, firm breasts.

Catching her breath at the burning desire that shuddered through her whole body, Randi's eyes flew to the lean features directly above her. His steady gaze slammed into her confused eyes and she knew he, too, had felt that shudder. And what was more, he knew what had caused it. Slowly he lowered his blonde head, placing his tongue teasingly along her bottom lip. Then as she made to turn her mouth away; he deftly parted the trembling lips and explored the inner softness of her mouth.

All sane thought fled under his new assault, to be replaced by the consuming sensations of desire. Her body burned under his. Came alive to the demands of his. As his thigh pushed in between hers, her body arched closer to his. Firm, warm fingers moved provocatively over the silky smoothness of the material that fitted her curves almost like a second skin.

The fresh, clean male scent of him, an intoxicating fragrance to the senses that were already high from the sensuous caressing fingers and tantalizing lips, sent her soaring to the heights. The fire of her own desire threatening to consume her. Then; Jay stopped. Leaned back away from her so he could see her face green fire met cold, determined gray and held. As a cynical smile came to the firm mouth of the man, Randi tensed. Her face draining of color, leaving it white. Lewis's voice reached her then; hard, cold and dangerously quiet. "Like I said, you enjoy it just fine."

Humiliation flooded through her as she attempted to struggle free once more. "Why? What kind of pleasure are you getting out of all this?" She demanded through tight lips.

"To be honest, quite a bit." He acknowledged quietly. "But, why?" A dry chuckle sounded. Not friendly at all. "Because of a certain, unfortunate misunderstanding and other equally unpleasant things, I've found myself in need of a wife. Hence, a small, red-haired, green eyed witch. You."

"A wife!" she gasped. "You are crazy if you think I'm going to marry you."

CHAPTER NINE

"I don't think you will marry me; I know damn well you will." He stated in a firm, quiet, very determined voice.

For a moment she actually believed it. But as common sense returned, so did her anger. "You can't make me if I don't want to. And I do not, Mister Jay Randal Lewis."

A dry chuckle rumbled down in his throat. "We'll see." His eyes never leaving her face.

"How can you sit there and say 'we'll see'?" she demanded furiously. "And let go of me."

He just grinned slowly. "No." White teeth flashed in a smile. "I rather like you just where you are. Under my control."

"If you try kissing me again, I'll...I'll scream this place down." She warned.

"Go ahead, there's no one to hear you." He replied quietly.

"But, what about Kim? How would you explain..." she whispered hoarsely.

"Kim left a good hour ago. And he won't be back until tomorrow afternoon." Drawled Lewis almost lazily.

"Tomorrow." Asked Randi warily. "But...but I've got to get back to my hotel."

"You no longer have a room at the hotel."

"What! My clothes…" stormed Randi as she suddenly jerked both arms forward. The move caught JR unaware and she took full advantage of it. Her hands formed into small fists, striking sharply on the rancher's chest. As one well-placed little fist caught his jaw an especially stabbing blow, JR grabbed her arms and held them to her sides.

"You little hellcat." He breathed through clinched teeth. "God, what have I saddled myself with?"

"You haven't yet." Reminded Randi shakily.

"Oh, but I will, Honey" smiled Jay.

"Don't call me honey. You, you ba…"

"Don't say it, Randi."

"I'll say anything I want. I want to know what happen to my room? My clothes, everything!" demanded the redhead.

"I checked you out of the hotel. Your clothes and everything else is here." Explained Lewis calmly.

"You did what?" she gasped aloud.

"You heard me." And then at seeing her indignant face, he continued, "Also our engagement will be in the morning paper."

Randi felt her mouth literally drop open and hurriedly snapped it shut. Dazedly she shook her autumn-colored head. "I don't understand why you are doing this. When I was at the station you could hardly wait to be rid of me. You were so worried about what your neighbors would think of you. And now you make a public announcement?"

"They, meaning the press, know you came here with me and also know that I have checked you out of your hotel and had your luggage brought here." He stated matter-of-factly.

"You can't be serious. This has got to be a joke. You wouldn't keep me here all night with…with you." Looking up into his face, her voice faulted.

"It's no joke. And yes, I am very definitely keeping you here with me, all night. Tomorrow we become husband and wife." His attractive voice had a hard ring to it under the silkiness.

"But, but why?" stammered Colon. Her small chin becoming stubborn.

"Because Starck informed the whole damn area about 'our little affair'. And everyone is in a first class uproar." He replied coldly.

"So let 'em be in a stinking uproar! There was no affair! I can't help it if they've got dirty little minds and want to believe a foul mouthed gossip such as Starck!" snapped Randi heatedly. Her dusky-green eyes afire with temper.

"I have to live there. My stockmen and their families, all the station employees have to get along with them. Without their friendship and trust; the station would die. Everything my family took generations to build would be gone, wasted; including their good and respected name. And why? Because some flighty woman decides to visit the outback." Growled Jay. His fingers unconsciously tightening around her slender wrists.

Randi frowned. Hell, what a mess. And he still believed her to be a wealthy (woman?) out for a good time at anyone's expense. She couldn't let all that happen to him or the station; but marriage?

Lewis watched the changing thoughts flick over her expressive face. He had almost told her he knew that her story had been the truth, as much as he knew of it, but at the last minute had decided to not say anything. She would be more apt to go along with his plans if she thought that she had contributed to (even though unintentionally) all the trouble.

As he felt her small body relax suddenly, he also heard her faint sigh of almost hopelessness. His own muscles braced into stiffness as he waited for her to speak.

Softly she asked, "Does it have to be marriage? Isn't there any other way?"

Silently he shook his head. As her eyes closed, he released her arms and moved slightly to one side. Instantly her eyes opened and she pulled herself up into a sitting position. Folding her hands nervously in her lap, she asked, "Really made a mess of things, huh?"

"Guess you could say that." Nodding his blonde head.

"Now..uh..how do we go about getting married? And what 'kind' of a marriage are you intending ours to be?" she questioned, barely able to get the words past the lump of fear in her throat.

Jay watched the color flood up over her cheeks and just managed to stop a faint smile. God, she was so small and yet, so very desirable. What kind of marriage indeed! But after seeing the fear that still shadowed the green eyes, he decided to keep a low profile, maybe easing the tension of the moment. "I've already talked to my lawyer. He's a very good friend and he will have everything all set up for us by tomorrow before noon. All that will be needed is your birth certificate and that sort of thing. You can give him all of that information before the ceremony. It will be a simple ceremony in the Registrar's chambers."

"Yes. I..I understand that. But concerning the, a well situation between us..." Randi muttered.

"We could keep it a marriage of convenience. Or, of course, we could have the real thing?" He stopped as he heard her gasp of incredibility. Then before she could say a word, he continued, "As for my feelings; or to be more blunt, my desires. I find you, well, should I say; I find that I am attracted to you. As you are to me."

"Of all the nerve! You presume quite a bit." Sputtered Randi, confused and at the same time knowing he was correct. She was. Very. Maybe that was what made her afraid?

"But, I presume right in this fact, don't I, Randi?" he drawled softly.

"Yes." Whispered Randi reluctantly. "It's only a physical reaction. That's all."

Lewis laughed softly, his smoky-gray eyes running over her embarrassed features. Then he leaned forward and kissed her mouth.

Instantly Randi felt the heat of desire curl somewhere deep inside her. She raised her hands in a futile attempt to ward him off, but as the cool fingers encountered curling, gold-tipped light-brown chest hairs and a solid, warm chest all thoughts of resistance seemed to die almost suddenly.

The firm lips traveled over her smooth cheek and jaw to just under her ear. His breath warm against her skin. Placing a gentle, soft kiss near the earlobe, he whispered, "Very physical."

Stiffening, Randi leaned back away from his overwhelming body. She had to think. And letting him kiss her was not the way. She was very definitely afraid of him. Of herself.

"You said that my luggage was here." Prompted Randi, keeping her eyes averted.

"Yes. They were delivered while we were eating. Kim placed them in the bedroom." Answered JR quietly, watching her expression.

She looked up then. "Whose bedroom?"

The teak-brown features softened slightly and a careful smile touched the firm lips. "Mine."

"But, you said bedrooms earlier. There are two bedrooms?" She set her lips mutinously.

"No." he stated quietly. "There is just mine."

"So." It came out on a sigh. "Well, I'll just sleep on the couch."

"No." disagreed Lewis. "You are sleeping in my bed."

Her delicate face hardened and she stated in a dangerously quiet, almost calm voice, "Then you are sacking out on the couch."

"I said my bed, meaning exactly that."

"Oh no; you said marriage of convenience!" she was on the very edge of shouting and had now rose to her feet. Her whole slender body stiff with rage.

"Seeing as I'm acquiring a wife and spending quite a little money on this, not mentioning the gray hairs I have more than likely acquired in this mess. I think I am entitled to, shall we say, check out the merchandise? For all I know, you might snore. Besides, I've changed my mind about the marriage. It's to be the real thing. It is time that I started thinking about a family."

For a moment Randi was speechless. Of all the conceited, egotistical males; he was the limit. "I am not your possession. I am not a brood mare you are looking to buy. And it won't make any difference if I do snore in my sleep; as I won't be sleeping with you." She declared chokingly.

"But you will be. On the station you'll be in my bedroom, and in my bed. I have no intention of the people around there to discover the reason for this marriage in the first place. And one night with us sleeping in separate bedrooms, it would be all over the district before noon the next day." He explained as if to a rather slow child.

At seeing her uncertainty, he added dryly. "I have no intention of making love to you tonight. I figured you had better get used to 'sleeping' with me. I didn't want a show of temper at the house. But, of course, I could be forgetting that you might be more experienced at sleeping around than I am."

Shock widened the darkening green eyes. What did he think he was marrying? A tramp? Humiliation swept through her and anger. Squaring her slim shoulders, she faced him defiantly. Her tongue could be sharp, too. If only he wasn't so damn tall. Or so sexy. "Never can tell. But, I happen to be choosy. Now, if you will excuse me. I'll go find 'your bedroom'." And with a toss of her head that sent the red, hip-length hair flying; she stalked out of the room.

Jay watched her go, anger and humor vying with each other. He waited for quite a while longer before rising from the couch and moving down the carpeted hallway to the bedroom. Quietly and carefully he opened the door and stepped inside.

Moving to the end of the queen-sized bed, he stood very still and stared down at the now sleeping girl. His lips twitched into a smile. The little redhead was curled into a tight small ball at the very edge of the mattress. To Jay she appeared like a very dainty, very lovely child. Except for the curl of desire that swept through his body.

Shakily he ran a hand through the sun-streaked blonde hair. Then hesitating briefly, he moved closer to the sleeping girl. Bending down over her, he reached across and lifted the pillow from beside the red-gold head. Taking it and stopping at the large closet, he pulled down a quilted spread and once again walked toward the door. With one more lingering glance at the small, oval face, he turned and headed back down the hall to the burnished-colored couch.

CHAPTER TEN

Chancing a look through her naturally thick, dark lashes; Randi studied the handsome profile of Jay Lewis. Her eyes slid cautiously to the tanned, strong hands resting easily and at the same time, confidently on the controls of the small aircraft they were flying in.

What a wild, confusing morning thought the red-haired girl with a sigh. One, she made sure to conceal from the tall man at her side. After a fitful night, she had awoke to find herself quite alone in the large bed. After taking a hurried shower, she had very nearly crept down the carpeted hall to find a sleeping rancher stretched out on the couch. But not for long.

Within fifteen minutes from waking up, the rancher had breakfast ready. After eating the simple, but nourishing meal; they had headed for the lawyer's. While she had gone in with Jay's friend to talk with him, Jay went to check on the other arrangements. Ray Proctor had been surprised to discover that Randi was not from Australia, but from the States. But as she had all her papers with her, they had no problems. The lawyer had assumed that Lewis had just forgotten to mention the fact. Ray Proctor was what Randi would call a real sweetheart. Older than JR by around three or four years, he had laughing brown eyes and a trusting kind of smile.

A faint smile touched her own lips now as she remembered the lawyer looking up at her and smiling. "Your birthday isn't far off? You will have to have a celebration. Everyone loves a reason to get together in the outback, and GetAway Station is one of the best. Be sure to remember to invite me."

Randi had nodded and soon afterwards JR had returned and then it was to the Registrar's Chambers for the quick, smooth ceremony. Everything had gone so swiftly. So easily. Almost like in a dream, only it was real. Very real.

Turning her burnished head to the side window, she looked down at the passing landscape. In a few more minutes they would be touching down at the station's own small landing field. Not the one that the mail plane had landed at. And she would be arriving at GetAway as Mrs. Jay Randal Lewis. RandiLee Lewis. She could not seem to believe it, even now.

Once again she glanced at the lean, tall rancher. Her husband. Through the entire flight so far, both had maintained an almost forced silence. Sunlight glinted on the pale hair, and without really realizing it, Randi found herself becoming increasingly aware of him. Aware of him a very virile man. As he had been last night. Her body had wanted him to continue. To eventually possess her? Was that what she had wanted?

Cautiously she let her glance settle on his strong jaw line and swung up to his mouth. . . ! She looked away quickly, her heartbeat fluttering a wild tattoo as she remembered the feel of those lips against her own. Heat seemed to sweep her body where he had let his warm, sensuous lips touch her skin.

Frowning with impatience, she looked down at her tightly clasped hands. Her glance catching the sudden fire of the sparkling emerald and diamond ring on her finger. It was a delicate, lovely ring and very expensive. Sometime either before or immediately after meeting her at the pool that day, he had purchased the rings. And amazingly they had fit, perfectly.

"We're almost there," Jay interrupted her thoughts and pulling herself back to the present, turned the dusky-green eyes on his teak-tan features.

"That's GetAway down there, isn't it?"

He nodded shortly. A certain amount of pride touched the handsome face, lending a warm fire to the steel-gray eyes. If only he would look at her with half the warmth. What was she saying? He meant nothing to her. Body chemistry, desire. Or was there more to her confused emotions?

Again his voice broke into her tangled thoughts. "How does it feel to return? And as the new Mistress of the station?"

Her eyes met his. Startled green and sardonic gray. He still thought she had done the first visit all for fun. She knew he did not suspect that she was an American. Anger stirred, making green eyes turn to liquid fire. Green fire.

"You've got me all figured out, haven't you? Well, coming back as the mistress is just terrific. It is definitely a very clever way to get to the outback, isn't it? Your outback. And I even got the almighty rancher, too."

The bronzed features of the man hardened and the lips formed a straight thin line. Jay knew he had asked for that. But he was still unwilling to let the slender, very defiant girl next to him know that he had found out about the newspaper ad and the mix up. Not just yet.

At his continued silence and inscrutable expression, Randi's temper exploded. Words of hurt rebellion tumbling one over the other. "I imagine I'll be the envy of all the females around. Oh, that's right; there are no white women around the station. But, what of Missy Darla? I'll bet she'll just spit nails when she finds out."

Somewhat taken aback at the stormy attack and then to find the girl knew of Darla, Jay was more or less speechless. Forcing his attention to landing the light aircraft and then what to say to the very indignant woman at his side was not a cheery thought. A sudden smile did flick across his mouth as he realized the little spitfire was jealous. She must have seen Darla when she had come about that fool party. Which was to be in a few days. That would be a sight.

What he would give to see the cool Darla lose her sophisticated air. Just once. Most of the district would. She was very good at cutting people down, putting them in their place or more to the point, the place she elected them to be in.

Looking down at the dirt runway, Jay could see Tom leaning against the jeep waiting for them to set down. As the slight jolt of the wheels striking the hard-packed ground, the rancher raised a hand in greeting. The wiry stockman straightened up, a wide smile on his rather handsome face.

Hardly waiting for the plane to come to a halt, Tom sauntered over to the passenger side of the aircraft. He was anxious to see the little fire-haired Missy again. And to think she was now the Boss's wife. There for a while he had been afraid the Boss would settle for that city lady. Missy

Darla. Even Tico, his woman, had little liking for the dark-haired woman. But the little Missy, now. Tico doted on the small girl. Tom, also. That girl could ride. He wished some of his stockmen could do as well.

As the plane touched down, Randi found she was still angry, but with herself for blowing up like some little spoilt child. She, too, had seen the jeep with the stockman near it waiting. The very same jeep she had left behind.

Seeing Tom's open, friendly face, Randi had the feeling of coming home. Tears filled her eyes causing her to blink rapidly trying to clear them. Quickly, so as to keep Lewis from seeing them trembling on her lashes, she pushed open the door and moved to climb out. To her relief, Tom reached up a hand to aid her in stepping down. In the activity of unloading the plane, she was able to find time to put a facsimile of a smile on her rather pale face.

Turning as she reached the jeep, she leaned back against its dusty side and through thick lashes watched the tall rancher as he carried two of her cases toward the parked vehicle. He moved like a large predatory cat; graceful, yet determined and dangerous.

The stockman, Tom, coming up beside of Lewis, flashed a bold wink at Randi, "Missy, it is good you come back. That roany horse has been missin' you plenty."

"Oh, Tom, I've missed him too. He's a super little horse." Grinned Randi. "How are your friends?"

"They are fine, Missy Randi. They are all glad to see you again." Volunteered Tom as he placed the packages he had been carrying in the rear of the jeep beside her suitcases.

Jay, who had remained silent through the exchange, now moved up next to the driver's side of the vehicle. He had seen with some surprise how excited his head stockman had greeted Randi. Surprised because Tom was usually so reticent. And even more surprising was the fact that it sounded as if everyone was more than happy to have the redhead as mistress of the station. He grinned to himself. Guess he had done a damn good job of it.

Flashing a smile at the wiry stockman, "Tom, climb in the back, I'll drive."

Then turning his gray eyes on the slim girl, "Hop in, Randi. Let's go home."

A lovely smile broke hesitantly on her face. "Yes, let's."

As they pulled up in front of the white picket gate, Tico appeared on the wide porch, a huge smile of welcome on her friendly face. Impatiently she fidgeted from one foot to the other as she watched them ease themselves out of the open-sided jeep and walk to the house.

"Welcome, Missy. Oh, Boss, you done bring her back shore enough. My man, Tom, say you would."

The boss tried hard to keep from showing the grin that was tugging at the corners of his mouth. Tom had no such worries, he just smiled ear to ear, dark eyes flashing.

Randi, closely watching all three people, did not know whether to laugh or cry. So finally settled on a quiet, demure smile. Mounting the few steps to the porch, she was completely engulfed within Tico's strong arms. Quite a homecoming, she thought. At least there were a few people who really were pleased to have her here at the station. And firming her mobile mouth, she decided that regardless of the reasons, she was glad to be returning to GetAway.

Easing her slight body back within the taller woman's embrace, Randi grinned up into the dusky-skinned face. "Oh, Tico, you're going to hug the stuffing out of me."

Tico's smile widened and she turned the girl toward the front door. Swinging open the door, she held it that way as first, Randi and then the two men carrying in the luggage and other packages followed close behind.

Jay placed the suitcases on the hall floor and straightened his tall, muscular form before turning to look down at the slim girl standing close to his side. "Tom will take the cases to our room. Let's go in the day room and have something cool to drink."

He had noted the becoming blush that stained the oval face at the mention of the shared bedroom; and firmly took her arm in a no nonsense hold and steered the girl into the bright, airy room. Just before stepping through the doorway, he threw over his shoulder to the hovering dusky-skinned woman, "Tico, how about something tall and frosty for two thirsty people?"

"Shore thing, Boss." nodded Tico as she turned toward the kitchen.

Her man, Tom, already on his way to the master bedroom with the little Missy's suitcases. A smile of approval on his dark, handsome face. The same look was on her own features.

Glancing up at the blonde-haired rancher, Randi remembered something that the housekeeper had said upon their arrival. "What did Tico mean when she called Tom her man?"

Jay smiled softly, humor flickering in the smoky-gray eyes. "Tom is Tico's husband. They also have a beautiful six-year-old boy named Kerry. You'll love him."

Astonishment darkened the green of her eyes. "But… but, I thought Tom was, well?"

The rancher nodded knowingly. "Old for being a father of a six-year-old? It was a surprise, a late, wonderful surprise. Oh, Tico and Tom have been together for a long time. In fact, they had pretty well given up any hope of having children then, there came Kerry."

"I'm glad it happen to them. I can't wait to meet little Kerry. Where does he stay when Tico is here and Tom is working?"

"They have a cottage down next to the lake. All the workers, stockmen, bore workers, etc. have cottages. There's even a store that stocks most items needed on the station. The others take care of the smaller children during the day. They are very clannish. Also very loyal. Very strong likes and dislikes."

A light laugh escaped her. A gentle, soft sound that Jay hoped to hear more of. "I saw that as I arrived. They sure have more or less adopted me. I love it."

Before Lewis could form an answer, Tico entered carrying the two tall, frosty glasses. "Here, Boss, Missy. Nice cool drinks."

Standing at the screened door of the bedroom that led to the verandah outside, Randi watched the blazing pinks and ambers of the sunset. The very glow of colors melting and firing anew in the rich brilliance of her own hair. She had been putting away her clothes in the shared bedroom when the beauty of the setting sun drew her attention.

As Jay stepped quietly inside the door, his eyes met the twin sunsets. The one on the horizon and the fiery aurora of his wife's silky fall of hair. At first he remained silent and still, just appreciating the picture she made. Her own slight frame motionless, intently watching nature's spectacular finale.

She was now dressed in slim-fitting, faded blue jeans and a white, knit vest-like top. In the casual clothes she looked no more than a young teenager. A slim, very sexy, young woman; and now she belonged to him. Almost, he corrected.

Just then she must have sensed his presence she turned swiftly from the now darkening sky. The green eyes dark and questioning. "Oh, I hadn't realized that you were there."

"I know. I just came in. Lovely sunset, wasn't it?" he questioned in a quiet drawl.

Randi nodded her head in agreement. "Very." Then moving away from the screened door, she asked hesitantly, "Did you want me for something?"

Carelessly he leaned his tall length against the doorframe and leisurely let his cool gray glance sweep over her.

"Yes. The evening meal is ready. Are you coming?"

A blush had crept up over her cheeks at the lazy intent stare, and she managed to stammer an answer, "Yes, yes, of course."

Leveling his lithe body up from the reclining position at the door, he let her pass through before moving up next to her. Together they walked down the hall to the dining area.

CHAPTER ELEVEN

Snuggling deeper into the plush, dark gold-brown chair; Randi rested her head against the large back cushion, her eyes closed. Quietly she listened to the soft, soothing music that drifted gently around her.

It was a relaxed atmosphere in the large, yet cozy, living room, with the lamps turned down low. Even with the unmistakable masculine presence of her newly acquired husband sitting in the chair just an arm's length away, she felt able to curl up in the warmth of the cushions and unwind from all the earlier tensions. The night sounds drifted in through the open patio doors, mingling with the soft tunes coming from the extensive CD collection.

Moving her head slightly, Randi was able to see the relaxed length of the blonde-haired man through the curtain of her lashes. He had his long, lean legs stretched out in front of him, his arms resting on either side of the chair with his hands folded carelessly across the broad expanse of well-muscled chest. Above the sound of the soft playing music, she asked quietly, "Jay, I've a question or two I'd like answered. If you don't mind, that is?"

His eyes opened slowly, yet she could see the smoky-grayness of them through the gold-tipped lashes. Stretching lazily, he questioned, "What do you want to know?"

"You might think it is silly, but well, here goes. For the very unliberated attitude of this area it seems to me that you sure know your way around the female anatomy. You sure as hell don't kiss like an inexperienced innocent."

A deep, very pleasant chuckle sounded. "You mean I don't act the part of a recluse? Well, I'm not."

Randi's dark-green eyes opened wider. "Okay, so you are not a recluse. But why was it so damn important that you get married? And to me? I just don't understand."

Leaning forward onto his elbows, Jay grinned. "Look, it's a whole different world out here. In the city I could have a harem for all anyone would care. Maybe a few raised eyebrows. But, that's in the city. Once in the outback, well, the code changes.

"I've had my share of escorting all the eligible neighboring daughters, cousins, or just visiting relations. When you own a rather large station and a bachelor, you end up having every assuming mother introducing you to their perfect daughters. But while out here it is strictly platonic until the situations change and become serious."

Stretching out her legs, she looked over at his shadowed features. "Okay. I suppose you have known quite a few desirable women?"

He eyed her carefully, but answered in a calm, steady voice. "Yes, I've had a few women friends. Affairs, if you like. Nothing to shock the world. I've had a few pictures in the magazines. It is hard to hide from the press. What's all this leading to?"

Resting her burnished head back against the chair, she smiled disarmingly. "If you had a close relationship going, why did you marry me? Wouldn't it have been better to have married someone you knew?"

With a swift, startling movement Jay hoisted himself up out of the chair and walked stiffly a few paces. His face hardening into ridged lines. "I don't have any close enough relationships to want to marry any of them. And if you remember; it was you that the rumors were about. Your name, what you look like. It would have looked rather phony to have turned up with a different woman as my wife."

She, too, rose to her feet; then immediately wished she had remained seated. His tall form seemed to tower over her much smaller one. "I'm sorry. I just didn't understand. I hadn't realized, that's all." Slowly she slumped back down into the dark, gold-brown chair.

Jay moved over to the large fireplace and leaned against the mantle, his smoky-colored eyes resting on her down bent face. "I can understand your confusion. But to clarify the reasons why I married you and then decided to make our marriage a real one are basically simple. Like I said I just didn't see any other way; and then well, about making it a real marriage in every sense, well you have to admit that there is a very strong attraction. On both sides. We were rubbing sparks off of each other from the very first. We were attracted to each other that night of the storm. Good old fashion healthy desire. Sounds like as good a reason to start my more mature life. Don't you think? Besides with lying in bed beside me it would have happen sooner or later. I'm a man and the attraction or desire is there."

Burning color swept over her delicate features and she avoided meeting his eyes. He was correct of course, for him. Before she could form any kind of reply, Jay was asking a question of his own.

"I know it is a little late in the asking, but is there anyone you should notify that you are married? Parents?"

Sighing shakily, Randi shook her head. "No one. My parents died in a car accident when I was fifteen. I have an older sister, Barb. She is married with a family of her own. I'll let her know. She'll be thrilled." And she laughed softly. Relaxing once again.

Jay watched her small expressive face. He liked the sound of her laugh. He liked her. Hell, he wanted her. Totally.

"I'm sorry to hear about your folks. Is your sister much older than you?"

Randi looked up from under the dark, thick lashes. "Quite a bit really. She is fourteen years older. Has two kids, Terry and Barry. Both boys. Her husband, Tim Nelson, is a real dear. But, I think she was more than glad to have me gone. Now she will be in seventh heaven." A smile touched her lips. "So you have nothing to worry about. No enraged father storming the gates."

He smiled. He was terribly handsome when he did that, Randi thought. Tilting her head to one side, she glanced up at him. "Don't get me wrong, my sister and I have always been fairly friendly, but we are as different as night and day."

Running his fingers unconsciously through the sun-lightened blonde hair, Jay asked curiously, "Are either one of your sister's boys red headed?"

Randi chuckled. "Nope. I was the only redhead in our immediate family. Guess you might say I was the odd one out. My mother once said that the red hair turned up around every fourth generation. My sister has dark hair and brown eyes. Not only are we different in personality, but also in physical appearance." Then frowning slightly, she asked, "What about 'Missy Darla'? How is she going to take the news of you acquiring a wife?"

A smile on the tanned face spread into a full grin. "We won't have too long to find out." At the questioning look that seeped into the dark-green eyes, he added, "Darla Russell and her brother, Carl, are having a large get-together at their station, Bangon, in three days. It is to be a bar-b-cue. Casual clothes during the festivities and then fancy clothes for the dance in the evening. Think you will be able to handle it? Darla is very sophisticated."

A hard glint entered the usually warm green-gray eyes. "Wouldn't think of missing the lady's party. Do you think Ray Proctor will be there?"

JR nodded slowly. "More than likely. Do I dare ask why you are wanting to know?"

"Sure. He was telling me how everyone out here loved any reason to get together. And then he made me promise to be sure to invite him to any of GetAway's. He said that GetAway always had one of the best in the county. Just figured he would want to be at this one too."

Lewis smiled again. "That sounds like Ray. When you see him, why don't you invite him to GetAway for the annual races and bar-b-cue?"

Surprise washed over her features. "Here?"

"Yes. It is a really big event. Stations for miles around and some from all over the country come and bring their best horses. Different stations have races throughout the year. It lasts two days usually and on the final evening we have a dance. Outside, unless it storms." Seeing the intent excitement registering on her face, he continued, "You will be introduced to most all the locals at the Russell's, so you will be prepared for the big event."

"Sounds exciting. Does GetAway have a horse in the races?"

"More than one. Any stockman can enter his favorite mount. If Tom could have his way, he'd have you riding. You really impressed him with your ability."

A blush warmed her cheeks. "Why that's nice. My ego has climbed tremendously. Could I? Ride, I mean?"

A frown touched his mouth briefly. "I don't know. It can be terribly dangerous. We'll have to see." At the mutinous expression, he remarked, "Now, don't go getting mulish on me. I said we would see. It is a good two month's off. Let's look to the Bangon party for now."

"Alright." She conceded. "Jay, can I see little Kerry tomorrow, do you think?"

Lewis moved over to where she was curled up in the chair. Reaching out his hand, the strong tanned fingers circled her slender wrist and gently pulled her into his arms. "Yes, Little One, you will see Kerry tomorrow. Tico asked if she could bring the little button with her in the morning."

"Oh." Randi breathed the single word through trembling lips. Then as Jay swung her up against him, she could hear the loud, fast pounding of her heart. Under her hand, she could feel the answering throb of Jay's heart. Afraid to look up for fear of letting him see the confused desire in her eyes, she kept her head on a level with his chest. Until, that is, warm strong fingers gently gripped her small chin and tilted her face up to meet the lips that took hers in a possessive, yet reassuring kiss.

A kiss that deepened, sending a warmth spreading throughout her body. Randi responded to the kiss, as it demanded she should. Her small, slender curves seemed to melt within Jay's embrace.

Moving slightly away from her, lifting his mouth from her desire bruised lips, he kissed her tenderly on the nose.

His voice deep and husky, he said, "You better head on to bed. You have had a very exhausting day. Couple of days, really."

Randi rested her forehead on his hard-muscled chest. "Yes. I am tired." Then with a faint sigh, "What about you? You must be as beat as I am?"

A tired grin flickered across the firm lips. "I've some paperwork to catch up on with the accountant, Ted, then I'll be able to hit the sack, too."

Randi stepped back and swept her glance over his face. A face she found very unreadable right then. Nodding slowly, she moved to the open doorway. "Okay. Don't work too long. Night, Jay."

"Good night, Randi." Whispered Lewis softly; but the girl had heard for she smiled, then walked out of the room.

For a moment, Jay just stood there staring at the vacant doorway. Then with a tired shake of his blonde head, he headed toward the study and Ted.

CHAPTER TWELVE

Bright sunlight drifted in through the partly shaded windows. Slowly and very reluctantly Randi opened sleepy gray-green eyes and stretched lazily. Then remembering where she was, she cautiously turned her head; but found no tanned male figure lying there.

Looking even closer she could not even be sure that he had slept there at all. Had he remained in the study all night? Leaning back against the pillows, the misty-green eyes gazed at the low, white ceiling. Last night she had waited what seemed like forever for him to come to bed. She decided that if Jay wanted to make the marriage real in every sense, she would do so.

She had been tense, scared; but at the same time excited. And when he had not appeared even after two in morning, she had reluctantly fallen asleep. Now she found that she was desperately disappointed.

Frowning, she glanced over at the bedside clock. Eight-thirty! Jay would have been up ages by now. He would even have had breakfast by now. Without her.

Closing her eyes against the sudden pain of rejection, she sighed sadly and moved to get up. Well, what had she expected? Especially after throwing a first class fit the first time he mentioned sharing the same bedroom.

Swinging her long, slender legs out from under the covers a soft tap sounded on the closed bedroom door. Thinking it would be the housekeeper, Tico, Randi called out quietly, "Come in."

As the door glided open, Jay's tall, muscular form walked through carrying a tray. His face was smooth and the blonde hair dark and damp from a recent shower. He was dressed casually in denim jeans and a soft shirt open over the broad chest. Looking up into the bronzed features once again, she found a gentle smile touching the very male lips.

"Good morning, Little One. Thought you might want some breakfast." Drawled the silky voice.

The gray eyes took in the confused flush on the small oval face and the tantalizing long length of leg that appeared over the side of the bed.

"Thank you. I had no idea….I thought you would be out…." Stammered Randi, her confusion increasing. "How did you know I was up?"

The smile widened and the lean figure stepped farther into the room, a booted foot effortlessly closed the door. "Just good timing. Now crawl back under the covers and lean up against the pillows. This tray will fit right over your lap."

As she hurriedly did so, she could feel him watching her every move. The gown she was wearing was soft as silk and very sheer. Thankfully as she glanced downward, she noted that the soft material gathered in filmy, but concealing folds over her small breasts. Looking up as the loaded tray was placed gently on her legs, her eyes met the amused gray ones. Warm color flooded her features.

"I thought I'd sit with you and have my coffee. You don't mind, do you?" he drawled easily, his eyes never leaving her face.

"No….no, not at all." Stammered Randi.

Instead of sitting in the nearby chair like she thought he would, he sat down on the bed beside her. His weight causing the mattress to give under him, bringing her closer to him.

Taking a swallow of the fresh, chilled orange juice, she let her glance run over his lean, muscled length. "You've had breakfast, I imagine?"

He nodded his head slightly. "Yes. Around seven. Had to go out to the far paddocks to check on some breed stock. So I was out earlier than usual." Throwing that cool gray glance at her again, he asked, "How did you sleep?"

Keeping her glance on the tray in front of her, she answered carefully, "Fine really. Took me quite a while to get to sleep; but after that I don't remember a thing until this morning."

Still not looking at him, "You must not have had much sleep yourself?"

"No, I didn't. Ted had to go over everything; and then by the time we had finished it was so late I managed on the sofa in the study. I knew I would be up early to look at that stock. Didn't want to disturb you. Your first night and all."

His voice was soft and she could not tell if he was laughing at her or not. Yet, she couldn't bring herself to look into the dark-tanned features. Her emotions were in a turmoil. Excitement coursed through her at the very nearness of him and hesitating at her ability to handle it. Would she let him down?

Her small, even, very white teeth crunched into the last slice of buttery toast. Across her line of vision, a dark-tanned masculine hand reached over and gently set the empty coffee cup on the tray.

"Are you finished?" drawled that same husky-male voice. At her nod, he took the tray from her and sat it easily on the carpeted floor at his side of the bed.

Before she had any idea of what he was about, he leaned over her and kissed her mouth. A firm, gentle kiss. Warmth curled up from her stomach to spread through her chest. His tongue flicked out and ran over his lips. "Mmm. You taste of butter."

"Oh." Her eyes still on his mouth, almost in fascination.

"Yes, oh." He murmured softly, in a husky whisper. The strong, warm hands slid over her shoulders, pushing her down farther onto the downy softness.

Dark-green startled eyes looked up into his very determined gray ones. Slowly as his head lowered to kiss her again, her eyes fluttered closed. The lean fingers moved up to hold her chin, leaving burning trails of pleasure behind.

Trembling started somewhere deep inside her. The kiss became firmer, more possessive and as he parted her lips, desire licked through her like burning flames. He was devouring her and she was responding. She could not help it. She needed him. Her slight, soft body seemed to melt and mold itself to his long, male length.

Her fingers tangled in the gold-tipped hair of his chest and she could feel the heat of his body through the thin layer of clothes between them. His heart was beating strong and pounding under her fingertips. As desire rippled through her slender, burning frame, she arched her body closer to his.

A dull thump reached her ears moments before the weight of his muscled leg curled over her lower body, pinning her closely to his lean, masculine shape. She could feel the growing hardness of his passion against her body.

His lips moved to her ear, his tongue traced the delicate-shaped lobe and sent shivers racing up and down her trembling frame. His voice, soft and husky, whispered against her hair, "I want you, Little One. I want to make love to you now."

A tremor rippled through her shaking limbs at his words, but she offered no real resistance. She was past the point of turning back. There was a growing emptiness inside her that only he could fill. How she knew this was beyond her, but know it she did.

As his firm lips again claimed her tender mouth, his hands slipped the filmy material off her shoulders; the fingers moving sensuously over her collarbone to the small, rounded breasts. Gently his thumb rubbed across the hardening pale rose-colored nipples, sending a breathless groan of pleasure and surprise escaping through her lips. As the havoc-causing fingers moved farther down to her ribcage, he lowered his head and softly kissed and licked the swelling young breasts. As his hand slid warmly over her flat, smooth stomach, she was lost to the swarm of emotion that seemed to engulf her whole being.

With his free hand he had managed to unbutton his own shirt and deftly slid out of the denim jeans. His body, hard, warm and at the same time comforting; slipped in beside and slightly over her under the coolness of the sheets. She felt the soft tickle of his body hair against her now sensitive skin. Straining to be closer, even closer to him, she mumbled words, words she did not even know she was saying. Words of longing, desire; of love?

Briefly panic threatened to overwhelm her and instinctively the slight frame stiffened, then as a husky, soft male voice reached her, she relaxed and once again melted against the strong, masculine body.

"I won't hurt you, Randi. But, God, I want you. I need you….."

With rising desire and passion his hands caressed her, bringing her to peaks of excitement and pleasure she never knew existed. Then with his mouth on hers. His body, his utter maleness, penetrated her very feminine, untouched body. Totally. With the briefest of pain that erupted into total rapture, she reached the peak of pleasure as he, too, laid claim to that same pinnacle of desire and fullest satisfaction.

Afterwards the strong, tanned arms encircled her, pulling her into the security and warmth of his body. His breathe stirred the hair at her temple and ear moments before his lips touched her cheek and then the firm, yet delicate jawline. A pleasing tremble shivered through her and carefully she peeked at him through the dark, long lashes. Only to find the gray eyes, a strange softness in their depths, staring gently back at her.

A shaky smile touched her lips.

An answering smile flashed on his. "You're very pretty lying there in my arms. Your face all flushed from being made love to."

Deeper color washed over the fine features, turning the green-gray eyes to emerald. The lips parted, but no words would come.

Hugging her close, he tucked her burnished head under his chin. Í didn't hurt you, did I?"

A swift shake of the head against him was his answer. Touching his lips to the bright, satin-smooth hair, he asked softly, "Did I frighten you? It was the first time, wasn't it, Randi?"

A smothered voice came somewhere near his chest. "Yes, the first time. And no, you never frightened me. Not really. It was…..it….."

"Never mind, I understand." Grinned Jay to himself. And for the first time in over forty-eight hours, he relaxed his tense muscled body and sighed, leaned back against the pillows and pulled the soft, warm woman closer to him.

Sudden mischief leaped in the now emerald-green eyes. Leaning her head back, she smiled up into his bronzed handsome features, "Was the sofa very comfortable?"

"Oh, yes. If you can imagine an over six foot frame on a five foot sofa? Ha!" came the quiet, drawling voice.

A soft chuckle sounded in her throat as she snuggled into his arms. "You must have looked real cute with your feet hanging out."

"You think so?" he chuckled also. Then twisting her under him, steely fingers flashed to her exposed ribs.

Laughter bubbled from her as the swift fingers sent shivers along her ribcage. Twisting and turning, she tried to get away from the teasing. "Jay, stop it. Ooh!"

Swiftly he leaned forward and covered her mouth with his. Her arms went around his neck as she kissed him back. Reluctantly taking his lips from hers, he shifted back and looked down into her small oval face. Then a soft smile touched his mouth. "We better get up and get dressed. Kerry will be here around eleven. I think Tico is just bursting with motherly excitement in being able to show-off her pride and joy."

"Then we better hurry." Grinned Randi, a small dimple appearing in her cheek. Realizing the state of her undress, a blush swept up over her cheekbones to her hairline.

Seeing her sudden embarrassment, Jay kissed her lightly on the nose and reached past her, picking up the filmy robe that matched the now discarded gown. "Here, I'll go first. Meet you on the patio, right?"

At her nod, he rose from the bed, his well-muscled body glowing tan as he moved with cat-like strides across the carpeted floor to the connecting bathroom. As he disappeared behind the closing door, a shaky sigh escaped through her lips. He wasn't the least bit embarrassed as he walked nude to the bathroom. Why should he be; he had a wonderful body. Every inch of that strong, lean sun-kissed body.

Swiftly she changed her thoughts to getting up and pulling on the robe.

CHAPTER THIRTEEN

Leaning back leisurely in the lounge chair with its dusty-orange colored terry covers, Randi let a pleased sigh softly escape. With a wide, brilliantly blue sky overhead and warm golden sunshine touching the creamy skin of her lightly-tanned face, she felt in a strange vacuum of security.

Jay lounged quietly not far from where she was sitting, his blonde hair appearing even lighter in the white glare of the warming sunlight. His features bronzed and healthy. Studying his clear cut profile through the thick fringe of lashes, she tried to decipher his present mood. Was he feeling as satisfied, as pleasantly aroused as she was?

Eyes, misty-green and thoughtful, swept casually over the long leanness of the man beside her. Traveling back up over the broad, muscled shoulders to the classic tanned face, she encountered smoky-gray eyes.

A smile touched the firm male lips. "Meet with your approval?"

Warm color flowed swiftly over the delicate features. Then before she could form any kind of answer, a very clear, young voice drifted to them from just beyond the tree-shaded verandah.

"Boss….I got uh dunkum fella…."

A moment later a small, curly-haired little figure came stumbling around the screened porch, his chubby arms trying to hang on to the bundle of multi-colored fur that was almost as big as he was.

Jay rose to his feet and approached the little boy. "Well, Kerry, what have you got there?"

Big wine-colored brown eyes gazed up to meet the gray. "Pup, Boss."

"Quite a bundle." Grinned Jay as he squatted down on his haunches to be on a more equal level with the boy. Glancing over a shoulder, he called, "Randi, come on over and meet my number one fella and his dog."

Randi uncurled her slender, blue jean clad form and moved the short distance to the young boy and man. A friendly smile came to her lips as she knelt down in front of the six-year-old.

The dark eyes watched the young missy and as she tilted her head to look at the wiggling puppy, the sun caught the fiery glow in the red hair; so it appeared as almost liquid fire. To the small boy, at least.

The little figure straightened. Stiff with awe and fear. The dark eyes wide and then with a chubby finger he pointed to the bright hair. "Mourra, mourra…."

Swiftly, yet quietly the man reached forward and grasped the boy's wrist, his voice soft and low. "Good magic, Kerry. See….." and with his other hand, tangled the lean fingers in the long, silky strains.

The wine-brown eyes lost the frightened look and shifted from the Boss to the little Missy and then back. "Sun magic? No burn?"

Jay grinned. "No burn."

Green eyes looked from the small boy to the man. "My hair?"

The rancher nodded. "Yes. With the sun hitting it, it looks like fire. The word has to do with sun taboo. Magic."

Slowly she nodded her head in understanding. Pulling the long, shining hair forward over her shoulder, she spoke quietly to the little dusky-skinned boy. "Kerry, would you like to feel?"

A hesitant hand moved and little fingers touched the shimmering silky strains. A smile flashed on the small, piquant face. "Good magic, Missy."

Unconsciously she felt herself beginning to relax. Looking down at the lively bundle of multi-colored fur that was trying to climb onto her knee, Randi smiled and gently lifted the tiny puppy up into her arms.

"He's adorable, Kerry. What have you named him?"

"Bandy, Missy."

Glancing at the rancher, Jay answered her unspoken question. "He's an Australian Cattle dog, sometimes called a Heeler. The mother is a red speckled. The sire is a silver-gray, blue speckled. His name is Smoke. He's been regional champion two years in a row. One of the best herding dogs around. You'll see him around; he's never very far away. I think he's down by the horse barns. There are two other pups. One is a red mottled, the other is blue mottled with black and tan. This is her first litter."

Then with a gentle hand, he reached out and rumpled the small boy's dark curly hair. "How 'bout we show Randi the other pups?"

The small head nodded and his tiny hand curled into Randi's as she got to her feet, still holding the bundle of warm fur. Once again she smiled, "Lead the way, men."

Jay matched his longer stride to their shorter ones. Every now and then his silvery glance would slip over the redhead's face. Taking in her unconscious pleasure of the small child's company. The young pup, too, had taken to her; snuggling in close to her side, pressing his dark nose in the hollow of her collarbone.

She was talking to the boy and listening to his answers with interest and giving the youngster a feeling of authority. A trait that many young adults seemed to lack. As they neared the corrals, a slender velvet-black nose swung over the top rail of the fence. A loud whinny shot through the morning stillness.

"He seems to remember you, Randi." Drawled the rancher with a dry chuckle. His gray glance shifting from the slender gelding to the equally slender girl.

"He does at that. He's a marvelous little horse." She replied with a smile in her voice. Though she had caught the seemingly doubtful chuckle of the rancher. But she chose to ignore it.

"I hadn't noticed at the time just which horse you had taken. I was surprised that Tom had let you ride that one. He's pretty and looks dainty, but he is noted for his; shall we say, bad manners." The masculine mouth twisted humorlessly.

Randi stopped, pulling the silent boy to a halt at the same time. Her face was stiffening slightly as she said, "I had no problem with him. Other than he's spirited and damn game for anything. I took him. I took full responsibility for any trouble that might have happen, leaving Tom with little choice in the matter. He isn't a mustang; he's too refined for that. So what exactly is wrong with him, not to meet with your approval?"

Jay straightened, a frown marking his tanned handsome features. "He's not a brumby. You've been reading too many American West magazines."

Angrily Randi interrupted. "A mustang is a wild horse. A wild horse is a brumby. So what the hell; the roan isn't a wild horse."

With tightened lips Jay continued, "No, he isn't one. But, he is on the small side for any of the larger men to want to handle; or for that matter some of the women who ride. And when anyone has attempted to ride him they've had nothing but trouble."

Without asking Randi had a good idea who the 'lady' was who rode, Darla? But the idea that the spunky little horse was branded as unmanageable was totally unthinkable. Then as she was about to tell this arrogant rancher so; a soft, clear voice sounded from beside her. Kerry, who had managed to hang onto her hand through the whole of the discussion and who had heard the words said, now spoke up in defense of the redhead.

"But Missy rode like top stockman. My Dad say so."

"Too right." Laughed Randi teasingly. "Sand is just a damn sight smarter than some of the riders apparently." And she threw an angry glare at the stubborn faced rancher. Then before anymore could be said, she added, "Now, let's go see the rest of Bandy's family."

Kerry did not wait on ceremony, but pulled Randi toward the closest barn. As they stepped inside a shadow seemed to emerge right out of the thin air. One moment there was nothing, then there he was. A silver shadow. His head was lowered, the hair along is back was raised. Then sensing that they meant no harm to his little family, the slender nose came up and the tail wagged briefly.

Gently Randi set the stocky Bandy on the straw-covered floor and at seeing his father, the pup made a rolling leap at the very dignified adult dog. Swiftly the grayish dog moved aside and with a decisive grunt had the pup by the ruff of the neck and was returning it to his mother. The three humans followed in behind the prideful parent,

The other two pups were sitting quietly in front of the red speckled mother dog, one a red mottled and the other a blue mottled with black and tan. Then as Smoke dropped his bundle gently on the straw, the multi-colored Bandy jumped on his two sisters. His little furry body sprawled out comically. In seconds all three were in a rough-n-tumble game.

Kerry squealed with delight and almost immediately was joining in with the playful pups. Randi glanced up and met the icy-gray eyes of the rancher staring at her. With a curt nod of the head, he motioned her out of the barn stall.

Stepping out into the sunlight, JR once again looked over at the red haired woman at his side. With a sigh he acknowledged that the submissive female of the morning was once again replaced by the little aggressive creature he had first met on the back of the bad mannered roan gelding. "I've got to go out to a bore hole north of the station about twenty miles. I'll be back at sundown in time for dinner. I'm sure you can find plenty to do within the house. The rest of the men will be out branding in the west paddocks all afternoon."

Randi halted and looked up at the tall rancher. A sudden sadness sweeping gently over her. "I think I might ride out to the branding for a while."

"No. I want you staying off the roan." Interrupted Jay in a stiff voice.

"Are you telling me I can't ride the gelding? Is that what you are doing, Jay?" she breathed through stiffening lips. Rebellion very evident on the delicate features.

Narrowing the gray eyes, he looked down at her flushed face and angry eyes. "Yes. Yes, that is what I am saying. No arguments, Randi, just stay at the house today until we can settle this between us. Now, I've got to get going. I'll see you tonight." Then with a decisive move, he turned her around and pushed her in the direction of the front verandah.

Without looking back, Randi marched to the porch. Tears blurring her vision. Tears of frustration and anger, also hurt. She felt let down somehow. Disappointed in Jay's strange attitude. Also the small fact that he hadn't even kissed her good-bye. Not even a brotherly peck on the cheek.

Swinging in through the doorway that led down the hallway, she came to an abrupt halt. Maybe the morning's lovemaking had not been what she had thought. Maybe it had been to put a seal on her staying so the Lewis name was in the clear? JR had not once said that he loved her only that he wanted her. Had she?

"Missy, are you lost?" chuckled Tico from the open doorway leading into the day room.

Pulling her features into a forced smile, Randi said as lightly as she could manage. "Well, sort of, Tico. Could you show me where the Boss's office is located? I'm supposed to type up some papers for Jay."

"Shore thing, Missy. It's right this way, down past the kitchen." Smiled the housekeeper.

"Oh, Tico, your son, Kerry is with the puppies in the barn stall."

"Thank you, Missy. He loves them pups." Smiled the dusky-skinned woman.

An hour later, Randi found herself mounted on the roan gelding and skimming effortlessly over the tall, pale grass. In the distance she could barely make out the forms of the gathered stockmen, but she could hear their voices and the lowing of the cattle.

Frowning slightly, she knew she was disobeying orders. But she was angry and more than willing to show JR Lewis that she wasn't afraid of him. Or that the gelding was in no way dangerous to ride. Getting closer to the branding camp, she could feel the excitement build. She would help with the roping of the calves. She was a first class hand. Oops, that was the American West showing through again. And she smiled to herself. Magazines, JR had said. Wonder what he would say if he knew it had been firsthand knowledge? Wonder what he would have to say when her saddle and equipment arrived from back home? She had emailed her sister, and after telling her briefly what had happen her sister had promised to mail her stuff to her right away.

Catching sight of the wiry-built Tom, she swung the roan in the stockman's direction. At hearing the sound of the gelding's hooves on the hard-packed ground, Tom looked up and seeing who it was, broke into a smile of greeting.

"Aah, Missy. Good to see you. We plenty busy, but time for smoko."

A look of puzzlement crossed over her delicate face. "Smoko? I'm sorry, Tom, but what is that?"

A grin split the dark handsome features. "It is a break. We enjoy billy tea." At her still confused expression, the head stockman searched for the right wording. "Hot tea in a tin cup."

Slowly Randi nodded her autumn-colored head. "Okay, I understand now, Tom. Can I join you?"

"Sure enough, Missy. Come on along." Nodded the lean-built man. At nearing the small cluster of men, Tom called to Ben to take the two horses.

Stepping down from the gelding, Randi smiled a greeting to the younger stockman. His equally dark handsome face smiling in return. Moving toward the campfire the head stockman made the introductions of the other stockmen that she had not met before. Their young curious faces watched her with reserve and a sort of awe. Respect, too, because she was the Boss man's wife.

In actual fact she was not far wrong in her assumption of their opinion of her. But they were more surprised at her slender gracefulness and the mere fact that she had ridden up on the roany horse. Their dark, liquid brown eyes were fastened on her face, the greenish eyes fascinating them. Then as she sat down among them and removed the hat, sending the silky hair pouring down her back like liquid fire; not a sound could be heard. At the sudden stillness, her green-gray eyes widened and she looked to Tom for an explanation. Then before he could open his lips, she remembered little Kerry's reaction to her fiery hair and she smiled.

"Tom, tell them its good magic. Not taboo. Please?"

Tom nodded and smiled. He gently explained to the men. Soon they were smiling and nodding in agreement. Turning back to her and handing her a billy can at the same time, he stated in a soft voice, "They think Boss Lewis got fine magic."

A soft pink blush rose up over her features as she smiled back. "Good."

The tea was hot and for coming out of a tin cup tasted surprisingly delicious. All too soon the break time was over and the stockmen started for their mounts. Glancing over at the wiry Tom, she rose and walked to where he stood. "Tom, would you care if I helped out with the muster? I can ride as you know and I have worked cattle. I could bring in the young calves for the branding and vaccinations. Well, how about it?"

Tom looked at her, a slight frown marring his dark face. He knew the boss would not appreciate her doing men's work, but she appeared to so want to. And yes she could ride. Maybe his stockmen would improve if they saw this slip of a girl ride? So with a firm nod of his slightly graying curly head, he let her join in.

As the afternoon wore on he came to admit that she knew quite a bit concerning cattle and horses. And what had really impressed the lean, wiry men was when she took out after a particularly stubborn, rather large calf. The dark-red roan gelding moving in with controlled speed and heading the calf off at every turn, then out came the long, coiled lasso. It slipped effortlessly over the bull calf's head and suddenly the gelding was sitting clear back on his haunches. And with a triumphant smile on her dust streaked face, she turned the ever willing gelding back toward the branding crew with the still protesting calf trailing along behind. The men gave signs of victory and some even cheered softly.

Randi, sometime later, pulled the red roan to a halt and rubbed an arm across her perspiring forehead, leaving a dust mark over one temple. She felt tired, but oh so happy. Tom rode up and grinned his friendly smile. "Time we headed in."

"Oh, is it that late already?" frowned the redhead. Until now she had forgot about Jay's order not to come out to the muster. A slight uneasiness curled in the pit of her stomach.

Seeing her pretty face sort of tense up and the green eyes cloud, Tom moved his own mount in closer. "The Boss not want you here?" At her slow nod, he shook his graying head. "Be a surprised Boss, huh?" And then he smiled at her, a conspiratorial smile. And she gently smiled in return.

CHAPTER FOURTEEN

The western skyline was a blaze with brilliant color as the small group rode into the homestead. Randi reached up and pulled the bush hat farther down, hiding her eyes. It was strictly a self-defense ploy. She had seen the angry-stiff form of her husband as he stood near the corral fence. His lean tanned face was also in shadow, just the stubborn jawline showing. That and the grim straight line of his mouth.

Once again Randi felt that curl of apprehension in her lower stomach. Only this time it seemed to spread throughout her slender body. Finding that she was actually holding her breath, she slowly let it out through stiff, almost colorless lips. Glancing sideways she met the sympathetic brown eyes of the head stockman.

A wan smile moved fleetingly over her mobile mouth. "I think the Boss is a little upset with me, Tom." Down right boiling mad, she muttered to herself.

Tom nodded and threw a glance in the direction of the waiting rancher. The dark-skinned handsome face frowned slightly. He knew his boss pretty well and the angry, stiff-legged man standing near the fence was totally out of character. Sadly he shook his graying head. "Keep your back straight, Missy. You can handle it; you done handled that bull calf. You one of my top stockmen."

"Ooh, thank you, Tom, but maybe we better not tell Boss Lewis everything just yet. He-uh-might not understand. Okay?" asked the redhead nervously.

The stockman just nodded, then they were pulling up beside the tall, displeased rancher. Slipping out of the saddle, Randi made to lead the roan toward the tack room; when a steely hand reached out and gripped her arm. Her whole body hardening in defiance, she stood with her face still partly in shadow, waiting.....

The quiet cool ring of authority simmered in the silky male voice as the rancher ordered Ben to take care of the gelding. The Aborigine youth silently nodded his dark curly head and took the reins from the girl's fingers.

Looking up and meeting his head stockman's questioning dark eyes, Jay remarked dryly, "That's all for now, Tom. I'll talk to you later."

A brief nod and the stockman moved on leading his own mount. The uncertainty still lingering in the velvet-brown eyes. Maybe he should tell Lewis just how competent the little Missy was with both cattle and horses. Besides the knowledge of the American way of cowboying that she had briefly shown them. But she had wanted him to not tell the Boss. Not yet she had said, so he wouldn't. Not that or the secret plans they had made concerning the up-coming races and the roan.

Watching Tom move away, Jay kept his fingers tightly around the slender-boned wrist of the redhead. His anger had continued to simmer ever since he had arrived back at the homestead to find that Randi had purposely disobeyed him and had rode the gelding and then had the audacity to go out to the mustering. Barely able to contain his temper, he stepped forward briskly forcing the girl to move with him.

Suddenly Randi felt the hot flare of her own temper explode and she firmly planted her feet and turned to face the tall, angry man. At the swift unpredictable move of the small-sized bundle of enraged female, the rancher came to an impatient halt beside her.

"I'm not a child to be hauled into the house. So you just take your mitts off of me!" stormed Randi, her face pale and eyes flashing green fire.

"You had me fooled." Came the cool rejoinder. "You are giving a damn good performance of a spoiled brat right now."

Stamping her foot in angry frustration, she tried to yank her arm free of his dominating hold. Her face that had been so pale with fury now became surfaced with hot color. Embarrassed color at how childish the hopeless struggle must appear to others. Tears weld up in the fiery green of her eyes. Damn him!

"It's your fault. All of it." She breathed through stiff lips.

"Just because you never grew up, don't take it out on me. To the house, Brat. Under your own steam or I'll pick you up and carry you." Ordered Jay with cool impatience.

At first numbed shock held her still and silent, but then as the words he had said sank in, she turned on him with renewed rage. "Oh you will, will you! You opinionated ass."

Dark embarrassed color swept up under the tanned features at her words, his lips thinned. With little patience and a lot of force he angrily yanked her slim shape up against his hard length. "I warned you, you little hellcat." Came the muttered threat.

With desperation Randi strained back away from the warmth of his chest and thighs, her hands against the hard muscled wall of his chest. Flashing a burning glance at the unyielding face above her, Randi planted a hard-booted toe against Jay's unprotected shin. A savage oath ripped from the man at the sharp pain inflicted on his leg.

With an exasperated groan, JR twisted her around and effortlessly slung her still struggling form up and over one well-muscled shoulder like a sack of grain. With clinched fists she plummeted his broad back and at the same time made to kick out at him, causing him to lose his hold on her. With a sharp, hard slap he smacked her on the bottom.

"You big brute! You are a bully, JR. Put me down at once."

"Not on your life. I'll put you down when I'm damn good and ready, and not before." Came the angry-stiff voice and the arm tightened around her.

He walked past the front of the house and around to the back verandah. Sweeping up the few steps to the enclosed porch, he turned and marched into the office/den, where she had been earlier that same afternoon. Stepping close to the leather couch that was set against the deep-wood paneled wall, Jay deftly lifted her and almost tossed her onto the leather softness. Looking up she met icy-gray eyes, the color of storm clouds.

A chill of fear rippled up her spine at the icy-hot glare in the granite-hard eyes. Her own face must be red from her upside down position, whereas his was pale under his tan, from anger.

Jay stood looking down at the slim slip of a girl willing his anger to subside. Taking a deep, steading breath, the muscles in his jaw bunching, he frowned and asked, "Why did you disobey my wishes and ride the gelding?"

Releasing a shaky breath, anger still glimmering in the gem-colored eyes, Randi countered, "Why did you order me not to ride the roan?"

With his features set in hard, uncompromising lines, Jay remained standing close to her sitting form. Almost towering over her, Randi thought angrily to herself. Still she managed to challenge the steely, narrowed eyes of the rancher.

"I don't think the roan is safe for a girl like you to handle. You should have waited until I could have talked more with you when I returned from the bore." Spoke the calm, low voice.

Taking a deep angered breath, Randi muttered in low simmering tones, "I couldn't handle the horse? How in the hell would you know? So far I've been the only one who has been able to handle him; but what gets me is that I haven't found him any sort of problem at all. Maybe whoever tried riding him before didn't know what they were about? And what do you mean, a girl like me?"

Jay paced irritably to the front of the desk and then back to where she still sat. "Darla is a very fine horsewoman. The horse just isn't trust worthy. And I was referring to your small size. You wouldn't have the strength to hold a bolting horse."

A dry humorless chuckle escaped through her tightening throat. "You are telling me I can't stop a bolting horse; because the fine classy Missy Darla couldn't manage a pint-sized spirited gelding? She might be a fine horsewoman when it comes to high class well-disciplined equine. I'm surprised she didn't try to ride the horse sidesaddle. I'm even more surprised that the lady would humble herself to ride a small, range-rough horse." At seeing the dark color stain the rancher's tanned neck, Randi jumped in with both feet. "She didn't like the idea, did she, Jay? Your high society lady friend is nothing more than an irresponsible snob!"

"That's enough, Randi." Thundered Jay. "Leave Darla out of this. It has nothing to do with her."

Rising up out of the leather softness, Randi challenged hotly, "I'm sorry but it sure as hell does. You condemn the roan on what she says. And me, too, for that matter. Get this Mister JR Lewis, that roan gelding is not a dangerous mount. And I'm not a child to be told to stay in my room until I can behave myself. I'm an adult and I have taken care of myself for longer than you have. And another thing for you to file away in that steel trap of a mind of yours, I'm not a rich citified little bitch. I'm not a rich anything! I've worked hard for my living and I've worked with horses and cattle. Even got my little hands dirty. That would really tear your lady friend up. You better face the fact that you are married to a tomboy. That's the way I am. Not a child playing cowboys for the thrill of it." Tears of anger, hurt pride and helplessness spilled out through the thick fringe of lashes, but she swiftly rubbed them away with the back of her hand.

Stiffening her slim shoulders, she turned and looked back at the unbending man. "I'd say that I was sorry, but you've done an awful lot of assuming. And I'm afraid most of it was wrong." Then she swung back around and disappeared through the doorway, softly closing it behind her.

Slowly slumping back against the desk for support, Jay still stared at the closed door. She sure had been angry. Managed to take a good strip or two off of him. A tomboy, huh? She was right though, he had done a lot of assuming. And from what had happen seconds before; a lot of it had been way off the mark. How could he explain to that fiery bundle that he had been worried that she would get hurt. Of the fear of losing her after just finding her? She'd never believe him. Not before and not now.

Why, too, had he brought Darla Russell into it? True, she had been the one to ride the roan and the horse had taken off with her. Even threw her. But, Randi had been very accurate when she had guessed that the roan was not the kind of horse that Darla rode. In fact, he still did not understand why she had been so determined to ride the little critter. Boy, she sure had used some language when the roan tossed her in the mud. True, too, he had not seen the actual ride. Just her version and later the stockmen. Though Tom had seen it, he had never said anything. Course he had never asked the head stockman either.

Moving to the closed door it suddenly opened. A young man in his early twenties, straight dark brown hair and almost amber-colored eyes, stepped through the doorway. Surprise lighting up his usually studious expression. "Lo' Boss. Just saw Randi storming down the hall. Don't think she even saw me. What's up?"

Jay chuckled softly. Ted had a way about him. Nothing ever seemed to cause him any undue anxiety. Maybe that was why he was one of the top accountants in the whole area. Not a bad jack-a-roo, either. "Just the person I wanted to see."

A grin spread across the young face. "Okay, so what can I do for you, Boss?"

The tanned face of the rancher dropped its humor and became quite serious. Jay motioned Ted over to the desk and seated himself in the nearby chair. "I need some information. I want you to see if you can find out anything concerning some people named Nelson. Barbara and Tim Nelson. They have two boys named Terry and Barry. And I think they might live near Sydney. For now just their address or phone number will do. Oh, and, Ted, don't let anyone know. Especially Randi. You might be able to get some added information from Ray Proctor. He handled all of Randi's papers and such for the wedding."

"Are you finding out more about Randi? Why don't you just ask her?" questioned Ted hesitantly, his amber eyes curious.

Lewis leaned back in the chair. His face thoughtful. "I don't really think that she would tell me much of anything right now, Ted. Things happened so fast that I didn't even stop to find out anything much. One other place you could check is the employment agency that I hired to find that added help. They should have an application form of some kind."

Ted glanced over at the rancher, then stated quietly, "You know, Jay, that Randi typed up all those letters for you this morning before going out on the muster." At the startled flash in the smoky-gray eyes he continued, "and she also emailed her sister. Then she asked me for our address and what would be the fastest way to get a special delivery. From the States. The United States."

In one surprised motion, Jay was up out of the chair pacing back and forth like a caged animal. Then stopping in front of the desk and facing the frowning young man, he asked in a strangely calm voice, "Maybe they moved there? She couldn't have been all the way from America. Could she?"

"I don't know. But I think you had better go talk to some of the stockmen that were at the muster today. They think Randi is really something special on a horse. Something about knowing all about 'cowboying'." Softly stated the accountant.

"Yes, I think I will, Ted. You go ahead and get ahold of the agency. They should have where she last worked and most of what we would need to know. I'll talk to Ray myself. He would have to have had the passport and other papers. He must have figured that I knew; if, of course, Randi is from the States." Replied the rancher carefully, still in thought. Then remembering that the accountant had been on his way to the office, he asked, "What were you looking for me for? Some trouble?"

Leaning back in the chair, the young man grinned slightly. "No big problem. Just I need your signature on a few papers for the sale of those steers to the buyers that are coming tomorrow to pick them up."

"Well, that's something I had better do first, don't you think?" smiled Lewis.

Ted nodded slowly. His amber eyes studying the rancher with respect and admiration. He was so very glad the girl he was going with was just a simple, lovely girl that he had known for years. But he liked the redhead the boss had married. She was straight forward and a person just wanted to protect her. It would all work out. They were both very nice people.

CHAPTER FIFTEEN

Wearily Randi leaned back against the rough wood of the tack room side stall and dejectedly down to the straw littered floor. The tri-colored pup clambered happily over her legs and then climbed up to plant a warm moist tongue on the stubborn chin. Randi tried to smile, but failed totally. Sighing sadly she glanced out through the open doorway. It was getting late, dusk was falling with the swiftness of night and still Randi remained where she was.

She knew that dinner had long since been over and found that she was not in the least bit hungry. Just the thought of food seemed to stick in her throat. The scene in the study kept flashing across her mind. Such a childish thing to do. And now she did not want to have to face JR and see the contempt in the ice-gray eyes; she just could not.

Soon the dusty-red pup joined the bluish one on her lap, the two playfully growling at each other. For once the male pup, Bandy, was sitting on the sidelines just watching. He was lying next to his mother, pretending to be grown-up. Smoke, the male dog, was out with Tom working some young steers that were to be sold.

For a brief while the girl had watched the dog and man work together. They were like one. Each knowing what the other wanted without either saying. Shawnee had been like that. Only she had been a top cutting horse. One of the best. And on the way to being a top reining horse, also. Randi had been able to compete with her without the aid of a bit. No bridle. In fact, people had been known to have come to some of the rodeos and horse shows just to see the brilliant pair strut their stuff. Shawnee had been a fire-red sorrel, almost the same color as Randi's own silky hair. And now there was a competition for No Bridle Cutting Horses.

A tear squeezed out through the tightly shut lids, slowly making its way down the now dusty cheek. Why had she thought of the filly now? After all this time? Because of her impending marriage to Rodger, she had to find someone suitable to take the horse. But the little mare never made it to her new home. Just as the horse trailer had pulled out of the guest ranch drive a speeding car on the wrong side of the narrow road plowed into the large four horse trailer. The expensive sport car tore the trailer up like so many pieces of paper.

A young child had been on her small Shetland pony, not five feet from the accident. Randi could still remember the terror on that small face and the screaming. So much screaming. Not just the child, but the horses......

Her own voice had added to the cries of shock and horror. After she saw the red filly twisting and turning in agony on the ground, a large piece of jagged metal ripped into her once silky side.

There had been four horses in the trailer, two had died out right, one was lucky and escaped serious injury; but not Shawnee. She had to be put down. And Randi would never forget the minutes of tortured agony the filly had to go through. The speeding car; no one had even suffered a scratch. The driver had been drunk as well as the other two passengers.

Yes, she had lost quite a lot with her involvement with Rod and Lynn. A job she had loved, friends, and a promising young filly. Even confidence in herself. The sad part being that Rod had known at the time that he did not love her, but really loved Lynn instead. So foolish and so very unfair. But mostly to Shawnee.

The red filly had been much the same size as the little roan. Much the same temperament also. Shawnee had been a handful to anyone who had tried to ride her; especially if they used a heavy hand. Something had clicked between the two of them, much like the gelding and herself now. Maybe that had been why she had been drawn to the red roan in the first place. The likeness or just the type? A gentle rebel? Like herself?

The little roan had potential. He was quick on his feet, able to gather himself well and had a lot of speed. Staying power, too. He also did not have a tendency to spook or become jumpy very easily like a high-strung mount might. But more than anything else, he was willing to try.

So deep in thought that she never heard the softly muted voices just outside the tack room. Nor did she hear the tall man walk into the outside part of the stall. The first she knew of another's presence was the slight stiffening of the adult dog as she rose to her feet to protect her family. Looking up to where the dog was facing, Randi found herself staring into Jay's tanned, closed face.

"So here you are. You missed supper." So soft was the voice.

"I know. I wasn't hungry." Muttered Randi quietly, her eyes shifting to the straw covered floor.

With a sigh, Jay bent down and put his arms behind her back and under her knees, lifting her slender weight up against his hard-muscled chest. Surprise held her silent at first, then with a slight stammer, "Where are....what are you doing?"

A brief smile touched the firm lips. "Looks as if I'm carrying you."

A firmness settled on the well-molded lips and the small chin lifted stubbornly, "Yes, I see that. I'm very capable of walking on my own. So there is no need for a show of brute strength."

The decisive steps faulted slightly, just for a fraction. The jaw jutting out just above her head hardened and she noted that a small nerve was jumping near the edge of the strong jawline. For a moment Randi hesitated, wondering just how far she should push him before he retaliated in kind. But when your opponent was far the stronger your best course was to attack. Wasn't it?

Shaking a sun bleached blonde head in puzzlement, he stepped up onto the back verandah and headed down its screened length to the door opening into their bedroom. Jay gently set Randi on her feet in the middle of the spacious room after shouldering his way through the screened door. The shadows covered her features effectively enough to hide her expression from him; his, too, if he but knew.

Looking down at her small figure so clearly weary that he offered softly, "A hot shower or bath would not come amiss. You must have worked hard out at the muster?" To Randi it sounded more like a statement than a question. Did he suspect?

Moving slightly away from him, she murmured hesitantly, "A...a bit. It was very dusty and warm. I think I will have that shower now." And she glared pointedly at the door. Waiting for him to take the hint and leave so that she could peel off the dirty, work-stained clothes.

The corner of his sensuous mouth tugged upward briefly, but the sardonic gleam in the smoky eyes was chilling her to the bone. Then as the hard, cool voice broke the silence, she actually flinched at the veiled barbs.

"Coy, all of a sudden? I'm your husband, remember? I know what you look like with no clothes on." A bitter laugh sounded from deep in his throat. "Don't worry, Brat, I'll not tease you now." And abruptly he turned on his heel and stalked out of the bedroom, slamming the door loudly behind him.

With tears burning from behind her eyelids, she turned blindly toward the bathroom. As she reached the door, she hesitated just long enough to lean up against the door frame and start pulling the boots and grimy clothes off. Bundling the discarded clothes into a ball, she flung them into the hamper.

The warm spray of the shower felt comforting on her chilled skin. Emotionally chilled, she added to herself. Pouring the thick, creamy shampoo on the wet hair, she vigorously rubbed it in to a lather. She was rubbing so hard that her scalp was beginning to tingle. Who was she punishing? Jay or herself?

Once again she moved in under the water. Absently she watched as the water ran down over the lightly tanned length of her firm, slender body. As the last traces of shampoo disappeared down the drain, she reached up to turn off the taps.

Suddenly a cool draft brushed against her wet skin, causing her to whirl around in confusion to face the now open shower door. Swiftly the door was pulled shut and the dark tanned arms of her husband encircled her wet form. Pushing her back against the wall, the spray falling on both the dark-red and beige-blonde heads as Jay's warm lips claimed hers.

Fire rioted up from the very depths of her being as the male fingers ran possessively over her body. With a soft groan of pure desire, Jay lifted her closer to the broad, hard length of him. Her own body moved against him, tantalizing and arousing him to a fever pitch. Deftly with one hand he reached up and the spray suddenly stopped.

With a push of a bare foot the frosted glass door swung open and he effortlessly picked her up in his arms and carried her into the still night-darkened room. With a fevered glance Randi noted briefly that the bed had been turned down and as he laid her wet form on the cool sheets, soft moonlight filtered in on them. He followed her onto the bed, his powerful frame covering her slender one.

As his lips burned a sensuous trail across her cheek, neck and again back to her parted lips, his hand tangled in the wet, silky waist-length hair pulling it around the side and gently twisted it over her creamy-smooth neck and shoulders. His voice husky with building desire breathed against her ear, "Now I've got you trapped. You are mine."

Once again firm male lips burned their fiery trail across her feverish skin. As the tongue licked over one of her sensitive areas and deftly went on to stimulate the others, her slender frame shook with the passion growing inside. She could feel his own desire building in response to the feel of her silky, tantalizing skin as it rubbed teasingly closer, even closer to the tanned firm, very masculine one.

Even as she thought the fire of his desire was going to consume her; she realized that she had unconsciously started to fight him. When, she had no idea, but somewhere along the line she had decided to at least show a token resistance. Something to show that she was not a pushover, a woman that all he had to do was kiss her and she forgot everything else. Even the fact that he more than likely did not love her, for he had never admitted to such a failing, even to the lessor that of liking her. He desired her, wanted her, he had said. And as these thoughts raced through her mind along with the worries of the roan and the interference of Darla Russell; even if indirectly, her slight resistance hardened determinedly.

Feeling the small figure stiffen under him and as tightly clenched fists pushed hard against his chest, Jay leaned back, just slightly, to have a better view of the mutinous, yet delicate face. Even in the moonlight he could make out the stormy green eyes that were still clouded with passion.

A dry chuckle sounded down deep in his throat as he leaned down closer to her again. Letting his desire hardened body rub up against hers and feeling the traitorous response of the slender, soft curves beneath him. Passion flared in the smoky-gray of his eyes as the same flame licked its way through his body.

Huskily his voice breathed against Randi's ear, "Showing a little resistance to save your pride, Brat? It won't work, you know. Your delectable little body is giving you away. You are a strong little thing, though. Wiry, I guess. Course anyone that ropes large bull calves had better be fairly strong, wouldn't you say, Randi?"

With his lips teasing the corner of her mouth, she was finding it hard to speak. And with the discovery that Jay knew about her 'work' at the muster earlier, completely silenced her. What could she say? What need she say? She had applied for the job of secretary-cum-do-all and she had told him then that she could work cattle. That was the reason for all the trouble now. Anger surged through her so that she choked out in a strangled voice, "I told you that I met all the requirements for your damn job except for the sex, if you remember? It was a rainy night in a little cabin, if you remember?"

"Oh, I remember alright. I also remember how we almost passed the time while we were." Jay taunted softly. "A very pleasurable way. Or it could have been."

Turning her face angrily toward him, a denial on her lips, she saw too late that she had done just as he had expected. His mouth was on hers, his hand curving around her neck and the thumb pressing firmly under her chin. No amount of twisting or turning would manage to evade his seeking kisses. Not even sure that she wanted to.

As the tip of his tongue probed against the tightly closed softness of her lips, she tried to ignore the pleasant sensation that quivered throughout her slender frame. Fighting silently, she twisted and shoved against him with her body, but only added to the hunger that screamed through her for him.

"Open your mouth." He growled against her tightly closed lips. "Open your mouth to me, Brat. You are mine and I'm taking you."

"No…." and as her lips parted on the words, his tongue forced its way into the warm sweetness of her mouth.

He seemed to drink the very life from her and still demanded more. Her whole body burned with an aching hunger for his lean, hard-muscled maleness. His fingers caressed and teased her body to a feverish ache. Bringing the small firm breasts to a swelling peak within his hands. Her slender frame strained closer against his male hardness, her palms rubbing over the blonde-beige chest hair.

With a shaky groan he took her. He had done so with force, but at the same time gently. The slight roughness something that they both had seemed to need. His breathing was still heavy and fast with the warm desire that still seemed to fire his blood. With another groan, soft and slightly caressing, he rolled to one side and pulled her down close beside him. Desire flamed into life once again as his senses recalled the feel of that sensuous body against his. The smooth texture of the silky skin, the faint clean smell of her.

Slowly his hand reached out and the strong tan fingers spread over the firm flat stomach. Moving his fingers across the satin smoothness to the gentle curve of her hip bone, he noted the slight hardening of the dusty-rose colored nipples of her breasts.

An answering desire hardened in his own body as he leaned purposely over her. His palm pushing gently against her hip bone, his mouth coming to rest on the stiffening nipple of her breast. As his lips moved over the swelling fullness; a soft, surprised groan escaped the now trembling girl.

The slender body arched up to meet his searching mouth and hands. With a shudder of desire he slipped over her, his mouth on hers; his body taking, conquering and consuming the slightness of hers.

Completely spent and with the soft warm glow of satisfaction seeping swiftly through their bodies; they lay quietly, still with their limbs entwined. With the sound of Jay's slow steady breathing declaring that he had fallen asleep, Randy shakily released a sigh.

A tear rolled down over her cheek bone to lay tangled wetly in the hair near her ear. If only he could love her. Not just want her body. She loved him so much. So very much....

CHAPTER SIXTEEN

Pale golden sunlight filtered down through the tall shade trees that bordered the patio and oval-shaped swimming pool, turning the clear blue-green water to dappled amber. A soft gentle breeze stirred the strawberry-red tendrils at Randi's temples and just in front of her ears. With a careless hand she brushed the few wisps of hair back away from her troubled young face.

In a pale-aqua bikini, her long hair braided into a long pleat down her slender back; she poised in brief hesitation before executing a neat clean dive into the cool, creamy depths at the deep end of the pool. For a timeless moment she almost wished that she could just remain in that pleasant, cool emptiness. But then her lungs began to burn with the need of fresh air and slowly she let her pale tan body float gracefully to the surface.

Laying back in a slow, leisurely back float, she closed her eyes against the bright sunshine. To-morrow was the Russell's party. Would she be able to pull it off? Would they believe that they had married because they were deeply in love or would they assume that they were forced into it. A faint pink washed over her features as the thought registered. Well, she was in love with Jay and if he kept to the possessive actions of the last couple of days then it should be very convincing. What were they going to think of his tomboyish bride? Would most definitely cause quite a stir with some certain people. And at that thought a totally pleased smile danced lightly across her lips.

It was then that she heard the voices. Strange voices, not that of Tico, but still a woman's. Not Darla Russell, either. That was one voice Randi would remember. There was the sound of at least two other voices. Male, though. Then they were almost to the pool area when she heard Ted's quiet voice cut across the soft murmurings of the others.

Deciding that she had better get out of the pool in case she had to meet these people; she was just coming to a stand in the thigh-deep water when she came face to face with them. It was a man and woman and a teenage boy. The woman came to a halt and stopped speaking in mid-sentence to watch the young girl come out of the pool.

Jewel Bellington was in her early forties with pale-brown hair and kindly eyes of a dark blue. She was slightly shocked to find this new wife of Jay's to be so young. Why, she could not be much older than their own son, Chris. Seeing the worried frown appear on the delicate features of the girl as she finished coming out of the water; Jewel smiled warmly and said in her soft, outback voice, "Hello, my dear. You must be Randi. I am one of your closer neighbors, Jewel Bellington." Then motioning to the tall man at her side, she continued, "My husband, Tad. And our son, Chris."

Randi smiled and walked forward, extending her small hand. They returned her handshake and the young boy, Chris, grinned back at her.

"Sorry, I didn't know that you were coming or I would have been out of the pool. You must want to see Jay. He isn't here right at the moment, but I'm sure that Ted can get word to him that you are here."

Ted smiled to himself. The young Randi did not lack in coolness. More of a calmness, he decided. There was nothing cold about the redhead's personality. Warmth and sincere friendliness shown in the smoky-green eyes. "I've already sent for JR. He'll be here directly. Randi, the Bellingtons own the Rockwood Station. One right place. They have some of the best horses here about. As you'll see at the races." Turning to the older couple, he continued with pride. "Our Randi, here, has quite a way with horses. The little red roan is putty in her hands. All the stockmen are convinced that she is part horse. A bright fire magic."

Chris, watching the slender girl, spoke up quietly, his young tanned face dimpling into a smile. "Speaking of red, Randi's face is turning just about that color. I ride also, Randi. I'll be riding in the races coming up. On my own horse, Cannon. Broke him in and did all the training."

Randi smiled and asked, "What kind of horse is he?"

"He is a buckskin with black mane and tail. A stallion, but he doesn't act like one. He is very well mannered. You have to come see him."

"I sure will, Chris. We'll set up a time." Smiled Randi. This was a very nice young man and his parents were great.

Ted glanced at a nearby table in the shade of the large trees. "Why don't we have a seat at the table over there and Tico can bring some refreshments."

Everyone seemed to think that was a good idea. Seeing her guests to their seats, Randi moved to one side and said in a soft pleasant voice, "I am going to go change and I'll be right back. I'll ask Tico to bring out the drinks on my way in."

"That's fine, dear. You go get changed." Smiled Jewel quietly.

As the redhead turned toward the house, she glanced once more at the small group, and then catching Ted's eye, smiled and disappeared into the house. She found the housekeeper in the kitchen and told her about the Bellington's visit and then headed for the bedroom to change.

The room was cool and she paused to catch her breathe. These were Jay's good friends and she didn't want to disappoint him or them. She pulled a pair of jeans and a soft pale-yellow top on and headed back out to the patio.

As Randi stepped out of the door, she saw that Tico had delivered the frosty drinks and some small sandwiches. Everyone seemed in good spirits and as she stepped closer, the boy, Chris looked up and saw her.

"Hi, Randi. Come and have a sandwich, they're great."

"I'm coming, I'm coming." Replied Randi with a smile and she sat down in the vacant seat next to the young man.

As Jay walked around the side of the house he could hear the murmur of voices coming from the patio area. He could pick out Tad Bellington's deep fatherly tones and those excited ones from Chris. They sounded pleasant. Hopefully everyone was getting along. He hadn't realized how much the older couple's opinion mattered; but it did.

When he stepped around the corner he realized they hadn't noticed his presence. Though, he noticed that Ted had seen him before the others. Glancing at the accountant's face he looked for some sign of how the Bellington's were getting on with Randi. What he saw caused him to breathe much easier. Though, in all reasoning he really had not thought that there would be any problem at all. Not when they met the red-haired woman.

Tad Bellington seeing Lewis walk up, stepped forward to meet him, his hand out-stretched in greeting. A true smile spreading across his weathered, yet handsome face. "Hello there, Jay. We have been talking to your dandy new bride. Quite the catch, Boy."

"Glad to see that you approve of my choice, Tad. Good afternoon, Jewel, and how are you, young man? You sure are growing, Chris. I'm betting that you end up taller than your father. How's that buckskin stallion of yours? He must be quite a handsome fella by now."

"He sure is, Jay. Can't wait to have you see him at the race. Do you think that you and Randi could come over by and take a look at him some time before?" questioned the youth.

Jay and Randi exchanged quick glances and the rancher turned back to the boy, "Don't see why not. We'll get over in the next few days. That alright with you, Chris?"

The young face split with a beaming smile of pride and excitement. "You bet!" Then facing the red-haired girl, "You'll love him, Randi. Wait until you ride him."

Randi hesitated briefly, noting the start of surprise on not only her husband's face, but also on the older couple. "I'd be very pleased to ride Cannon. If you are sure that you want me to?"

"Oh, I'm sure. It's alright, isn't it, Jay? If she rides Cannon?" questioned Chris with a moments' doubt.

The rancher shook his blonde head in wonderment, chuckling as he did so. "I've no objections, Chris. I was just surprised. But come to think of it I'm not sure why I would assume that you would not want Randi to try out your favorite mount. If anything she doesn't even have to ask to get what she wants. Must be that little-girl look of yours, Randi. Everyone wants to protect and pamper you."

A fine green glitter came to the smoky eyes as Randi met the gray ones head on. "Or browbeat."

"Not you, my sweet. Tad, come on down to the corrals and I'll show you that yearling colt that I telephoned you about. Chris, want to come along?" Grinned the rancher.

After a brief indecision, Chris decided to join the two men. Besides they were going to look at his favorite subject, horses. With a smile he fell into step between the two tall men.

Watching her son and husband walk toward the horse corrals, Jewel turned slowly back to the young woman at her side. "You sure won Chris over. You are the first person he's ever asked to ride the buckskin, little else get close to. Even Jay has never had that privilege. I like you, Randi Lewis."

A faint pink color tinged the pale-gold cheeks as Randi met the older woman's kindly eyes. "You know, I like you, too. In fact, I'm hoping we'll be very good friends." Slipping her slender hand through Jewel's arm, she directed her toward the house. "Now about this get-together at the Russell's? Is there anything I should know before turning up over there? Other than she (meaning Darla) seems to think that Jay belongs to her."

Mrs. Bellington smiled softly. "I'm glad to know you have placed that little number in the right category. I'm not very sure of her myself. Neither of them, if rights be known. Can't say as why I don't trust them; but there's something that just isn't right. Maybe it's just the way they pretend to be so uppity, so much better than everyone else."

Randi nodded slowly and reached out a hand to open the rear door to the house. "I think I know what you mean. I've only seen Darla once and that was from some distance. But then I've never pretended to be sophisticated." Laughed the autumn-colored haired girl.

Easing onto the sofa, Jewel eyed the slender girl that had more or less stolen her heart as well as those of her family. "My dear, I for one like you just like you are. Randi, just how long is that gorgeous hair?"

"Don't know for sure, but I can sit on it. To tell the truth of the matter, I was thinking of cutting it. Oh, not a lot. Just a trim. It gets so hard to take care of." Sighed Randi with a lop-sided grin.

Jewel Bellington smiled in return. "I can understand what you mean about upkeep, but don't touch it yet. Wait until after Russell's party. Besides, what does Jay think of the idea of you cutting it?"

Randi gave the older woman an almost sheepish grin. "I haven't even mentioned it to him. And I don't intend to. He can voice his opinion afterwards. At least that way he can't change my mind."

They were still softly chuckling over the hair when the three men walked into the room. Looking down into the redhead's face, Jay questioned in an almost idle voice. "A joke or just women's chatter?"

Jewel laughed and answered instead. "I'd say a little of both. Now, young man, dwell on that for a while because that's all we're telling."

Leaning back against the cloth seat of the large pickup, Randi eyed the swiftly scudding grayish clouds. True, there were only a few dotting the cobalt blue of the late morning sky. "Do you think that it might rain?"

Jay threw a quick glance in the girl's direction, then said with barely concealed irony. "And spoil one of Darla Russell's parties? Good heavens, we'll hope not or we'll never live through the tantrum. Did you bring a dress or something fancy for the dance later?"

A smile touched the delicate lips. "Yes, I brought something fancy for the festivities later. But you'll just have to wait until later to see what. That is if it doesn't rain or anything like that."

Lewis chuckled deep in his throat. Never a dull moment with the little spitfire he married. "I hope you'll enjoy yourself. The Bellingtons will be there of course. You sure got on well with Jewel. All of them, really."

"They are nice folks. They are real easy to get to know. It's too bad that Ted and his girl couldn't come to this shindig." Sighed Randi sadly.

The rancher's tanned features hardened slightly. "Darla and Carl just invite 'certain' people to their parties. Ray Proctor will be there. You like him."

Randi almost snorted, then laughed dryly instead. "You mean they only invite wealthy people. And you remember, Jay Randal Lewis, that this invitation was only for you. I remember hearing it, and she came all the way over to GetAway just to give it to you. In person. Talk about tantrums; I'll bet there will be one hell of one when you show up dragging your little wife behind."

CHAPTER SEVENTEEN

Leaning his lanky frame against the rough-barked tree trunk, Carl Russell sipped his third or fourth drink and gazed disinterestedly at the gathering crowd of people and animals. Station owners, all of them. Wealthy, superior-thinking and arrogant. If you would ask them; that would be their own opinion of themselves. To the dark-haired man they were more in the line of opinionated braggarts. Real stuffed shirts.

In his late thirties, only a few years older than his sister, he appeared older in a dissipated sort of way. Too much liquor and late nights, or possibly early mornings of coming in. His dark, almost black hair was fairly free of any gray and the equally dark eyes had about as much expression as an opaque stone. And as warm. He liked fast, expensive sporty cars; money and all it could buy, but not the kind you had to work for. Work was not part of his vocabulary. He felt the world in general owed him a good time. And since his sister, Darla, had come across this land holding, things have been fairly productive.

Now if Darla's plan for latching on to the GetAway Station owner would pan out they would be on easy street. She had tried everything to get her claws into the man, but he was hard to nail down or to fool. The talk of a redheaded girlfriend visiting the station awhile back had put her into a real fit for a while, but Darla was a gambler like himself. And she figured the odds would still be in her favor. Maybe even more so. Especially because of the breath of scandal.

Hearing yet another vehicle pull up, the dark eyes shifted to the general direction of the parked cars and horse vans. At seeing the GetAway pickup come to a halt, he straightened his tall form and made to go greet the blonde haired rancher. Drawing nearer he saw a small figure step out of the passenger side of the vehicle. A female figure at that. And with long red hair. Could this be the same girlfriend that the pilot, Starck, had told tales about? What was this? And where was that sister of his? He wanted to see the expression on her haughty face when she found that Lewis had brought himself a date. A redheaded date at that. What a laugh. Carl had no illusions concerning his sister. They were too much alike.

Looking again at the newcomer, he decided to go on over and make his introductions. The perfect host. Ha! Besides from what he could see, Lewis did not have bad taste in women. Even in blue jeans and silky pale-pink shirt, the girl was good looking. And next to fast cars, Carl enjoyed the weaker sex and if they were good looking and easy, then who was he to complain? What gorgeous hair. If the sun hit it just right it could blind a man. Beautiful.

"Well, well, Lewis, I see that you made this little shindig. And brought along a….a friend?" questioned Carl slowly as he pointed with his almost empty glass at the redhead.

Glancing up at the greeting, Randi watched the dark-haired man come closer. She could almost feel the leer in his glance; and she felt uneasy, almost frightened.

She did not like him. And she did not even know him. Unconsciously she moved closer to Jay's side where she felt more secure.

Jay stood quietly until Carl came to halt a foot or so away. "Hello, Carl. I see you have been at the shindig awhile." And nodded to the drink in the man's hand. "Don't want to drink too many of those in this heat or we'll be carrying you inside before long."

A dull red crept up the unhealthy pallor of his face. "I haven't had many as of yet, JR. Now, who is this friend of yours? A mighty pretty little thing, too, I might add."

The sun tanned features turned stony. "This is Randi, my wife. And, Randi, this is Carl Russell. He is one of the owners of Bangon. And of course, this is Bangon Station." And he motioned around at the large holding.

Randi smiled carefully and hesitantly held out her small hand for Russell to shake. His hand took hers and it tightened fractionally longer than necessary before releasing it. Randi had a hard time of it not to wipe her fingers off on her jeans, but stuck them behind her back instead.

Turning his head sideways, Carl looked first at the girl and then back at the tall rancher. "You are quite the sly guy, JR. No one had any idea that you were interested in anyone in particular. At least not that seriously." Then turning to Randi, he continued, "You made quite the catch, Red."

Anger flared briefly in the dusky-green eyes as the small chin raised ever so slightly. "You could say that, then again you could say that Jay is the one to have made the 'catch'." Her smile was forced, but she would not look away.

Jay's arm came around her slim shoulders and he gave her a quick hug. "Too right. I most certainly got the better of the deal." Flicking a swift look in Carl's direction, Jay caught sight of the tall, dark headed Darla coming their way. "Hum….Carl, here comes your sister. In all her glory."

Turning around as to get a clear view of the drama that he knew would be unfolding within moments, Carl leaned back against the truck door smiling to himself. In moving to the side the small redhead came into his sister's view. Darla's steps slowed momentarily, then with a hard gleam in the dark eyes, she came on toward them. She moved in next to Jay and had her fingers locked onto his arm before turning the forced smile to the slender girl at his other side,

"Why, darling, who do you have here? This can't be the little 'friend' that Don Starck was talking about? Is it?" drawled the smooth tones of the dark-haired woman. Her thin lips curved into a tight smile, never reaching the eyes, eyes dark and sharp as chips of ice.

Before Jay could offer any information, Randi spoke up in her quiet, yet firm voice. "You could say that I am the same 'little friend' that our very talkative pilot mentioned. I am also the wife to the man whose arm you are so firmly clinging to."

The taller woman's face paled with surprised shock. At first she did not, or could not believe that this little bit of bright red could possibly be married to Lewis or that she could so calmly tell her, Darla Russell, to get her hands off her husband. But nonetheless, Darla removed her hand and even stepped back slightly. "You are JR's wife? We never heard anything about it." Then looking spitefully at the tall, blonde man at her side, she added stiffly, "You did it secretly. Must have been some motive for all the speed?"

The teak-brown features hardened and the gray eyes turned cold. But Jay's voice when he spoke was cool and very calm. "The very best motive ever, Darla. I believe you call it 'love'. And besides it wasn't all that sudden. Took me a good month to convince Randi. And it was in the papers. Our engagement and marriage. But maybe they haven't been sent out this way yet. The wedding ceremony was only this week. A quiet, simple affair."

"No, we haven't received the latest mail. In fact, the mail will more than likely arrive with Don Starck when he flies in for the bar-b-cue." Piped up the older Russell, his dark eyes bright with curiosity. Carl was enjoying himself to no end. And at his sister's expense. In all truth, it was about time she had her sharp tongue spiked and it sure appeared as if the slender redhead could manage the job just fine.

Apparently the tall woman felt vaguely the same way. Enough anyway to bide her time until she had herself more in control. Also without the tall, domineering man standing within range of what she had to say. She would see just how tough the little hussy was without her protection standing next to her.

"I hope you enjoy the party. You didn't mention your name, my dear." Darla spoke with just a trace of the anger apparent in her voice.

Just as Randi started to answer, Carl interrupted, "The lady's name is Randi. Quite an unusual name for quite an unusual and delightful person."

Darla threw her brother a sharp glance before saying, "Randi? That sounds like a boy's name. Still, I suppose someone as….uh….uh….dainty as yourself doesn't get accused of being masculine?"

A dry laugh tinged the soft huskiness of the slender girl's voice as she eyed the very sophisticated woman. "On the contrary, I'm as close to being a tomboy as you can get. But you are right I don't get thought of as being able to do physical things. In fact that is one of my biggest problems. Everyone thinks I'll break if handled a little roughly. Like a china doll or something. Ha!"

Just then a young, very excited voice broke through the afternoon stillness; causing all four people to turn in that direction. The dark-blonde hair on the tallish young man proclaimed him to be Chris Bellington, to Randi's relief.

"Randi! Hi ya', Randi. I was hoping you would get here. I've got to show you the cutest little foal you've ever seen." Then as his blue glance landed on the rancher, "Oh, hallo, Jay. Is it alright if I take Randi for a few minutes?"

Jay laughed easily at the boy's enthusiasm and if it were to be known, at his extremely good timing. "If the lady doesn't mind. Go ahead, I'll catch up in a moment."

Randi smiled warmly at the excited youth before glancing up from under long dark lashes at her husband. At seeing the pleased glint in the gray coolness of his eyes, she answered softly, "Let's go, Chris. What is this foal? Is it one of yours or one of another station's?"

The boy chuckled deep in his throat and took ahold of her hand. "She is one of ours. We brought her along with the mare today. Snowfire is competing in a few of the games this afternoon."

Watching the two disappear around some paddock fences, Jay grinned to himself. It was then that Darla's stiff voice reached him. Turning his sun-lightened blonde head in the slender woman's direction he asked, "What did you say? I wasn't paying attention. Sorry."

Tipping her head slightly, Darla looked up into the tanned features. "I said they look about the same age going off together like that. Where did you find such....uh... delightful little creature, darling?"

Jay was fully aware of the barely concealed anger and tried to hide the smile tugging at his firm lips. "Actually, I met Randi right out here. Riding that little red roan that threw you awhile back. She seems to have taken quite a shine to that scalawag. And come to think of it, him to her. Funny, she doesn't seem to have any trouble at all with the fellow. Wonder how that is?"

A dull red crept up the elegant neck and professionally made-up face at the wondering look that Lewis was sending in her direction and at the chuckle she was receiving from her brother. "Shut up, Carl. You can't even stay on the back of a sway-back broken-down mare." Forcing a smile of sorts on to her lips, she added to the rancher, "I'm just not used to range-rough little broncs. Or maybe it hasn't decided to act up just yet on your little... uh...wife."

"Humm....yes, I suppose you could be right. Are you going to be competing in any of the games this afternoon?" Jay asked with a show of tact.

"Oh yes, of course. In the jumping event. What about yourself and Randi?" questioned Darla with a steely glint in her very dark eyes.

"I'm not sure. We didn't bring any of our horses along this trip. But, maybe we could use one or two of the Bellington's? I know that they brought a number of theirs." Jay answered unconcernedly, as if tiring of the subject.

At the mention of the Bellingtons, Darla shot up a dark, slim eyebrow. "I take it that Jewel and Tad have already met Randi? It's too bad that you didn't let the rest of us know. You don't realize how much of a surprise it was to us, darling. I can't see how your wife can put up with that gangly young teenager. He'd drive most adults right up the wall. But of course they must be of a very close age? You didn't rob the cradle, did you, sweetest?"

Darla failed to see her brother's warning glance. A frown touched his dark, careless features. She was stepping on the man's ego talking like that. But at the same time he would like to see just how Lewis answered the question.

Having glanced past the two Russells, Jay had just caught a glimpse of the elder Bellingtons approaching at the same time hearing Darla's spiteful question. Turning slowly back to face the stern, unfeeling face of the otherwise elegant woman, Lewis frowned his displeasure. "I have every respect for Chris. He's very mature for his age. And I, by no means, have robbed the cradle. Randi is over twenty-three and in no way acts like a child of Chris's tender age. They seem to be able to communicate; maybe you should try it sometime, Darla. Now, if you will both excuse me, I see Tad and Jewel." Stiffly the tall lean man walked away from the two dark-haired people. Displeasure written in the very straightly held shoulders and proud head.

Shifting his feet, Carl ventured carefully, "I don't think you asked the right questions that time, sister dear. He was one angry man. You stepped on his ego when you assumed that he would stoop to marry a child."

Anger blazed in the almost black eyes as they swung on the man at her side. "Oh shut up, Carl. Why don't you go have another drink. You had better not let JR catch you drooling over his sweet little redheaded bitch or he'll hang and quarter you."

"Temper, temper. That might be just the thing for him to come running to you, dear sister. Especially if I make it look like the girl is playing up to me. Jealousy is a wicked too, but if used right…. But it's your play, sister dear. At the same time if you are smart you will get on the good side of friend rancher and let his wife think that he is in fact seeking you out. If you catch my meaning?"

Darla had leaned back against the GetAway pickup, resentment in every line of her tall, slim body. But as the words and sense of what he was saying penetrated, she began to listen. And then a very frail plan began to form. "You know at times, brother mine, you do come up with some good ideas. Must run in the family?"

"Being smart?" He questioned doubtfully, a frown forming between his dark brows.

Darla laughed harshly. "No, dear brother. Trickery. Purely selfish motives and a lust for money and power. Ha! Don't look so damned surprised. I've always known the way you gamble and was slightly surprised to see just how much we were alike. Quite a bit from the looks of it."

Carl shook his dark head and then offered his sister his arm in a show of grandness. A sly smile touched his thin lips and the ebony-colored eyes almost managed to smile. Oh, he knew just how important it was that his sister should get in good with JR Lewis. They both needed the money that the wealthy rancher could provide. They were very nearly out of ready cash and the station had not been run on a money making income since they took over. He also knew about the ore samples that Darla had sent in from Lewis's property.

They were a striking couple and as they walked past, many of their quests would not imagine that they were not from a wealthy or a family of class. Or that most of their air of sophistication was assumed, pretense; but with a single hidden purpose to obtain the wealth that they seemed to represent. And by any and all means they deemed necessary.

CHAPTER EIGHTEEN

Following the boy into a tree-shaded lane where rows of horse vans stood harboring many horses, they came to one of the most unusual and beautiful horses that Randi had ever seen. It stood there, delicate and slim with an almost gray-white body. But it was the flame-red mane and tail that drew your attention. So unusual with the almost white coat. The face was slender and the velvet smooth muzzle had the same, yet muted red color running almost to the dark-brown doe-like eyes. The ears, too, had the softened flame-red color and again it appeared around the tops of the hooves and up the slender, straight legs.

Randi stopped and just drank in the lovely creature. So utterly lovely in her unusual coloring. And then peering out from under the silky belly of the mare, a strawberry nose appeared. Followed by two dainty reddish feet and legs. "She's wonderful, Chris. And who is this playing peek-a-boo from under her?"

Chris laughed softly as not to startle the two horses. "The mare is Snowfire and the little one next to her is Sunfrost. Better known as Sunny. She is the foal I wanted you to see. Here, let me bring her around so you can get a good look at her."

Sighing in wonder, Randi grinned and watched as the youth went to the far side of the mare and returned leading the dainty filly. The little foal was extremely like her mother, yet the red was more of a strawberry and of course more muted in color. Then as Chris brought her closer, Randi saw the small rump with its soft plume of a strawberry tail and a dappling of roan spots of the same strawberry shade. Almost like that of an Appaloosa. The body and structure of the little filly and the mare were definitely that of an Arabian. How?

"She has the markings of an Appy. Almost, anyway. What was the sire?" questioned the red-haired girl with a slight frown.

The boy grinned. "A large honey-colored buckskin. He's almost a roan. That's where the blanket on the rump comes from, I guess. Well, Randi, what do you think of her?"

"I have every belief that the filly is the cutest foal that I have ever seen. If not the most unusual." Stated the girl calmly. Pleased to note the pride and respect showing on the boy's face and in his stance.

Stepping closer so that she could rub her hand over the silky smoothness of the mare and then touch the soft muzzle of the filly, she could hear others coming closer. Turning her head she saw that it was Chris's parents and her husband. Flashing a welcoming smile to the three, she remarked to the tall, blonde-haired man, "How do like the filly, Jay? Isn't she the most gorgeous thing you have ever seen? I just can't get over the coloring. Especially the mare. I've never seen anything like it before."

Jay leaned against the fence and watched the girl as she ran her hand expertly over the back and legs of the filly. He noted, too, that she checked the neck and head and all four of the tiny dainty feet. She knew what she was about. Then catching her green glance on his face, he smiled and replied, "Yes, one of the most lovely. Sunny, there, has just about the same strange strawberry color as you do, Randi. Did you notice?"

At her start of surprise, Jewel spoke up softly. "You are right, Jay, they are about the same lovely shade. So unusual."

Tad grinned slowly before saying, "I imagine that is one of the reasons that Chris made sure that we brought the little stinker with us this afternoon. He mentioned the sameness in color yesterday after seeing Randi at the pool."

The boy was blushing at the looks he was receiving from them, but managed to smile in return. "I could see how alike they were and I wanted to see if I was right. You have very pretty hair, Randi. And such an unusual color of red that I was surprised that Sunny could have almost the same color. You aren't mad or anything, are you?" His blue eyes narrowed at the thought, sudden uncertainty in their depths.

Randi saw the confusion on the boy's features and hurriedly assured him that it was an honor to be so well noticed. Besides the little filly was lovely and she could not find anything to make her think that it was other than a compliment to be classed with such a high-bred filly. Glancing around at the faces surrounding them, Randi asked, "How about something to eat? I don't know about the rest of you, but I for one am hungry. Isn't this supposed to be a bar-b-cue?"

It was decided that everyone was indeed hungry and so they moved off in the general direction of the outdoor cooking. As they walked along many neighboring families made their introductions and carefully eyed the small, red-haired wife of one of their respected landowners. Apparently she seemed to pass their close inspections. Outwardly Randi appeared calm and unaffected, but inside she was a tight ball of nerves. But pleased that most of Jay's friends and neighbors seemed to accept her at face value. Most were nice and very welcoming. Not at all like the Russells.

Just before they reached the wooden tables that were set up for the many folks that would be eating, Jay said lightly, "The Bellingtons have said that we can use some of their mounts to compete if we are a mind to. But it is up to you?"

Catching the pleading look from Chris, Randi found herself saying, "Sure, don't see why not. We'll see what kind of events are on the agenda. Okay?"

Jay nodded slowly and made to sit down next to the slender woman and the dark-blonde haired Chris. "Good, we'll check after we eat. What horses did you bring along besides Snowfire and the little one?"

Swallowing his first bite of the juicy bar-b-cued beef sandwich, Tad Bellington answered for his son. "We brought those two dark bays that you like the looks of so well. And then I'm riding Sinbad and Chris is planning on showing good speed in the youth race with Tucker. You know which one, Jay, the flashy black and white?"

"I'm going to win, too. Just you watch. Next to Cannon, Tucker is one of the quickest mounts around. And the youth race is a short one." Piped up the boy excitedly, his blue eyes alight with challenge. A sheepish grin touched the mouth, and he shook the dusty-blonde head slightly and chuckled softly. "Well, I will. At least I'm going to try darn hard."

Randi reached over and ruffled the boy's hair. "I bet you will. Now, look who is coming our way? Hi, Ray." And she smiled up at the brown-haired man as he reached the wooden table.

Setting his plate and coffee cup down across from Jay and Randi, he smiled warmly in return. "Hello, Randi, everybody. How goes things?"

Jewel looked over at the lawyer and spoke softly. "So far everything has been pretty smooth. Even the sandwiches are good. How have you been, Ray? It's been awhile since we've had the pleasure of your company."

"Yes, I guess you are right, Jewel. Just the everyday loads of paperwork mostly. Nothing very exciting really. Randi, are you getting ready for your birthday? It's coming up pretty soon, isn't it?"

A soft pink washed over the lightly tanned features as the redhead carefully eyed the lawyer. But she smiled and replied jokingly, "And I thought you were my friend, Ray Proctor. Haven't really done anything about it. To tell the truth, I had almost forgotten about it; until you mentioned it.

Thanks, Ray."

A wide grin spread across the lean face and reached clear up into the warm brown eyes. "Did I let the cat out of the bag? Sorry about that. Well, just sort of. I like parties, and a birthday is a good excuse for one. At least in my book. How about it, Jay, are you going to throw a bash for the little half-pint?"

The gray eyes had fastened on the blushing features of his wife and as Ray finished talking they slowly turned in the older man's direction. A slight frown marred the firm lips, but the voice was seemingly unaffected. "Well, I don't really know. As I didn't know that it was Randi's birthday; but just maybe we can set it up. We have the annual races and picnic coming up shortly. We'll just have to see what can be arranged. You'll be coming to the races, won't you, Ray?"

Most of the afternoon had gone by slowly and finally the last of the events were coming to an end. Good thing, too, from the looks of the increasing number of gray clouds that were gathering over- head thought Randi to herself. Pushing the long, dark-red hair back off of her face she could feel the coolness of the stronger breeze as it blew in off the mountains in the distance. Lightning, too, was flashing in the area above the mountains. Maybe with any luck at all they would not have the dance and light dinner. She felt that she could do very well without that. It had seemed that she just could not keep out of Carl Russell's way.

No matter where she was or what she was doing, he would turn up. And she was becoming very tired of trying to fight off his unwelcome advances. The man was like an octopus. Randi didn't like the nagging feeling that it was all for Jay's benefit that the dark-haired man kept latching onto her. It was becoming rather apparent that it was happening just when Jay would be looking in her direction. That and the fact that every time Randi would look for the familiar figure of her husband he would be talking to the other Russell. Always conveniently close together; almost like lovers. They (meaning the two Russells) were up to something. No doubt about it as far as Randi was concerned. Yes, the Russells were planning something besides the party.

The youth race had just ended a few minutes earlier and Randi was heading toward the vans where Chris would be getting ready to unsaddle the latest winner. The boy and flashy black and white gelding had just about flew past the rest of the contenders.

Rounding the square-sided horse van Randi could hear the raised voices of two people. Then looking up from her temporarily shaded position near the van, Randi made out the angry-stiff figure of Chris and also that of Darla Russell. Both were mounted and the horses were shifting nervously under their angry riders. The little filly, Sunfrost, was standing pressed back against the wood-planked fence, fear apparent in the dark eyes. The mare was standing as close to her offspring as she could get. Only the bridle and reins stopping her from getting closer.

Starting to move toward the two, Randi could hear what was being said. And because of the loudness, very clearly. Sensing something dangerous in the very aggressive attitude of the tall woman, Randi broke into a run.

"You little spoiled brat! You dare try to tell me what I can or can't do?" Sneered Darla with barely controlled rage.

Chris was so angry his lanky body was shaking with emotion, his young face tense and white. "I will when it comes to mistreating my horses! You had no reason to hit the foal, she wasn't hurting you. Now get away from her, you are scaring her."

Then just as the tall young man went to swing out of the saddle; the Russell woman urged her mount into Tucker and with blind rage savagely struck the smaller horse across the hindquarters. With a surprised squeal of pain the horse reared and pivoted; tossing the youth off-balance. Then with the other horse crowding in from behind, the black and white took off at a dead run; with Chris, his booted foot still caught in the stirrup, dragging him on his back alongside of the flashing hooves.

At seeing the dark-haired woman lean forward, Randi had changed from a jog into a full run only to come up just short of reaching the gelding as he broke and ran. Turning to the only available mount there, the unsaddled Snowfire, she pulled the reins free and sent the mare off at a full gallop, not yet mounted. Using the forward motion of the now flying horse, Randi swung onto the satin-whiteness of the smooth back.

The mare stretched out into a land-eating pace, closing the distance between the terrified mount and the boy and herself. Randi leaned low over the slender neck and flowing mane to urge the mare on in a soft voice that sent the mare even faster. As she and the mare flashed by, Randi had caught the surprised and startled faces of the guests; including her husband and that of Jewel Bellington. Jewel's eyes held fear for her son and an almost pleading in their dark-blue depths.

In what seemed to the racing girl like forever; but was in reality only moments, the mare closed in on the gelding and Randi grabbed the flying reins, and gently as possible pulled the horse to a halt. The gelding's sides were heaving and trembling with fear and exhaustion, his slender head hanging low. Slipping off of the still moving mare, Randi reached the boy helping him to remove his foot.

"Are you alright, Chris?" breathed the girl in a husky voice.

A faint smile touched the strained features. "I think so. But I think my ankle is a bit twisted." Then looking into the green eyes, his hand came up to her face. "Thank you, Randi. Thank you."

"Don't mention it, Sport. Here come the others. Your dad and mother." Smiled Randi with a forced lightness that she was far from feeling. And rising to her feet she turned to meet the worried glances.

Jewel Bellington reached her first, her hand coming to grip the slender redhead's arm. "I can't say how thankful..."

"Don't even try, Jewel. He's a bit shaken up and I think that he might have sprained his ankle." Interrupted Randi.

As Jewel bent to her son, Tad Bellington appeared, his tanned face seemed aged. "That was some mount you did, young woman. But thank you."

"It's called a flying mount, Tad, and no thanks are needed." Answered Randi her green gaze going past the tall man and searching the crowd for the tall woman on a blood-bay horse. And seeing that she was not there, Randi turned and swiftly headed to the mare.

As she was swinging up on the graceful Snowfire, she thought she heard Jay's voice calling her name; but chose to ignore it for the time being. The important thing at that moment was to locate Darla Russell. The woman was going to have to account for her actions. She could have killed the Bellington boy.

Hearing the fast tattoo of a horse racing into the hard-packed yard, Darla turned away from her mount and glanced idly at the oncoming rider. At seeing the flash of white and red, she knew it to be Jay's redheaded wife. A dry smile touched the thin, almost cruel lips. Let the little bitch try something. It would be her outsider's word against a Russell's. No contest at all.

Stepping away from the tethered horse, she carelessly walked toward the shaded grassy area near the side entrance to the long, low house. The red-haired woman seeing the move turned the mare in an intercepting course that would put her directly in front of Darla's retreat to the sanctuary of the house. Stopping just short of the trees, the dark-haired Russell waited for the girl to dismount. At seeing the white, stiffly-angry features of the girl's face; Darla felt the first quiver of apprehension feather along her backbone.

Randi walked with stiff, angry strides straight up to the taller woman, her hostility threatening to spill over if she did not force it down. Eyes the color of green fire narrowed on the owner of Bangon. "That was a cruel and deadly thing to do to a child. To anyone, for that matter."

A blankness settled over the other's features. "Whatever are you talking about, Randi honey?"

"You know damn well what I'm talking about, Darla. You deliberately struck Chris's horse. And I can't understand why you would pick a quarrel with a sixteen year old boy to begin with. Do you like hurting things that can't hurt you in return? Like the little filly that Chris accused you of hitting." At seeing the slight start of surprise wash over the otherwise expressionless face, Randi added bitterly, "Yes, I not only heard, but also saw. I heard the two of you arguing and I saw the way the filly was backed up against the fence and scared clear out of her wits. And then I saw you hit Chris's horse and push your own mount into the rear of the gelding. By the way, Chris is safe. No thanks to you. But I doubt if you were even the tiniest bit worried."

The dark-brown eyes turned a frosty black as Darla stepped in closer to the redhead. "You meddling little bitch? You don't know what you saw. You don't even know that your husband is in love with me and not with a poor, child-like creature like you. Before you showed up we had an 'understanding' and if you think that just because you are married to him that he is going to stop seeing me you're a fool."

"Not as much of a fool as Jay is if he can be taken in by a grasping, scheming, cruel fraud as you. If he believes in your pretending, then you are more than welcome to him. But right now all I'm concerned with is that you make an apology to young Chris. The rest of this conversation has nothing to do with what happen." Seeing the grim twist of the thin lips, Randi raised a gold-tipped brow. "Or was it? You did it to get back at me. That's it, isn't it?"

"I'm not about to apologize to that snot-nosed kid. Where does he get off giving me orders and on my own Station. And as for you, you little nobody. Even if I did you couldn't prove it and who would believe the likes of you?" spat the thoroughly aggravated woman. And seeing the momentarily dismayed sadness that clouded the green eyes, Darla raised her fist to strike the younger woman. A false sense of triumph urging her to make a move.

The blow landed hard on the smaller woman's shoulder, sending her back a pace or two. Instant blind rage coursed through Randi's slim frame. Stepping forward and bringing a low hard swinging fist up from her hip to connect with the dark-haired woman's jaw square on, Randi felt the force of the swift uppercut all the way up her slender arm and shoulder. But the once gloating woman was now lying flat on her elegant back and looked anything but sophisticated.

A crowd of some size had gathered at a distance, but had been able to see the climax of the heated argument that had been going on between the two women. The outcome was to say the least a surprise. How anyone as small and delicate-appearing could haul off and land a punch like the one the redhead delivered to Russell was astounding and something that the outback people would not forget for a long while to come.

Looking down at the woman, Randi slowly dusted off her hands and made to turn away. Looking to where she had left the mare, she saw Jay's tall figure moving towards her, his lean face dark with anger. Not giving him a chance to reach her, she vaulted onto the mare's back and reined the horse in the van's direction. She by no means wanted to be taken to task in front of that gathering crowd of guests by Jay. She really did not want to be hassled around at all.

Carefully she slid down off of the mare and absently rubbed her fingers over the little filly's nose. At the same time as she looped the reins over the fence, she heard Jay approach. Stiffening her back unconsciously, she turned to face him. "Jay? I suppose you want to know what that was all about?"

A dry laugh broke from his throat as he faced her small figure. "You do, huh? I'm so mad that I would love to shake some sense into that silly head of yours. What do you think you are trying to do? You just cold-cocked the owner of this station in front of her guests! Do you understand just how embarrassed I am?"

Thunder rumbled over the flats and clapped loudly as it slammed up against the station buildings. The suddenness of it caused Randi to jump nervously and before she could lose her nerve, she raised her small chin and answered with a sharp note to her voice, "You are embarrassed? You, the almighty J.R. Lewis? Well, isn't that just too bad. I'll tell you something, Jay. If I had it to do all over again, I'd do it the very same way; only sooner. You haven't even bothered to find out the reasons or what happen. Now, if you'd like to know, you can go ask your elegant 'lady friend'. I'm sure she will tell you just what you want to hear."

Before she could make a move to get by him, his hands snaked out and grabbed her arms, just above the elbows. "Oh, no you're not. You've got an awful lot of explaining to do." Just then the wind kicked up and the heavy clouds opened up and dumped what seemed like gallons of rain on them. A cold, drenching downpour.

Shivering and not necessarily from the rain, Randi turned her face away from the cool gray glance. The fine molded lips set in a tight line of rebellion. Jay bent his head, his lips close to her ear; but whatever he had planned to say was halted as the Bellingtons strode up to them in a flurry of rushing.

Jewel taking one look at Randi's mutinous features, placed her arms around the slender girl as if protecting her from the grim faced man beside her. "Come inside the van out of the rain. You both are getting drenched. Ray Proctor is bringing a thermos of hot coffee."

Once inside out of the pouring rain, Randi moved away from Jay's tall rather threatening figure and turned to the boy, Chris. He had his foot propped up on a makeshift box, but other than that he appeared fine. "How's the ankle?"

Chris glanced over at the silent rancher then back to the redheaded girl who had saved his life. "It's doing fine. Randi, what you did to…. Well, I think you were fantastic. Where did you ever learn to hit like that?" demanded the youth with a smile.

"You saw, huh? Some friends I once knew showed me a few different moves to protect myself. I imagine that they would be rather pleased with it, too." Answered Randi with a soft sigh.

Chris, who had secretly been watching the tall rancher, caught the slight frown that touched the weather-tanned features. The blue eyes narrowed and hardened as he pulled himself up taller in his awkward position. "Jay, did you see Randi save me from being dragged? I wondered as you didn't ask how I came to be in that situation. Anyway, I'll tell you now. Darla was hitting on Sunny and then she turned on me. After some heated words; well, as I was dismounting she struck Tucker and I got my foot caught in the stirrup." He glanced quickly at the silent girl before continuing, "The rest, I imagine, you saw as well as my Dad."

Jay remained unsmiling as he faced first the redhead and then the boy. "How do you know Darla caused your horse to bolt? That's a pretty serious charge to level at someone without proof."

"I saw it. I came in on the argument and then I saw her hit the gelding with her riding crop and most definitely not by accident, and then she very deliberately rammed her own mount into the rear of Tucker. The horse could do nothing else." Quietly spoke up Randi from the corner where she had more or less hidden herself.

No one said anything, not a word, the silence seemed to grow until Ray Proctor broke it as he handed a hot mug of coffee to the chilled-appearing girl. She looked up and smiled thankfully. "It sure smells good, Ray. Thanks."

"You look as if you could use it. That flying mount that you did was really something. I've never seen anything quite like it before, except maybe on the television or the movies."

A faint smile barely touched the redhead's lips as she replied quietly, "I learned to do that when I was twelve or so. I can also do a flying remount. That's where one rider that is riding in a race comes toward you at a full gallop and as they go by they reach down and take ahold of your arm and the forward motion of the horse pulls you on behind. It's a lot of fun. I've done both positions. When you get better, we'll try it, Chris. If your folks don't mind. How does that sound?"

The boy's eyes grew large and round with excitement. "You bet."

Jay sat silently watching the boy and then eyeing the young woman that he had married. And realized once again just how much he did not know about her. Damn little. Turning to the lawyer, he commented lightly, "Ray, I've got some business that I will need to see you about. Sometime soon. When you can spare some time."

Ray glanced over at the tall man that had been his long-standing friend, noting the frown between the sandy brows. "Sure thing, anytime, Jay. Give me a call in a few days and we'll set up an appointment."

CHAPTER NINETEEN

Pulling the tan felt hat down low over her forehead, Randi squinted through the bright hazy sunlight to the far distance. The red roan moved nervously under her in impatience or possibly from the heat of the day. It was warm, conceded the girl to herself with a faint grimace that tugged gently at the fine molded lips. Almost a week since the disastrous party at the Russell's. So long and yet, not nearly long enough. Jay was still rather distant with her. The fact being that he has not touched, nor kissed her since returning from the Bangon Station.

Running a slender hand over the back of her hot neck, she looked once again over the uneven range that she was beginning to love. Heat haze danced across the tan grasses before her eyes, bringing tears to them. Or maybe it was more of a case of sadness. Randi was finding it hard to love someone and have them lying next to you in bed, but not really be there at all. Jay no longer made love to her, not even touching her accidently.

With a sad, lonesome sounding sigh, she turned the red roan gelding toward the group of tall shading trees nearby. A small, but deep waterhole was nestled within their coolness and she had decided to seek out its soothing tranquility. Bending down she touched the silky dark-reddish neck of the gelding, "How about a cool drink, Sand, and then a little time in the shade?" The little horse snorted his acceptance and trotted easily through the stand of trees.

Suddenly, without warning the gelding stiffened and came to an abrupt halt; his small ears moving frantically back and forth. The dark eyes were wide and the head bobbed up and down. Leaning forward Randi once again touched the now lathering neck, "What's the matter, fella? Something wrong, huh?"

As she turned her head to look in the same direction as the excited horse, she heard or was it felt something whiz past? Not a second later a sharp crack broke the stillness. Then as she straightened, something slammed into the trunk of the tree nearest her head; sending bark and debris flying. Gunfire! Bending low, Randi sank her heels into the roan and sent him off at a full gallop. She didn't know who was firing at them or why, but she knew that she had to get out of range. And quick.

Just about to the pond, the game little horse stumbled then once again lunged ahead; only to suddenly give a sharp squeal and started running crazily. With a savage buck that almost unseated the girl, he plunged into some thick trees, their low branches blocking the way out.

Again hearing the unmistakable sound of rifle fire, Randi looked up to see a rough-barked tree limb rushing to meet her. Aware of the impact, a swift shooting pain and then darkness.

Pushing her weight up from the boulder that she had just moments before rested the high-powered rifle across; Darla smiled thinly as she caught sight of the roan horse streaking out of the stand of trees near the waterhole. With no rider in the saddle. After throwing one more quick look at the timber just to check for any movement, she turned and calmly walked to the large thoroughbred bay horse standing a few feet away.

Unlocking the high-powered telescope from the rifle, she slipped the weapon into the case and hooked it back onto the saddle and turned the horse toward the Bangon property. Funny, she thought idly to herself, her palms were all clammy now.

Once again a lean, tanned hand went through the sun-bleached blonde hair as Jay walked again to the verandah and looked out over the paddocks to the distant mountains. Where was she? She should have been back over an hour before. He should have never let her ride that temper mental roan horse. If he threw her in a fit of unruliness and she was hurt; he'd…. What would he do? What could he do?

Hell, more than likely she had just forgot the time. Besides why would she want to return to the house any sooner than she had to? Not lately at any rate. Not the way he had been treating her. The silence, the coldness. But he had been so angry with her over the brawl she had been in with none other than the hostess. And to lay the lady out flat! A rueful smile tugged at the tense mouth. She packed a wallop when she got mad.

Hearing the rapid thunder of a fast running horse entering the yard, he looked once more in the direction of the barns. With dusk settling in he found it hard to make out who it was. But at the same time as he noted the empty saddle, the worried yell from Ted reached him. "Jay, it's the roan! Randi isn't with him and the saddle is all scratched up."

Lewis was already through the gate and nearing the young man before Ted had finished. Together they turned and headed back to where Tom was trying to calm the excited and thoroughly frightened horse. Branches clung to the saddle and it in turn was setting at an angle, one rein dangled and the other was completely gone. Stepping back a pace from the rear of the gelding as Jay and Ted came up, Tom frowned and remarked in a quiet voice so as not to further excite the mount.

"Boss, this horse has a gunshot wound on his rump, just behind the saddle. See, the long red welt with plenty of dried blood along the end where the bullet hit first."

The tan face turned pale as he eyed the graze that was on the mount. No doubt about it, it most definitely was that of a bullet. But where was Randi? Why would anyone take a shot at her? Maybe she came across some rustlers and they in turn shot her? Could be, but usually they were at it during the evening hours or at night.

Running a shaky hand along the trembling neck of the roan, Jay stared toward the far distant mountains. Another hour or less and it would be dark and they would never find her. They could not look again until morning.

Glancing back at the two worried faces of his friends, he noticed for the first time the gathered stockmen. Their faces somber and just sort of waiting. Waiting for him to make a decision.

"Which way did the roan come in? And then what direction had Randi gone in earlier today?" questioned the rancher with desperation shadowing his husky voice.

Ted glanced quickly at the head stockman then faced the man next to him. "The horse was running from the north, near the foothills, Jay. From the way he was high-tailing-it, I imagine that he ran a pretty straight course for home. Maybe we can back track him?"

Tom bent his lean frame and rubbed a dark hand down the slender front leg of the gelding. Straightening up again he turned to the tall blonde man. "Boss, this is mud. But not the red sandy stuff found around most of the usual places. See, it's darker in color and has reeds and grasses sticking to it. You find that over near the Bangon borderline. The Stillwater Billybog. I'd bet my woman on it." Breathed the dark-skinned handsome Aborigine stockman.

Ted nodded agreement with Tom's findings and Jay turned to the gathered men, "Get your mounts and we'll search the area near and around Stillwater and the Foothills. Be very thorough when checking through the timber near the waterhole. The roan has branches stuck all over the saddle, so it's a good place to start. Let's go!"

Tom eyed the keyed-up Boss and then bent quickly to the little roan. With deft, swift movements he pulled the beaten saddle from the damp back and then eased the ruined bridle from the scratched head. But instead of running into the open corral, the little roan backed away. His whistling call shattering the silence. With jerky, quick steps the horse moved in with the other mounted horses that were about ready to leave. Throwing a quick pleading look at Jay, Tom mounted his own horse and reined it up next to the Boss's black. "He wants to go too. He'd jump the fence if you force him back in."

Swinging his horse around, Jay nodded agreement. A faint warm glow appeared in the smoky-gray eyes. "Let him be. Never know he just might lead us back to Randi."

Pale golden sunlight floated before her eyes as she slowly forced them open. A dull, persistent throbbing was clouding her thinking. Her head ached as did most of her slender body. She found that if she breathed very deeply, a sharp pain pierced through her right side. A soft moan escaped through her tightly clinched teeth.

By moving her head slightly she could look around the room. Her bedroom back at GetAway. They must have found her. Silly, of course they had or she wouldn't be lying here in her very own bed. She must have been hit harder than she realized for her to be so confused. A quick, yet thorough glance around showed that no one was in the room other than herself. But after listening for a moment or two she discovered the softly muted sounds of voices coming from the other side of the partially closed door. Two voices, both being male. She could not make out the words, but knew one of them to be Jay. His voice sounded wonderful to her, even if soft and barely distinguishable. There for a brief while yesterday she had doubted whether she would ever see him again.

Easing herself back onto the pillows, Randi closed her eyes and her thoughts returned to the side of the tree where she had lain in the tangled grasses and reeds. Oh, yes, she had returned to consciousness for a very short time yesterday. Long enough to hear what at first she thought was Sand heading for home; but had quickly realized that it could not have been. For two very good reasons. The horse was heading away from the station buildings and at a sedate walk. Shortly after the sound of the hoof beats could not be heard a certain blankness had seemed to envelop her. Her mind seemed fuzzy and it was hard to think clearly, yet she had tried to move and found it all but impossible to do so. The pain in her side had made even the simple task of breathing hard and painful; her vision, too, had kept blurring until finally unconsciousness had once more claimed her.

From the direction of the corrals a familiar shrill ringing whinny floated to her with the gentle breeze that blew in through the screened verandah door. Could it be Sand? Was the little horse alright? With a soft sigh she once again closed the smoky-green eyes.

Pushing open the door, Jay peered in on the resting girl. Her face was pale and a bruise garnished the right side of the small oval face. A rather deep cut was near the hairline, but the doctor had assured him it was nothing to worry about now. It should not cause any more problems. Among the scratches on her arms and assorted other bruises she had come off with only two cracked ribs and a mild concussion. It could have very well broken her neck. Yes, she had been very lucky.

At seeing the slight wince that the slender form made and then the slow opening of the cloudy green eyes, Jay moved further into the room to halt at the foot of the bed. "Morning, Randi. How are you feeling?"

At the sound of his voice the small figure stiffened. Then looking up and seeing Jay's concerned face, a gentle, yet hesitant smile touched the fine lips. "Hi."

The tall man moved around to the side and then eased himself down next to her, being careful not to touch her for fear of hurting her. "Is it painful to breathe?"

"Not too bad, now. I'm more stiff than anything." Sighed the girl carefully. But lifting her gray-green gaze to his face she asked, "Sand? Is he…."

A smile touched the firm male lips. "He's fine. I think that horse is part bloodhound. He more or less led us back to where he had lost you."

"Really?" Chuckled Randi, but stopped almost immediately at the quick pain it caused to the injured side.

"Yes, really. He is scratched up a bit and has a rather deep mark where a bullet grazed his rump." Answered the man as he watched the expressive face of the redhead.

A frown touched the center of her brows. "Jay, why would anyone shoot at me?"

"I haven't been able to figure that out as of yet. Do you want to tell me what exactly happen? Maybe we can figure it out from the bits and pieces." Jay replied quietly.

Randi nodded then started to relate what and how the events lead up to getting hit by a tree limb. "I knew that someone was shooting at us, but just couldn't seem to get out of their range of fire. You know though, Sand sensed something before it had happen. I mean he started acting up just before the gunfire started. Not bucking or anything like that; but he just stiffened and stopped. Very abruptly. And his coat was wet with lather and minutes before he was dry. He knew." And she glanced up from under veiling lashes to see how the silent man was taking this last bit about the gelding. To her surprise he was not laughing at her or her suspensions.

Leaning back he let his thoughtful gaze rest on her upturned face. "It sounds like it could have been instinct, some sixth sense that warned him? Maybe he sensed other horses?" Jay sighed tiredly. "Anything else that you can remember? Just anything at all?"

Randi closed her eyes for a moment and then as she remembered the hoof beats. "Yes, I do. I think. Possibly only one person. I heard a horse walking away from the waterhole area shortly after I must have fallen. I came too briefly and at first I thought it had to be Sand, until I realized that it was going the wrong way and the roan wouldn't be walking. Another thing, just before I heard the rifle shot I looked up in the same direction as the roan and

I didn't see anyone, but I did see a flash of light; like that of the sun reflecting off the barrel of a rifle?"

"Where?" asked the watchful man, his gray eyes never leaving her face.

"Why…..uh….short distance away from the wooded area. Just up a slight hill from the waterhole. There's a few trees that stand up on it and a number of boulders strewn around. It was just in the shade of the trees and a little behind the larger boulders. I only got the one quick look, then I was too busy trying to get out of the way."

Raising up in the weathered saddle to ease his stiffness, Tom pushed back his tan felt hat and once again studied the ground and surrounding boulders. A deep frown marred the dark handsome features as once again he looked down over the stand of trees and waterhole where they had found the little Missy the night before. He could make out the figure of Ben, the Aborigine youth that took care of the stables and most of the horses, as the youth moved around near the still, deep watering hole. He could easily make out the whole terrain and every move that the boy made. Tom had brought the youth with him to look for some kind of sign of who had taken pot-shots at the Missy.

Seeing Ben wave his arm to catch his attention, Tom motioned him to come on up to where he sat his horse. The dark-skinned youth nodded agreement and swung aboard his own mount. While waiting for him to reach him, Tom quietly studied the signs before him. He had not said anything to the Boss about coming out here, he wanted to check it on his own first. To be sure. Now he had found more than he really had planned to. Hearing the buckskin's hooves strike the rocky ground near where he stood; he motioned for Ben to dismount and slowly followed suit, being careful not to get too close to the large boulder and the ground near it.

Turning his head in the boy's direction, he pointed to the soft soil near his feet and also beside the grayish-colored rock. "Take a good look, Ben, and tell me what you see?"

The dark liquid-brown eyes scanned the area where Tom motioned. A frown tugged at the sensitive lips, then he faced the older man. "Those are shells from a high-powered rifle and that boulder over there is where the rifle was fired from. The footprints are made by a boot, a riding boot. But….."

Tom's mouth tightened. "Yes, but what?"

Taking a deep breath, the youth continued. "The boot marks are those of a woman. And the imprint near the soft dirt by the large boulder is that of a knee. They were made from whoever had fired the rifle and she wasn't hunting she was aiming at a target. The little Missy? But why?"

"It sure looks that way. Did you notice in which direction the horse's tracks lead off? Yes, toward Bangon. Remember that the left hind shoe has a brace bar across it. We'll know who it is for sure if that horse shows up; say, at the races that are coming up. Not a word to anyone just yet, not until we have proof. Did you bring your camera? Good. Take pictures and then gather up the shells."

Ben glanced at the head stockman, the features were tight with anger and a promise of violence if his suspicions were proved correct. Ben and Tom both knew pretty well who it was, but were not sure of the motive. But they would find out. The Aborigine people were very loyal to each other and to those that they respected. And there were a number of stockmen at the station who would do anything for the Boss's little wife.

CHAPTER TWENTY

Pushing the heavy fall of copper-bright hair back away from her warm face, Randi looked out across the paddocks toward the distant cloud of dust. A large van-type vehicle was coming along the drive at a steady clip that would put it at the homestead in a matter of minutes. Turning her head back toward the stables, she called softly into the shaded darkness, "Hey, Tom, could you come out here for a second?"

Stepping out of the partial shadows and into the bright glare of sunlight, Tom raised a hand to his dark brown eyes so that he could see. Moving up next to Randi, he asked in his rather soft, slightly husky voice, "What is it, Missy?"

Turning a smile on the stockman, she pointed a finger at the oncoming vehicle. "What or who is that coming our way, Tom? Looks like some sort of van."

Tom looked up in the same direction, screwing up the far-seeing dark eyes so as to make out the vehicle through the fine dust. At seeing the van, a slight smile touched the usually serious mouth. "That, Missy, is the mail van. It delivers packages and goods from town that the mail planes can't always carry. Maybe your special package will be on it, you think? If so, just in time for the races. The little roan is just about ready and you, too, I think. Think maybe you will be able to run in the big race as we plan?"

Wrapping her arm around the slight frame of the wiry man in an affectionate hug, the redhead grinned in return. Tom had become one of her best and most trusted friends in the time since she had arrived at the station and into their lives. "Yes, Tom, I sure plan on riding in that race. And also to be able to give that special demonstration we discussed. You bet'cha. Oh, Tom, I sure do hope that my saddle is in that van today. Don't forget, not a single word to bossman Lewis. Let's go meet the truck. Isn't Ted doing the books at the store this afternoon?"

Moving the girl forward with the palm of his lean, callused hand he agreed with the redhead. "Yes, he is. But Ted will not say anything if we ask him not to. He wants to see you ride in the race as much as the rest of us. It's just that the Boss is worried about you. He's afraid you get hurt, I think."

A slight frown touched the fine lips, Randi wasn't as sure of the reasons as the head stockman but she decided to remain silent about how cool the boss man was to herself. It was her problem and she would have to work it out on her own.

She decided too, that even if her racing in the upcoming race would cause Jay to become upset he could not get much more distant with her than he had been in the last few weeks or so. At first she had thought that the reason he never touched her or slept with her was because of the shooting accident and her injuries, but she had healed fairly well and hardly had any pain left to speak of.

The cracked ribs still caused her a twinge every now and then if she tried to do too much or moved too quickly. The bruise on her face had almost disappeared from view. She had hardly seen him at all since she had been allowed out of bed. The better she became the farther away he seemed to withdraw.

Hopefully her saddle and other equipment that she had asked her sister to send had arrived. It would at least give her something to do that would not make her think of her distant, cold husband. Maybe he did regret marrying her now? Maybe the snooty Darla Russell was more like the wife of a wealthy station owner? Well, if that was what he wanted he could have it. Darla would be more than pleased. Besides who was she, little miss nobody, to cause the mighty to change their minds if they so choose?

Just then she heard Ted's soft drawl call out from the van side. He was signing a set of papers that belonged to the delivery man. "Hey, Randi, got some things for you. Came all the way from the United States. Some place in the mid-west? I'll need some help getting them out of the van, could you help, Tom?"

Grinning, Tom moved forward to give the lanky young man a hand with one of the large cardboard boxes. Then the two moved back into the step van and each lifted out another box a piece and finally the tall truck driver handed a brown-paper wrapped package to Ted and started up the van and was once again on his way. Ted then turned to Randi and asked, "Where do you want this stuff?"

Glancing over at the head stockman and then back to the young accountant, Randi replied, "How about in the stable next to where we have Sand's stall? It should be out of the way and still easy and convenient to get at. I'll take one of those smaller boxes."

"No, why don't you take this smaller package and leave the heavier stuff to us. No need to set those ribs to hurting when you have two healthy, strong men around to carry them for you." Stated the handsome sandy-haired Ted.

A soft blush rose up over the delicate features and she smiled her thanks and then carefully took the smaller

171

package from Ted's arms and started in the direction of the stalls. Sighing softly to herself, Randi thought that there were quite a few very nice people on the GetAway Station and the Australian outback. And she felt very lucky to just be associated with them. Most of them, anyway. Not including the Russells or Don Starck.

Within a few days she would be twenty-five years old and the race was due to start on or about the same time. She wanted Sand ready for that race and herself too. Her lightly tanned body still showed signs of the bruises and was still slightly stiff. But no matter what she was determined to compete in that race and if she had her way about it; winning. This was one time that Jay Randal Lewis was not going to stop her from doing exactly as she had planned.

So deep in thought was she that she had not realized that they had reached the stables. Looking up as the silvery dog touched its cold nose into the palm of her hand, she spoke to the dog first and then to the two men as they followed her inside, "Just put them anywhere near the corner and I'll go through them a little later after lunch. Oops!" Tripping over a thick clump of straw, she dropped the brown paper wrapped package to the floor.

The wrapping tore as it hit the wooden planks and the magazines and folders spread out at their feet. Ted set his box down and bent to help retrieve the spilled articles before the pups got into them. Picking up a brightly-colored horseman's magazine that was published in the U.S., he flipped through the pages quickly and then turned to the redheaded girl. "Randi, could I borrow this for a while and look through it? I haven't seen this one and I'd love to read some of the articles that are in it. Would it be alright?"

Straightening up from picking up the small bundle of folders and such, she smiled disarmingly at the accountant. "Sure, go ahead. I don't think that it is a new one, but you are welcome to read it. Any of them. Looks like my sister sent everyone she had, ha!"

Glancing at the stockman, Randi's grin deepened. "Go ahead, Tom. You can take your pick also. Here, this one has a special section on reining and also calf roping. Okay, you guys scoot so that I can get this sorted out and head for lunch or Tico will serve me up cold beans."

The two men disappeared through the tack room door and as they did so, Randi leaned against the wood wall and looked through some of the folders and papers that her sister had sent. Some were old clippings from when she had been on the guest ranch and she and Shawnee had competed in the reining events and other horse shows. Yeah, there was a bright-colored picture of the red horse and herself as they accepted the top ribbons for the trail classes. With a sudden sad mistiness clouding her vision, she flipped the magazine closed and set them on the top of a box and determinedly headed outside into the bright sunlight.

She did not really feel very hungry but supposed that Tico would have something ready for her. She had no worry of finding Jay there as he had went over to one of the out-stations to check up on some new calves from a newly acquired bull. He shouldn't return to the homestead until evening and maybe not until morning. He had said that he might just stay over at the Burton's. The Burtons were a couple that managed the out-station for Jay. She would have plenty of time in that case to go through all that had come from home.

After leaving Randi at the stable, Ted made his way back to the store and then after closing up headed for the office located at the back of the house. He had to finish up a few folders of important papers that needed his signature before he could mail them out the next day. In hardly any time at all he managed to complete the task and settled down to leaf through the few magazines he had borrowed from the Boss's wife.

The one he had seen at first was that very month's edition of a top western magazine that was not only very popular in the States, but also in the whole of Australia. Western type events from the American west was becoming more and more common in the outback. Even to the extent of competing in the rodeo circuits internationally; and by the American Rodeo rules and regulations. The United States had some very good opinions and ideas concerning horses and the running of the different areas of the horse business. And most of their magazines carried the articles that Ted felt would benefit their own station.

Picking up the second magazine he started to just sort of thumb through the pages almost absently. Until, that is, a brightly-colored photograph caught his attention. A glossy red horse that he had seen in other magazines before and a slim rider were pictured boldly across the two pages. The horse, a mare, was in the act of 'cutting out' a calf from a small herd, and she had no bridle on the slender, sleek head.

The photographer had caught the graceful, yet powerful movement of the dainty horse to perfection. Also the quick alertness in the dark eyes. Head to head, shoulder to shoulder with the calf.

But there was more. Something about the slim rider sitting the moving horse that attracted his attention and held it. It looked vaguely familiar. The style, the way the body seemed to become part of the horse. As if one.

Frowning slightly, he glanced down below the caption and skimmed the following story.

TOP CUTTING HORSE – THE FINALE!
SHAWNEE FIRE and owner/rider RANDILEE
COLON Demonstrates their winning style in working
cattle. To prove the point – NO BRIDLE was used.

Continuing on down the column, Ted read also that the two had been a top item in the States. Especially in the New Mexico area where Colon had worked as a wrangler on a well-known guest ranch. Not only had the mare ranked in the top best of cutting horse greats, but also in Western Pleasure, Reining, and in Trail Class.

Shaking the brown hair back off of his forehead, Ted grinned to himself. No wonder the little roan had been no problem for the slender girl. Reading further, he discovered that Randi had also rode in Western Cowboy Races. Real tough stuff. Almost an endurance-type race. Quite the mystery girl, their Randi. And most decidedly; she was an American. Had been an American.

Towards the bottom of the editorial, a few brief words seemed to leap out at him.

IN TRIBUTE

To a gallant horse that gave her all and an equally elegant woman, who we the western horse lovers will (along with her) miss the loss of the red mare that stole our hearts and our imaginations of a dream.

It went on to say that the mare had been seriously injured in a trailer/car accident and had to be put down. Turning the page there were more photos; most in black and white. But they along with the words told a very sad story. One that, Ted felt he must show to Jay. As soon as the rancher returned from the out-station.

Placing the informative magazine on the desk top, Ted sighed and leaned back in the leather-bound chair. Just to think that right here on GetAway was the owner of Shawnee Fire, all round cattle horse. The versatile champion that every horse breeder wants to have happen within his own stables with his own horses.

Even knowing the redhead for only a short time, Ted knew that the shock of losing the beloved mare like that had most surely shattered the girl. She was so loyal to the roan and he in turn was loyal to her.

CHAPTER TWENTY-ONE

Pushing the tan bush hat back from his warm forehead, Jay let the big blue-black stallion rest.

Gray eyes, cool and remote, swept over the early morning vastness. Already a faint heat haze was hanging over the lower valley. Maybe another storm was shaping up? He was not far from the station house, just a few more miles that the stallion could make disappear in no time at all. Part of him was in a hurry to reach home; aching to see, touch or just be near Randi. But another part was hesitant, uncertain, finding small excuses to delay the arrival.

For a man so strong in most ways, this weakness when it came to the mere slip of a girl he had married was totally unsettling. He was angry, short-tempered, and unreasonable with her at times (more times than not) and then could not really figure out why.

The shooting accident (if it was an accident, which he doubted) still bothered him and he felt that in some way or for some reason it had to do with or because of him. No matter how indirectly. True, no real proof; except maybe a nagging, gut feeling. But as long as that feeling of unease persisted he would find it terribly difficult to get close to Randi or show his feelings for fear that something would happen to her. Instead he seemed to get angry, almost cruel with her. Fear was something that Jay had never had much trouble dealing with, but this was different. It was not himself that he feared for; but the slight red-haired woman.

He had talked to Ray Proctor about the shooting and the lawyer was astounded as himself. He had planned on asking Ray about Randi's papers and with all the other worries it had totally escaped his mind. Proctor had been angry and could not understand how or why such a thing could happen. Ray had not been the only one. The Bellingtons wondered also. He was also wondering what his head stockman had found. He was fairly certain that Tom and B**en had gone back to where they had found Randi. But other than an intent, closed face Tom nor Ben had related what, if anything, they had found. And no amount of probing seemed to make** them more likely to say anything. In fact it seemed to make them even more closed-mouthed than before.

Straightening in the saddle, Jay decided to move the black on toward home. But maybe he would swing past the Stillwater Billybog just to check things out. If nothing more than to ease his mind. Also it would delay him reaching home too soon. Another excuse? Could be. The signs, if any, would have been washed or blown away by now.

Sinking his heels into the now refreshed stallion he turned instead of to the waterhole, back to the out-station. The stallion moved with nervous uneasiness that seemed to reflect Jay's own feelings exactly. Nervy, tense and completely unreasonable.

For the umpteenth time Ted paced to the front verandah to look out over the station drive toward the direction of the Burton's out-station. Wishing for some sign of the boss's coming. The young man had very nearly radioed the Burton's when he had realized that Jay would not be returning last night. But had later decided to wait until morning. The information was just about bursting inside of him and he needed to tell the Boss. Surely he would be coming soon? He should have left fairly early that morning, so where was he?

Frowning slightly the sandy-haired young man glanced at the watch at his wrist. Still fairly early; he was just excited and maybe a little anxious so that it seemed longer than it actually was.

Just as he was about to turn back to the house, he heard the distinct sound of hoof beats. Looking up once again, he saw to his relief the Station Boss pulling up at the corrals.

Pulling his hat down farther on his head he stepped down off the porch and headed for the tall blonde man. His own long legs taking him swiftly to the large black horse and still mounted rancher. "Hello, Jay."

With the black tossing his head with impatience, Jay swung out of the saddle. Turning to face the accountant, he deftly handed the reins to Ben as that young man appeared. "Hello, yourself. How goes things?"

Ted grinned. "Not bad at all. What did those calves look like? Were they worth the price of that new bull?"

Jay wiped a hand over his damp forehead, then smiled. "You could say that. Some of the nicest looking stock we've had in a long time. That new blood line is just what we needed." Then glancing casually around, he asked quietly, "Where is everyone?"

"I think Tom is over at the south paddock sorting livestock. And Randi is over at the stables where the pups

179

are, sorting through some packages she received from her sister."

Jay halted and started to turn in the direction of the stables, when Ted's quiet voice spoke up. "I've got something that I think you will be interested in seeing. Why don't you come on over to the office now and you can see Randi at lunch." At seeing the frown appear on the handsome face, Ted added with a smile. "I think you will be, should I say, pleasantly surprised. At least you will be once the shock wears off."

Jay hesitated for just a few moments longer, then with a slight shrug of his shoulders nodded in agreement and started for the office at the back of the house.

Randi stood at the shaded stable entrance and watched as Jay rode in on the black. She felt her stomach tighten and the slender hands trembled just a bit. What kind of mood was he in today? What would he say when he saw her saddle? And he would see it, no doubt in her mind about that. More than likely be angry with her about it. As of late, he was always angry with her. Maybe he just could not stand to touch her any longer; maybe he found that the attraction he had for her was now gone? Unlike herself who had foolishly fallen in love with a man who did not love her in return. What a fool. Oh, well, no use in brooding about it now, first things first. And right now it was the race. Nothing was going to stop her from riding in that race. Nothing or no one.

With a faint sigh of relief, she watched the tall rancher walk toward the house with Ted. She had not wanted to confront the stern man now. She was too much on edge. And not just because of the upcoming races either. At the back of her mind the shooting still lingered, haunting her when asleep and slipping into her thoughts during the waking hours. Why? Why would anyone take a pot-shot at her? Something kept nagging at the idea that it was rustlers. It did not figure that a professional rustling ring or for that matter, an amateur gang would try to steal cattle during the daylight hours. Besides, why would only one person do the shooting? And it had been only one person. Randi had been around rifles and guns too long not to know when it was coming from one place and one rifle. And whoever it had been had meant to kill her.

Shaking the long red hair back over her shoulder, she turned back into the shadowed interior. The saddle needed to be oiled and she had it mounted on a rack and had been doing exactly that when she had heard her husband ride up. The saddle was not a very fancy one; yet it was an expensive stock saddle. Very light-weight, very strong and durable and most important, it was comfortable. Smooth dark-butterscotch colored leather, with no tooled designs made up the whole of it, except for the rough-out brushed padded seat and nylon breast strap. The stock saddle was the universal model with two cinches, one tight one behind the shoulders and a loose one behind the stirrup. The second one was used in calf roping and anything to do with pulling or holding. It would keep the full pressure off the shoulders of the horse, helping to keep the saddle from pulling off or injuring the mount. The cantle was reinforced to strengthen it for the purpose of roping.

Sitting down on an over-turned bucket, Randi once again started to lovingly work the oil into the saddle. Her friends at the guest ranch had got together and bought her the saddle when she had first won the reining horse state competition. They had wanted to show their appreciation and friendship.

Deep in thought, humming softly to herself she did not hear the little red convertible pull up in front of the house. Not until, that is the red speckled dog rose to her feet and a deep rumble sounded from her throat. The smoky-red fur ruffled and standing up on the neck and back. "What is it, girl?"

Then the sound of a car door slamming shut reached her and she idly moved over to the entrance and looked out. At seeing the car, she turned curious green eyes toward the house. The tall, dark-haired Darla was just about to the front door. A heaviness settled around Randi's heart; but it was the hackles on the back of her neck that caused her to move out into the sunlight. A nagging secret feeling that she felt that she should know the reason of, but seemed to escape her.

A shrill ringing whinny sliced through the air, sending birds flying in every direction. With a startled glance Randi watched the roan pace back and forth and then stop and snort. Tossing his head and pawing frantically at the ground near the fence. His dark eyes were flashing and the teeth were bared. The small pointed ears laid back close to his blue-black mane, the fevered eyes glued to the tall woman as she was disappearing into the shaded interior of the house.

Once again the hair at the back of the redhead's neck seemed to stand on end. A sign of fear; or a warning of danger? Quietly Randi moved over to where the little horse stood still pawing the ground. As she reached him, Tom and Ben came to stand at the corral next to where the roan stood.

With a frown marring the delicate features, Randi questioned softly, "Has Sand acted like this before when Miss Russell arrived?"

Even before the man shook his head, Randi knew the answer. "No, Missy. Only this time. Some-thing is upsetting him."

A hardness had settled on the handsome features of the older stockman as he spoke. The warm liquid-brown eyes had become icy and hard. Randi felt a chill run lightly over her body. For the first time she was seeing the serious side of these loyal, usually easy-going people. With a grimness settling around her own mouth she was silently thankful that these men were her friends. They would definitely make tremendous enemies. Just as she was about to mention that maybe she should go in and see if their guest needed anything; the very guest appeared with Jay and Ted.

Cool gray slivers flashed across the distance to ram full charged into the equally cool green. Straightening up from the fence Randi watched the three walk toward her and her two companions. At a slight inclination of the dark-handsome head, Tom motioned the young Ben back to the stables. Then with the slightest movement he somehow positioned himself protectively between Randi and the oncoming guest. A fact that Randi noted and from the steely look in the gray eyes, her husband had noted it also.

Shrugging slightly as if to throw off an unwelcome burden, the slender redhead stepped forward to meet the three. The smile was stiff and not very friendly, but was as good as she could manage. Remaining silent until one of them decided to speak first. She doubted if she could even force a friendly note out through the stiff lips. So she waited.

Ted sensing the tension that effused from the three people around them was almost tangible, slowed his pace and let the boss and Darla Russell proceed slightly ahead of him. He, too, did not care for the tall, regal woman and for some odd reason he felt that he should be ready to protect the small, still form of the red-haired girl that was his boss's wife. Surely Jay wouldn't let any harm come to Randi? And why would he think that Darla Russell would be capable of harming the girl? He didn't know, but he felt it just the same.

Jay came to a halt a short distance before the slight figure of his wife. "Morning, Randi and how are you, Tom?"

Randi nodded, but remained silent. Tom stepped forward a little more and then answered softly, "Just fine, Boss. How were the new calves? Any good qualities show up special?"

Jay smiled slightly. "A few. What's the matter with Sand? He seems to be very unsettled."

And even as the words were falling from the handsome lips, the small red roan lunged at the confining fence. A squeal ripped forth as the horse was not allowed to get to whomever it was he seemed to want. Darla stepped back as if the roan had indeed sank his teeth into her. A sneer marring the elegant perfection of her face as she hissed, "I told you, Jay darling, that he is dangerous."

Randi could remain silent no longer. Her small oval face hardening. "He was fine just a little while ago. It's just been within…uh…oh, a few minutes. Actually about the same time you arrived, Miss Russell. Wonder why that would set him off? Any ideas?"

The older woman stiffened. But before she could answer, Jay spoke up. "Maybe it's an odor that's on the vehicle or maybe it's that garment you are wearing, lovely though it is. Some animal, isn't it, Darla?"

The garment in question was a brown suede jacket-like top that the dark-haired woman was wearing. True, it was some sort of pelt. But secretly thinking, Randi felt that it was more likely to be the pelt inside the top that the horse took a dislike to. A faint smile tugged at the mobile mouth, but she forced it to remain hidden.

With a narrowing of pitch-dark eyes, Darla decided to agree. "Yes, maybe you are right, JR. I just heard about your accident, Randi dear, and thought I should come over and see how you were coming along."

Tipping her head to one side in doubt, but refraining from voicing anything contrary to what the smooth woman had implied, Randi murmured dryly. "That was thoughtful of you. It was an unusual incident."

Jay frowned. He seemed to feel that there was more being said than actually was being heard. "Randi, don't you think that maybe you should apologize for your actions at the bar-b-cue?" His voice was tight with anger. Hidden and just waiting for the slender woman to flare into a temper.

Randi stiffened, but held her ground without hitting out in anger. Inside she was alive with molten hot rage. But she vowed not to show it. And then without really committing anything, she replied stiffly, "Yes, I suppose my actions were a bit inadequate." And to herself she added 'I just didn't move fast enough to stop it.' Yet her lovely face remained unreadable, only hinting at the anger just simmering beneath the surface.

With a hard smile, Darla turned away from the red-haired woman and back to the tall rancher, her arm going through his. "Good, I'm glad that little disagreement is over. Now, darling, am I invited to your station for the races? After the disagreement….uh….well…"

"Yes, of course the whole Bangon Station is invited, Darla. Everyone comes and everyone is welcome." Jay answered quietly. His hard smoky eyes still lingering on the delicate face of his wife.

As they moved off in the direction of the red convertible, Randi turned swiftly toward the corral fence. Her slender fingers grasping the rough top board of the fence so tightly that her knuckles showed white.

The little roan moved gently up to the girl, his soft dark nose ruffling the red hair near her cheek. His love for the girl very evident in his actions as he blew soft air through his nose.

Both Ted and Tom watched in silence as she almost sagged against the fence. Her strong will was getting a work out. But suddenly she straightened her slim shape and leaned back against the fence, her back rubbing up against the horse that stood with his head hanging over her shoulder.

With a flickering glance at the head stockman which was answered with a slight nod, she once again looked to where the two tall people had gone. Then very softly, almost in a whisper her gentle voice reached the two men standing close to her. "It wasn't the jacket nor an odor. But something that only Sand knows. At least for now; but believe me I'll know sooner or later."

Then she turned and walked back to the stall and the saddle. Shortly after Tom followed. Ted watched them move away and suddenly wondered if he wanted to tell Jay about the magazine article or to wait. Maybe he should just wait. A few more days shouldn't hurt.

CHAPTER TWENTY-TWO

Sitting in front of the dressing table mirror, Randi took the comb and ran it through the long silky red-burnished hair. The hair had grown since she had been at the station. She could actually sit on the ends. Pulling it all over to one side she once again ran the wide-toothed comb through it. With deft, nimble fingers she quickly braided it down her back, leaving smaller tendrils framing her small oval face.

With a small sigh escaping through slightly frowning lips, she finished the braiding and gracefully stood up. She had changed into a clean, fairly new pair of blue jeans; slim and fitting snugly over hips, waist and thighs. The legs were of the straighter variety that showed off her long, slender ones to perfection. The soft white sweater had the palest of soft colored pin-stripes running through it; with three-quarter length sleeves. It was definitely a feminine appearing top that caused her to look much more delicate and softly sexy.

Pulling on a pair of butterscotch-brown leather boots with a slightly taller heel than she usually wore, she made a turn and looked one last time in the mirror before heading for the patio for lunch. The taller boots made the slender legs look longer and the sweater did things for her slender, supple figure. Made the waist look pencil-thin and the small, firm breasts slightly larger; even without a bra (which she hardly never wore or the sport bra she wore when riding). She did wear a silky camisole that had hidden support, but was much more comfortable.

Darla Russell had decided to stay for lunch and Jay had also decided to make time for the meal when usually he implied that he was far too busy. So it must be the lady in dark red and gold chains that drew his attention. A firmness touched the soft mouth, let him; better yet, let her. Maybe they were made for each other! At least they were both hard individuals; hard, unfeeling and sometimes cruel. A sudden burning flooded the gray-green eyes, but she managed to blink the offending tears away. Unconsciously she raised the small, stubborn chin a fraction higher.

Walking with a swinging grace down the narrow, long hallway; Randi turned the last corner and stepped into the day room that led onto the patio. Through the partially open doors she could see the two tall elegant people standing rather close together, the woman's arm linked through Jay's and her fingers gripping the soft material of his silky shirt. Even while she watched the dark head leaned against the broad shoulder. Stopping briefly in stunned shock, she suddenly noticed that someone else had entered the room and was standing close behind her.

Turning slightly she found herself looking into Ted's sympathetic amber eyes. Her small oval face paling, she forced a brittle smile to her lips and lifted the shoulders in helpless confusion.

Seeing her hurt and suddenly very displeased with his boss's treatment of his young wife, Ted moved forward and placed a warm, rather protecting hand on her elbow and escorted her out into the leafy sunlight. His voice as he noted the rancher's start of surprise was harder and just that bit colder. "Afternoon. Sorry if I've kept you waiting but some business came up and though it made me a few minutes late; it enabled me to find Randi here just about to enter the day room. It's always a pleasure to escort a lovely lady. Have a seat, Randi."

The green-gray eyes shined their thanks to the young man as she slipped into the chair at her husband's left. Ted seated himself at her other side and left Jay to pull out the chair for the dark-haired Darla. Without looking up, Randi murmured quietly, "Hope I didn't keep you waiting too long either? At the last minute I decided to change. Took a little longer than I planned. What have you been up too, Miss Russell?"

A dull red crept up the women's features, turning the face hard and unfeminine in an unexpected way. The accountant just managed to stifle the surprised chuckle that rose to his lips and then almost blew it as seeing the hard glint and equally surprised expression pass over Jay's tanned handsome features.

It was then that Randi looked up directly into the eyes of her husband and then to the dark-eyed woman. Nothing but innocent inquiry appeared in the grayish-green eyes as she smiled softly and said on a note of surprise, "Oh, dear, that didn't sound quite right. What I meant to imply was, what have you been doing with yourself these last few days?"

For once the dark-haired woman was at a loss for something to say. With apparent difficulty Darla finally managed a tight, yet weak smile in the rancher's direction first, then in Randi's. "Oh, I've managed to keep busy with some riding and of course visiting friends and such. I am trying to get Shadow Mink ready for the races. She's a jumper, you know. Very high-class. Oh, and, Randi darling, you must call me, Darla. Miss Russell just sounds too formal."

Clear green eyes settled on the aristocratic features. For a moment a faint gleam of hardness shot through their depths, but only for a moment. So quickly that Darla thought that she must have been mistaken.

Then the soft and slightly seductive voice sounded from the girl as she answered, "If you think so. Do you have a horse competing in the main race to represent your station?"

Leaning back in her chair, the other woman's face and body seemed to relax. "Yes, we have entered Sailor Boy. He'll be hard to beat."

Ted grinned to himself, but turned a very disarming look in the Russell woman's direction. "He is good. When did you purchase him from Green Plain's Stable?"

A faint anger crept into the hard eyes. "You do your homework, Ted. Actually I managed to buy the horse a few weeks ago. Maybe, just maybe GetAway won't walk off with the prize this time. What horse is running for GetAway?"

Before the accountant could answer, the redhead's husky voice sounded softly, "We have more than one horse in the races, as you know. But the favorite might be called a 'dark horse'." And then she smiled.

It was a secret smile, full of meaning but only to those who she wanted to let in on the secret. With narrowed silver eyes, Jay glanced at the young accountant and then back to his small wife. Apparently Ted knew what the smile was about. And because he felt suddenly left out, he felt the anger stir within him. Or was it jealousy? Before he could sort the odd thoughts out in his mind; Darla's cool voice sounded from beside him. "I say, Randi dear, you seem to have an ace in the hole?"

A faint blush rose over the smooth cheekbones. "Yes, you might say that. But no more until race day." Then turning her attention to the sandy-haired young man, she asked in her husky voice, "Ted, didn't you say that Ebony Warrior will be running in one of the main races?"

Throwing a quick glance at his still silent boss, Ted frowned to himself. "Yeah, I sure did. Everyone else had better watch out for that black horse. He can really move if the conditions are right. Isn't that right, Jay?"

Ted had decided that it was about time that his boss got into the conversation. So he deliberately rounded on the tall, blonde man; leaving the older man no alternative but to speak.

Jay knew that the accountant was uncomfortable with his own attitude toward Randi and now with the Russell woman, so he answered with a more normal voice. "That's right. He just seems to get better every time he runs. But of course he comes from a long line of champions. Much like Sailor Boy, Darla. He must have cost you plenty?"

A hardness tightened the thin lips. "Enough, darling. But if he wins it'll be worth it. But he won't he running in the same class as your Ebony Warrior. Will you be riding the big brute?"

"Of course, who else?" drawled the male voice softly.

A dark gleam sparked in the almost black eyes as she turned the classic face in the redhead's direction. "Oh, I thought that your little wife just might. I mean she is so…. uh….well, should I say boyish?"

The young accountant straightened up to his full height, anger apparent on the handsome features. "I think, capable would have been a more true description." Then turning disappointed amber eyes on the blonde rancher, he added stiffly, "I've got some important papers to see to. If you'll excuse me."

Randi silently watched him walk away, her gray-green eyes wide and mobile mouth tightened with anger. "I have some business to attend to, also. Excuse me."

But as she went to rise a steely hand reached out and held her wrist. "Randi, I think you could let the 'business' you have go until after our guest has gone."

The small oval face paled, but her husky voice remained cool and just slightly impatient. "Our guest is really 'your' guest and I'd much rather leave now, if you don't mind? So, let go of my arm and I'll be on my way. Miss Russell, have a nice visit and do drive carefully on your way home." Still her slender wrist was locked in that strong one of her husband. Slowly though he released her and with a graceful pivot she turned and made her way toward the stables.

Darla watched with humorless eyes as the redhead walked away, the shapely back straight with some kind of indignation. A slight grin lurked about the thin lipped mouth. Maybe she had contributed to the disquiet that was very apparent here.

"Jay darling, let her go. She seems a bit upset. Might be better to let her get over her uh…temper tantrum alone." With a quick glance at the hardening features of the man sitting next to her, she added dryly, "I wouldn't be surprised if your young accountant doesn't have a crush on her. I wouldn't be too hard on him; she's so young appearing and what with no bra on it would excite almost any young man. Even though she doesn't seem to flaunt it. But you know these young people, always rebellious."

Jay listened in silence, he didn't really care for the opinions of the older woman, but still he was doubting.

Almost angry with himself, he forcibly pulled his attention back to the dark-haired Darla. Absently he made what amounted to small talk. "What is Carl up to?"

Darla let a dry smile wash over the dark-red painted lips. "You know Carl, he doesn't do anything if he doesn't have to. But he has been working out with Sailor Boy and the new rider I hired to ride him. You know, Jay honey, I think that my dear brother has been 'favorably' impressed by your little wife." A dry laugh, "Must be that long red hair."

A frown marred the handsome features. "Oh, really? I thought that Carl enjoyed his women fast like his cars?"

"Yes, most usually he does. Maybe it's because of her outgoing personality that gave him ideas. It's very possible that she doesn't even know how her actions sort of….. uh…..invites reactions from men."

Randi frowned in concentration, her hands working swiftly and almost unconsciously on the leather of the saddle sitting before her on the saddle rack. Sighing, she slowly covered the saddle. The frown was not from the work she was doing, but because of the thoughts that were stumbling over each other in her mind. That Russell woman was up to no good and the way Jay had treated her had very definitely upset Ted. A sudden feeling of gratitude washed over her. That young man had made her feel protected. And right then she had definitely needed it.

But because of it the young accountant was at odds with his boss and worse, his friend. She did not want to be in the middle of anything like that, nor to be the reason for a disagreement between the two men. It was not fair for the Russell woman to come along and make silent accusations that a person could not refute, but that someone else would believe. Why was Jay so willing to believe anything that bitch had to say or do? If Darla kept sticking her sophisticated nose into their business nothing would ever get straightened out only more muddled. But of course that was exactly what Russell wanted.

Learning back and then with her arms raised over her bright head, she stretched her stiff muscles to ease the ache of sitting too long in one position. Just as she arched her back to get rid of the last of the kinks out; a hard, slightly insolent voice broke through the stillness, causing her already taunt nerves to spring in reaction. Twisting around with startled green eyes, she came face to face with the frosty gray ones.

"Such a waste with no one here to appreciate your young, sexy body. Or maybe you were expecting Ted to come down here?"

Vaguely she shook her head as if to clear it, confusion running wildly through her. "What do you mean?"

A dry, unpleasant chuckle sounded as he stepped inside the stall. His eyes were hard and yet his body was tense with a longing. The handsome face was stiff and unyielding with his anger. "Don't play the innocent with me. That little exhibition of showing off your enticing young body, the firm rounded breasts and flat stomach would totally demoralize any young man, even our level-headed accountant."

Now standing, Randi narrowed the sage-green eyes with an anger of her own, but also to conceal the hurt that his accusations had inflicted. "You are crazy! Absolutely off your bean! If you think that poorly of your friend to think that he would sneak around behind your back; you don't have any sense at all. Ted would never do anything to hurt you, you big dumb fool. And referring to my 'innocence'.

You, my dear husband is the one who took it!" Then with uncanny accuracy she added, "Or maybe it's your guilty conscious that's playing on you? You haven't been taking your 'pleasure' so maybe you figured that I would go find someone who would? Is that it, Jay?"

Suddenly hard, strong fingers were biting into the soft flesh of her upper arms. The force of his move brought her up against the rough wood of the stall wall. Fear flared through her slender frame, but she tightened her lips over words of pleading.

"You, who go around wearing enticing clothes and no bra, advertising your availability; has the gall to accuse me of not living up to a man's ability to satisfy his wife's needs! Well, we'll just see...."

"No, Jay!" stammered Randi, her slim body shaking with tremors. "You can't!"

Once again that dry chuckle sounded as his mouth ravaged hers. His lips were hard and cruel as they forced her softer ones against her teeth. She could taste the salty flavor of blood and tears of humiliation squeezed out through tightly closed lids. His body moved in closer to her smaller one, pushing her firmly back against the wall. Randi could feel every bone and curve of his lean form, panic rose to her throat as the strong tan hands cupped the firm roundness of her breasts. Not caressingly as he had done the few times before, but roughly as if he were punishing her.

"You should know by now never to tell me that I can't do anything. You know very well that I will." Sneered the tall man against her ear.

Once again Randi tried to make him see reason. Her husky voice coming out in a hoarse whisper, "Jay, stop you are hurting me."

Taking his hand and placing it roughly against her jaw, he pushed her tear-stained face up so that he could look down into her misty-green eyes. The hardness and cold hostility that appeared in the gray eyes caused her to gasp and try to shrink back away from his cruel touch. "I don't think you have, Randi honey. Not nearly enough." He muttered harshly.

His intent was clear, he planned to make her plead and then he would go ahead and take her anyway. His male ego had suffered and now she was to pay. He was showing no tenderness; only harshness and animal instincts. His way of humiliating her. And it was working, only she felt as if her very heart was being ripped out of her.

Then as his hand grabbed ahold of her long red hair and forced her slender body to the straw-covered floor did she start to fight him. Silently at first, just twisting and turning so as to keep her now bruised body from becoming totally trapped by his heavier one. Suddenly she caught a faint whispered oath come from him, his face near her ear. At the same time he made a stretching move toward where one of the boxes lay that she had received the day before. An old pair of scissors lay on top of a brown paper wrapped package that Randi had not yet opened. Panic, pure and simple rushed through her slender body. He wouldn't!

But even as the denial flashed across her mind, his body had moved to an almost sitting position a top of her. His knees pinning her slender shoulders to the rough floor, he took up a handful of braided hair and cut into the thick silky strains of red. Pain ripped through her tender scalp as the old, dull scissors tore at her hair. The cut was uneven and had pulled most of time. More tears welled up into her eyes, but she tightly kept them closed. She wanted to scream. It was there at the very back of her throat, but as anger swelled she clinched the small, even teeth shut to keep it locked up inside.

Then as the man on top of her finished with her hair, he eased up just enough. Just enough for her to twist and bend at the waist into a half-sitting position. Her small fist came up from the floor; all the hurt and anger was behind it, and she took the rancher completely by surprise. Hit him squarely on the jaw with a blow that racked her arm and shoulder with pain. Her small face was pale, almost a grayish-white; the green eyes just dark haunted circles in the tense face.

With a shaky breath, she demanded harshly, "Are you satisfied now, Jay? Have you humiliated me enough? Get away from me! I don't want you touching me; go back to your high-society slut and play your little games. Me, I've had more than enough."

Slowly Jay stepped back, appalled at what he had done. He started to say something, anything to let her know that he had not meant it. That he had been angry, jealous, hurt too in his own way. But seeing her standing there deathly pale and her slender body shaking uncontrollably; yet very defiant with her tear-stained chin lifted stubbornly, he decided that now was not the time. With broad shoulders sagging, he turned and moved quietly out of the stable.

Randi stood where she was for what seemed like hours until she could no longer hear his footsteps. Then she looked down at the shorn strawberry-red hair that lay in profusion about her feet. It was then that she fell to her knees and started to cry; sobs that seemed to tear themselves out of her very body. She cried because she loved him and he had hurt her so. Cried because he had so little trust or respect for her. Such a joke! A rotten, evil joke.

CHAPTER TWENTY-THREE

The low roll of thunder swept up over the valley and the rumble grew in volume until it ended with a loud clap that seemed to shake the stable and grounds. Randi slowly sat back and leaned against the stall side, a soft sigh escaping through stiff swollen lips and with a shaky hand wiped the hair out of her face. Looking up toward the open doorway, she could see the gathering darkness settle on the outside corrals and grounds. Not from evening, but from the building storm. And from the sounds of the thunder it would soon be emptying the cloud's moisture.

Suddenly out of the shadowy grayness a small, dark, curly head appeared. The dark eyes grew round and soft at seeing the red-haired Missy sitting there in the stall. Beside the small Aborigine boy appeared the smoky-gray father dog. Smoke moved up next to her and stuck his cold nose against her neck, a whimper coming softly out of his throat.

"Hello, fella." And glancing up at the small boy, she managed a trembling smile. "Hello, Kerry. What have you been up to?"

The boy stepped farther inside and then came over and sat down beside her on the floor. "Hello, Missy. I been workin' with me dad doin' bull-locks. Smoke some good fella. What the Missy doin' here? It's gon'a rain plenty soon. Me dad says so."

"Sure does look like it." Agreed the girl with a nod of her burnished head. "I was working on my saddle over there and was going to start on some boxes my sister sent me. But I sort of lost track of time. Have you seen Boss man Lewis around?"

Kerry shook his curly head. "No see Boss. Him left while ago with some um…buyers. Ya' know, men?"

Rubbing her fingers through his silky hair, she answered, "Yes, they were supposed to be by today to look over some cattle that Jay had wanted to sell. I imagine that they will be staying over for dinner. I had better get to heading for the house and you, my little man, had better be getting back to your mom before it starts pouring."

Kerry grinned slowly and replied, "Rain won't hurt me, I'm tough, me mom said so." Then as his glance touched the stable floor, his lips formed an 'O'. "Fire magic." He breathed softly.

Forcing her gaze to the burnished pile of cut hair, she made herself smile, "My fire magic was getting too heavy. So cut it off a little."

With large, dark eyes still fixed on the red-gold hair, he asked in almost a whisper, "Could I have some of your magic, Missy?"

Seeing the pleading softness in the coffee-brown eyes, Randi nodded, "Sure, Kerry, you take some. It'll be your Good Magic from me."

A big smile lit up the small boy's face and then he grabbed up a long bunch of the copper-red hair in his little fist. Then with a soft 'thank you', he disappeared through the stable doorway.

Randi sighed and picked up the rest of the shorn hair and scattered paper off the floor. Putting everything in an empty box, she turned and looked at the blue-gray dog still standing beside her as he watched her every move. She rubbed the silky pointed ears and before she could reach the door the thunder cracked and the dark-gray sky opened up and rain came in a down pour.

"Well, Smoke, we better make a run for it."

Both raced out the door and headed for the verandah of the house. Deciding at the last second to go directly to her room, she turned and went down the side of the house. As soon as they were on the verandah, out of the rain, the wet dog hung back. Seeing him hesitate, Randi grinned, "Come on, Smoke, you deserve a good dry off and some tender care." She smiled with a gentle light in her eyes. "Believe me, Smoke, old boy, no one is going to say a word about it."

She was soaked through and the once fluffy, warm sweater was now cold and clinging. A real mess. Almost to the screened door of the bedroom, a tall striding form stepped hurriedly around the corner of the verandah. He had his dark-sandy head looking down and did not see her slim body until he had almost walked into her. A menacing growl curled up from the dog's throat as it moved closer to Randi. "Ooh, Ted! Quiet, Smoke."

The young man stammered in his surprise, "So sorry, Randi. I just didn't see you. I wasn't looking where I was going." Then with amber eyes narrowing, he took in the wet clothes and then seeing the shortened hair, he gasped, "What happen to you?"

Ignoring the subject of his question, she remarked rather off-handedly, "Didn't leave the stables soon enough. Got caught in the downpour. Both of us, you see. Now don't tell anyone, but I'm taking old wet Smoke into the house with me. He deserves to be dried off in luxury, don't you think?"

A dark-tanned hand reached out and touched the dark-red water soaked hair. "No, I meant what happen to your hair?" Looking into the now dark, yet expressionless greenish eyes, he had a feeling he would not get a direct answer. "Randi?"

With a slight shake of the pale face, she whispered, "Nothing happen, Ted. I just decided to uh…well, I cut it. It was becoming too long and terribly hot. Now, I've got to go inside and get out of these cold uncomfortable clothes and finish up the trimming job. Oh, Ted, how many will be at dinner?"

Not totally believing her story, but unable to do anything about it, he silently shrugged his broad shoulders and turned a half-gentle smile her way. "Two buyers and Tad Bellington with Chris. They showed up as Jay went to show the calves to the breeders. Tico is already preparing something special, but light, she said. That's where I was coming from. Well, suppose I better get to the front and get these papers to the Boss."

Randi nodded and turned to go inside, first letting the silver-gray shape of the dog precede her. "We'll see you later, Ted. And thanks."

For a moment or two, Ted waited and silently watched the girl and dog until they entered the bedroom and the door closed behind them. Then and only then did the young accountant turn and head to the front of the house where his Boss and guests were waiting for him. He had an uneasy feeling that the redhead had not been the one to cut her hair. At least not on purpose, but for what reason? Or more to the point, who would do something like that?

Surely not Jay? With a sad shake of the handsome head, he dismissed the unsettling thoughts from his mind.

Even though, he did acknowledge that he had decided to wait to show the rancher the magazine article concerning Randi. For no other reason than because of the shabby attitude he had shown to his young wife at lunch earlier. Hell, with that viper Darla Russell curling herself all over Jay; and even more unsettling the rancher letting her, someone had to protect the younger woman.

Ted was finding the association between the rancher and the Russell woman more and more confusing, especially since Jay had hardly ever acted at all affectionate toward either of them before. In most instances the rancher had treated them rather on the cool side; very polite except in the few times that the Russells had talked down their noses about one of Jay's friends or employees. Then it was barely civil.

Closing the screen door, Randi went into the adjacent bathroom and grabbed up a large, fleecy bath towel. Turning back into the bedroom, she sat down on the plush carpet and called the wet, bedraggled dog to her.

"Come on, Smoky fella. Let's get you dry, huh?" she smiled at the almost frowning expression on the blue-gray dog's face.

As the dog laid down in front of her and then let her rub his wet fur until it was almost dry, she leaned back and sighed softly. Draping the now dampened towel around the heeler's head and neck, she tiredly pulled off the soaked boots; grimacing at the sodden damp jeans and sweater. But with a slight shrug of the slim shoulders, she tossed the pair of boots out of the way and turned her attention back to the very patient Cattle Dog.

It was as she was about to finish rubbing the dog's short coat dry that the bedroom door suddenly burst open and Jay's tall figure sort of exploded into the room. Startled, Randi leaned back, her misty-green eyes wide with apprehension.

Sensing the fear or uncertainty in the girl, the blue-gray dog rumbled a warning deep in his throat and moved closer to the girl's still form. Most of the silver, very tense and alert body was under the large towel; but the almost yellow-brown eyes were narrowed and fixed on the rancher.

In one quick glance, Jay had taken in the dog's protective move, his wife's defensive behavior and the fact that she was soaked to the skin. The sweater was clinging to the youthful shape like a second skin; so sodden that the water was dripping off the edges onto the equally damp jeans. The chopped red hair hung in wet strands around her small oval face that was deathly pale and all eyes. Eyes that once were gray-green fire were now shadowed with a darker green, less brilliant showing her hurt and fear.

Anger stirred within him, at himself for causing the girl such anxiety. Looking at what he had done to the glorious hair caused him to wince with pain and bitter humiliation that he could let jealousy and anger get such a hold on him. Taking a step toward her, he halted as the dog stiffened and the lips pulled back to expose the hard white teeth, softly she touched the dog's head. "Jay?"

Pulling the handsome features into a closed expression that would not give nothing away, he coughed and said, "I heard that you had got caught in the storm and came to find out if you were alright. I see you are except for your wet clothes and….uh…..hair. Don't you think you better get yourself taken care of? Before you catch a chill."

Randi lowered her head, her slender fingertips tracing imaginary lines on the dog's silvery coat. "I plan to." Then looking up from under long wet lashes, "Just as soon as you leave and go back to your guests."

The gray eyes narrowed and the male lips hardened into a firm line. "Just as you wish." Then with a very stiff, upright back he walked out of the room, pulling the door closed with a soft click behind him.

Randi leaned forward onto her arms, arms that shook ever so slightly. As the misty-blue dog came up and laid his nose against her cheek, she sighed and whispered in a lost voice, "What do I do now?"

Wiggling closer, the dog whined softly as if trying to answer her desperate question. Slowly Randi wrapped her arms around the dog and just sat there for minutes hugging the warm, silky fur to her. The large gray-green eyes slowly filled with tears and then trickled unheeded down the pale cheeks.

Standing to one side of the room, Ted found himself watching the stiff, uncompromising movements of the tall, blonde-haired rancher. The man had been very silent since returning from checking on his wife; and even though Jay hadn't said that was where he had gone, Ted had known. The other two men, both very carefully dressed and had city written all over them had given the now taciturn rancher a couple of confused, if not puzzled glances at his change of manner.

The Bellingtons, too, had favored Jay with worried looks, but had refrained from saying anything. The younger of the two, Chris, kept glancing at the door waiting for the redhead to appear. After having done so with no sight of the girl, the dark-blonde youth moved to stand near to Ted. "Ted, what has Randi been doing with the roan? Do you think she will get to race him like she wants?"

The accountant grinned slowly, his teeth showing white. "Oh, I'd say so. That girl usually does as she wants. And I think a lot of people are going to be very surprised when they find out just how good she really is." Then catching the intense look on the boy's face, he changed the subject, "How are you coming along with the training on your stallion, Cannon?"

The young face brightened. "He's doing just great. The best. If Ben races Ghost he's going to have one good race on his hands. Do you think he will enter the gray-white gelding?"

Nodding, Ted answered confidently, "Oh, I imagine so. That boy has been running that horse every chance he gets. The Ghost is good, too. You'll have a tough time beating him, Chris."

Just then the boy glanced once again toward the door and seeing the redhead coming down the hall, said softly, "Here she comes. But...but there's something different? Her hair! Ted, she cut her hair."

Once again the accountant nodded. "Yes, this afternoon. She said that it was getting too hot and hard to care for." Hesitating, then quietly added, "Chris, don't talk about it too much. It might... uh...well, it might upset her some. Okay?"

Glancing quickly into the warm amber eyes, the youth agreed. "You bet." Then with a flirting grin, he added, "I think I like it."

The accountant had to agree. It looked totally different than the wet, chopped mass that he had seen earlier. Now the slight curling of tendrils that had appeared around her oval face was more apparent throughout the unusual colored hair. She had it parted on the side and the hair fell in a swingy bob cut to just below her chin, a long bob he thought they called it.

Coming to the day room doorway, Randi stopped for a moment and took a much needed deep breath, before entering the bright room that was adjacent to the dining room. Stepping inside she looked through long lashes to where her husband stood, his broad back to her. In a swift sweeping glance, she found the two city cattle buyers and then Tad Bellington standing near to Jay; Chris and Ted off to one side by themselves. Not sure of her reception if she went next to her husband; but afraid of stirring up his temper if she went over near to the young accountant, decided to walk near to Jay but speak to Tad Bellington.

Almost afraid that her voice would break from the strain, she whispered huskily, "Good evening, Tad. Hope I haven't kept everyone waiting?" Chancing a quick peek at the silent man at her right, she just as quickly lowered the troubled green eyes. His face was as withdrawn as a sphinx in Egypt and as closed. With a sigh and a tightening of her own lips, she asked, "Jay, you must introduce your friends from the city. They must be the cattle buyers?" And she turned the small oval face in their direction, a small smile on her mouth.

Tad Bellington frowned his confusion at his friend's conflicting attitudes. Placing an arm behind the slender back of the red-haired woman, he turned her in the two gentlemen's direction and made the necessary introductions. Just as he was finishing, Ted and his son came up to them. "Ah, Ted, have you noticed anything different about our Randi girl?"

Smiling broadly. "Yes, I have. And I must say that both Chris and I agree that the new hair style is delightful."

A faint red appeared on the fine-boned features. The smile Randi turned on them was trembling slightly. "Why, thank you, kind Sirs." With a trace of her old spirit flaring up, she turned challengingly to the tall man on her right. His gray eyes mere slits as he noted the raised chin. "And you, dear husband, what do you think of my new hair cut?"

With everyone waiting and watching him, Jay forced a smile to his hard lips. "I have to agree with the majority. Looks quite delightful."

One of the buyers laughed lightly, completely ignorant to the undercurrents that were flowing around them. "You mean to tell me that this lovely lady had longer hair?"

Chris stepped forward slightly, his manner one of protectiveness. "Oh, but it was. So long in fact that she could sit on it with it braided. Isn't that right, Jay?"

Lewis nodded shortly. "Yes, very long indeed." Then with a look toward the dining area, his frosty-gray eyes encountered Tico at the doorway. "Well, gentlemen, looks as if dinner is ready to be served."

Extending his arm toward Randi, he stated quietly, "Shall we go in?"

Silently she nodded and gently touched her hand to his arm. Even so she could feel the muscles tense under her fingers. Slowly and sadly she lowered her burnished head and fought to keep the tears at bay.

As they entered the dining room, Tico moved to one side to let everyone file by to their chairs. As the Boss and the little Missy moved near, her gentle brown eyes widened and flashed to the tense, pale face of the girl. Why would the little Missy cut that fire-bright hair? Why her little son, Kerry said it was fire magic. Good magic. Something happen, the dusky-skinned woman would bet her beloved Tom on it. Pulling the now frowning eyes away from the still bright hair, she set about placing the salads before the seated people. If anyone noticed her unusual silence, no one decided to remark on it.

The buyer who had spoken up before concerning the length of Randi's hair once again asked a question of the quiet woman with the small oval face and large eyes. "Randi, are you much of a horse woman? I've heard that GetAway Station has some of the best horses and the best races in the district."

Before she could form an answer, Chris Bellington spoke up, "You had better believe she is. As Tom, GetAway's head stockman says, she's one fine fella. And from an Aborigine stockman that is a compliment to end all compliments."

Speaking up from next to his son, Tad Bellington added quietly, "You should have seen her at the Bangon Bar-b-cue. She did a 'flying mount' and saved my son from being dragged. She definitely knows her way around horses."

Randi laughed nervously. "Well, I couldn't let that happen, could I? Who would have been able to race his stallion?"

"Speaking of my stallion." Interrupted the dark-blonde haired youth. "What about coming over to the station and seeing Cannon like you promised?"

"Well….uh…I…" stammered Randi, glancing toward her silent husband.

"Well, nothing. You are coming to the house with us tonight. I promised Jewel that we would bring you.

You'll stay the night, of course." Commented the older Bellington.

"I guess it is settled then." Smiled Randi. She definitely needed to get away for a while. She didn't like the look on Jay's face, but he had no real say. Thank heaven.

CHAPTER TWENTY-FOUR

Pinks, lavenders and the palest of bluish-lilac danced across the valley with the darker green of the trees outlining the foreground like a painter's watercolor wash. It was early, very early and slowly Randi let the pale, sheer curtains drop back into place. The Bellington home was quiet and not even the birds were up as of yet. So why was she? The bed had been comfortable, and needless to say she could use a good night's rest; but she hadn't slept. Instead she had tossed and turned until she had finally gave up and got up.

With a last look at the beautiful, pale colored dawn through the shaded windows; the slender girl sat down on the edge of the downy-soft bed with a snort of disgust. She had wanted to get away from Jay and all the conflicts and tense emotions, and what does she do the minute she finds herself alone? Think about him. Answers to the many questions that whirled around in her head from one thing to another. But eventually it all came back to what would she do? What should she do? Stay on even though it seemed to tear them both apart? All they seemed to do to each other was fight and hurt one another. She was still hurting; both physically and mentally. But what was worse, was how much would she hurt if she were to leave?

Hell, she could not even go away for a few hours without thinking about the man, wondering what he was doing, if he was missing her. Like a thorn in his side more than likely.

Suddenly remembering last night when they were just about to leave. The look of remoteness on the handsome, yet hard features had sent a pain shooting deep into her heart. Maybe he wished that he had never decided to marry her? She sure had caused enough trouble to last for a long time. But if he did not feel something, why the fits of anger? Shouldn't there be sort of an indifference about her wanting to race, or ride a certain horse, or even what other people had to say about her? Unless of course, it hurt or damaged his respectability.

Twisting the edge of the silky nightgown, a frown marring the otherwise smooth forehead; she suddenly straightened and then caught a glimpse of herself in the dresser mirror. She could still see the bruises along her back and on her arms, but the ones from the cracked ribs was almost gone. She had to stop thinking about Jay Lewis. The man could damn well take care of himself.

Standing and walking over to the dresser and lazily picking up the brush, she ran it through the shortened strawberry-red hair. A slight smile touched the fine molded lips as she remembered last evening when they had arrived at the Rockwood Station homestead. Jewel had just about dropped her mouth in surprise at the hair cut. At first she had thought it had to be cut because of the accident; but Randi had then told her that she had just decided to cut it that very afternoon. At first the older woman was shocked, then as she looked at the changed hair style, she had revised her opinion and said that she actually liked it better.

Now looking in the mirror, Randi turned her head slightly sideways and thought that she, too, liked it better shorter. Well, at least something good came out of the humiliation of Jay's attack. From the look on his face when he invaded the bedroom and found her drying the dog; he, too, had experienced some form of blame for unnecessary harshness in retaliation for what he assumed she had done.

Once more looking into the mirror, her defiant expression stared back at her and she smiled to herself. She planned on having a good time while she was at the lovely Bellington home. This morning she was supposed to get her first glance at the stallion, Cannon. Chris had been so excited she wondered how the boy had slept.

The Bellington house was an older version of the typical outback homestead. Instead of all on one floor like the GetAway home this had two floors with a verandah around the first floor, much like at home. The second floor held mostly bedrooms and each one had its own balcony. The homestead itself was laid out in an open flat that rose gradually to meet the purple and wheat-colored foothills. The foothills surrounded the triangle shaped valley and the house was at the top point of that triangle. Surprisingly large sturdy trees graced the front and most of the sides of the pale-cream colored home. Vines climbed up the latticing of the verandah to the balconies above. Sweet smelling blossoms gracing the dark-green foliage; leaving a faint, pleasing perfume on the air.

With a shake of the burnished head, Randi decided to forget trying for more sleep and rising, went over to her case that was sitting on the table at the foot of the double bed. Pulling out blue jeans and a pale-yellow knit pullover, fresh underthings; she headed into the adjoining bathroom for a quick shower. Maybe by the time she was through the rest of the household would be up.

Chris turned the corner of the kitchen and almost knocked his mother off her feet. "Oh, sorry, Mom. I was in a hurry."

Chuckling softly the older woman turned to the silent form sitting at the large table buttering hot toast. "See what I mean, Randi? Always in a hurry for somewhere." Then looking at the tall, lanky youth, she added, "Breakfast will be ready in a jiffy, Chris. Sit down and stay out of the way. Your father should be down in a minute or two."

Helping himself to the stacked toast, Chris grinned around a mouthful of buttery crispness at her. "Good morning, Randi. Did you sleep well?"

The slender redhead leaned back and looked at the dark-blonde teenager from under thick lashes. "Yes. Do you like toast, Chris?" At the nod, she chuckled huskily, "I thought so. At least it looked that way. Do you want to go take that look at Cannon after breakfast?"

Swallowing down the last of the buttery morsel, he answered, "Yep, sounds good to me. You'll really love him. He's some looker. Morning, Dad." Grinned the boy with a definite twinkle in the blue eyes.

Watching the two male members of the Bellington family, Randi could see the companionship as well as the respect that they held for each other. It was good to see a family so together. Just then Jewel brought over the hot plate brimming with sausage and bacon, eggs and flapjacks.

Randi offered to pour the fresh squeezed orange juice in the glasses at each plate, and as she did so she could hear the friendly banter between son and parents. Yes, it was a very nice family.

Leaning against the corral fence, Chris nodded his head toward the girl and the buckskin horse. "See how she rides, Dad. Just like she was part of him. I've seen Jay do it and I try, but she's really special."

Tad Bellington moved his forearms higher on the top rail of the fence next to his son. A frown of concentration furrowed his weathered brow. "Yes, I can see what you mean. It was like that when she did that flying mount on Snowfire. Never have seen anything like it."

Both men looked at the swift, smooth moving stallion and the slip of a girl setting easily on the broad back. She was riding the shiny coated horse with no saddle and the horse was stepping out as if he could walk on air. The black mane and tail flowed out and matched up with the copper wave of the woman's gleaming hair. With a deft, slight movement of the slender hand the large stallion did a quick turn and headed back the way they had just come. Smiling softly, the redhead pulled the large horse in next to the fence near the two men.

"You were right, Chris, this horse moves like a dream." Declared Randi with an even wider smile. "Don't you agree, Tad?"

The older man chuckled gently. "Yeah, especially with you on him. What was that last little turn you did?"

A frown touched the smooth features for a brief moment. "Oh, I know what you mean. That was a pivot. In cutting out cattle the horse has to learn to maneuver with the least amount of distance. The front end turns while the hind feet stay in place. It is also used in reining trials during competition. Also a roll-back. That is when the horse almost sits down and turns in one move. You have to have a very well balanced animal. One that can get his legs up under him very swiftly. And from the way Cannon moves I'd say you have a darn good horse here. He's fast no doubt about it. Especially for such a large horse, but he's well put-together."

Gracefully the redhead slid down off the wheat-colored horse. As she did so, the elegant head turned and nuzzled her neck and cheek. Unconsciously lightly tanned fingers reached up and touched the velvety nose. Laughing softly she joked to the horse, "You better not let Sand catch you doing that my boy. Or you'll see one jealous small-sized package of dynamite."

Chris glanced at his father, then eyed the slender girl before asking, "Sand is that roan gelding that Jay talked about when we first met you?"

"Sure is. Quickest thing on four legs that I've seen in a long time. Why? What have you heard?" she asked as she looked from one face to the other.

Tad Bellington decided it was his turn to speak up. "Well, we had heard that the roan was unmanageable. A rogue. True, Jay hasn't had much to say about him lately; except that he would surprise a few people. But the Russells have been saying plenty. You aren't thinking of riding him in the endurance race, are you, young woman?"

While the older man had talked Randi had steadily kept her eyes on the dusty toe of her boot, but as he finished she slowly raised the wide green eyes to meet the lighter blue ones. The tiniest of smiles tugged at the corners of the fine mouth. "I sure am, Tad. And if all goes right, I'll be riding the winning mount. Jay doesn't say anything about me riding Sand anymore. Not since the shooting. He finally realized that it hadn't been the horse that had been untrustworthy, at least not when it came to me. He doesn't know that I intend to enter Sand in the endurance race, but he does know that I plan on racing. And as far as the

Russells telling tales, well, seeing as how it was Darla that took a fall from the pint-sized roan, there's no surprise in hearing that they are talking. You should see the way that little roan bares his teeth when she comes around."

Chris snorted slightly and moved a short way from the fence that he had been leaning against. "I'd like to do more than bare my teeth at her myself. She is one dangerous sort of lady. But, what you just said about the way Sand reacted to Miss Sophistication? I was talking to Tom for a few minutes last evening and he made almost the same statement, except that it only started acting like that since the shooting. Now I wonder why? Did they ever find out who had done the shooting?"

Randi shook her head. "No. But I heard that Tom and Ben had gone out to look around and whatever they found or didn't find they are keeping it to themselves. Not even Jay can get anything out of them. Just between you two and myself, I think it was one person and had nothing to do with rustling." Frowning suddenly, she added, "I have done some shooting myself. And I'd swear that it had been a high-powered rifle, more than likely with a scope. Like I said, I've done some shooting. Not with handguns; my hands are too small to be accurate. But, I'm damn good with a saddle gun. Especially a .30--.30 lever-action. In fact, I've done some competition shooting. I don't go in for the high-powered stuff or scopes, but I had watched some experts. And they were really something. I asked a few questions and some of what I learned applied to the style of shooting that whomever had tried to do me in used. Almost did it, too. Would have except for the horse I had under me. That little critter saved my bacon."

Both Bellington men looked at each other, puzzlement in the very alike blue eyes. Chris cocked his dark-blonde head and asked, "What is a 'critter' or 'saved bacon'?"

Laughter bubbled out in a clear, almost musical note. "I'm sorry. A critter is a small animal and referring to my bacon means the same thing as myself. I guess you'd call it slang. What races are the Rockwood horses running in?"

In unison all three turned toward the large house. Chris walking right next to her and Tad slightly behind. Chris volunteered the first of the information. "Well, Cannon is entered in the two-year-old flat race. The same that Ben is riding the Ghost in. And our head stockman, Daniel Robertson is riding Creeper in the endurance race. He's a darn good horse. He is a dark palomino with no early speed, but is great in the long race. The longer the race, the better he likes it. Then Snowfire is going to be in the jumping with one of our Aborigine stockmen on her. His name is Handker. Just a little fella, but very good on the horses. And Dad, there, is going to ride the sorrel stallion Sinbad in the relay doubles along with me and Cannon. Not too bad a line-up, huh?"

"No, not bad at all. Sounds like I might have some good competition with Creeper. You'll never guess who is racing in the endurance race for Bangon? Alright, I'll tell you. Darla went and bought a horse called Sailor Boy from the Green Plains Stable." Imparted the girl quietly, yet watching the passing expressions on both faces.

Surprise lightened the younger Bellington's eyes before the realization sank in, which turned them hard. The older man had no such lapse. His features tightened with anger. His normally friendly blue eyes turned every bit as icy as Jay's own gray ones could get on occasion. The smile turned to a straight thin line as he bit out sharply, "Leave it to Russell to take the sport out of friendly competition. She is doing this on purpose. I'm surprised that she didn't enter him in the flat race against Jay on Ebony Warrior. Do you know who is to be in on the relay doubles?"

Dark red hair tumbled around the small oval face as she shook her head in negative to his question. "No. Tom and Ted were both hoping that Jay would participate in the first half, but so far he hasn't said one way or the other." Then lifting the slender shoulders in a faint shrug, Randi added, "I think they thought that I would be the last half. But like I said we haven't heard from Jay as of yet. As much as I hate to, I suppose that I better get back to GetAway. I have a saddle to finish cleaning up. And some special equipment. I'll be seeing you guys in two days. Seems like it really crept up on us fast."

Tad grinned his open friendly way, placing a fatherly arm about her shoulders, "It couldn't be coming too fast because of your birthday, could it, Randi?"

Laughing lightly, Randi answered, "You could just be right. But I don't think anything has been planned."

CHAPTER TWENTY-FIVE

Leaning with his muscled forearms against the rough wood-topped counter, silver eyes narrowed against the glare of the bright afternoon sun as it blared through the open doorway of the stock store. Tiredly Jay ran tanned fingers over the beige-blonde hair and then pressed them to the warm back of his neck. Earlier, right after lunch, the store had been fairly crowded; mostly with stockmen and some of their families gathering the last essentials needed before the races. Squinting once again into the harsh sunlight, a small figure suddenly appeared at the door, momentarily blocking the stream of glare and throwing shadows across the suntanned hard face.

"Hallo, Boss. What ya' doin' in here?" called the small Kerry, his dark cherub face split wide in a white-toothed smile.

Jay smiled back in return. "Oh, nothing much right now. What are you doing here? Where's that dunkum fella, Bandy at?"

The dark curly hair gleamed as the sun's rays struck it. His dark eyes grew wide as he placed his little chubby hands on the counter. One was clamped tightly around a bright narrow object that in the shaded interior was hard to distinguish. "Me dog is at the stable with Missy Randi. Me mom, she done send me over here to get a ribbon for me 'good magic.'" And he held up the clinched hand for him to see.

Jay drew in a sharp breath as the burnished bronze bundle of Randi's hair glinted copper in the sunlight. His chest felt tight with a raw pain that the sight of the shorn hair caused. Looking down into the pleased round face, he managed to ask quietly, "How....where did you get that?"

"Missy Randi, Boss. She said had too much fire magic and she gave it to me before rain storm night. Boss, I need ribbon. Me mom say so."

The blonde-haired man nodded his head and came around the counter to show the small boy where the different colors of ribbon were.

"Well, let's see what we've got. Yes, here they are. Just about every color you could want. Do you see any that you like?" grinned the rancher, his smoky eyes sliding carefully over the small boy with his 'fire magic' clamped securely in his chubby fingers.

Looking at the over foot long length of copper-red hair, his hard features paled and uneasily he looked away from the small boy with the precious possession of Randi's hair. To the child it was his 'fire magic', his good luck; but to Jay it was the humiliation of what he had done in the terrible grip of jealousy.

The curly dark head turned first one way then another trying to choose the perfect color for his 'magic'. Slowly the short fingers reached up and touched a roll of pale yellow satin-like thin ribbon. Firming the youthful lips in sudden decision, the clear soft voice piped up excitedly, "Boss, that one, that one."

Jay nodded and took the roll of silky colored ribbon back to the counter and brought out the scissors and cut off a generous amount. Folding it neatly, he put it carefully into a small sack before handing it to the small boy. "Here you go, Kerry. It is a very pretty color. Did you say that Missy Randi was at the stable?"

Absently, his mind on the 'magic' in his hand, he nodded agreement and steadily headed for the door. "Yep, Boss. She there with Bandy and pups. She was….uh….'greasing'….a saddle." His little face wriggled in a confused frown, not sure about the word that was unfamiliar to him.

Lewis followed the dark-skinned boy to the doorway and then leaned his shoulder against the door frame; watching as Kerry disappeared around the corner heading as swiftly as his short, stubby legs would go to his parent's cottage near the shaded stream that ran the length of the property. What had Kerry said? Oh, yes, she was 'greasing' a saddle. How? What? Could he have meant oiled? Shaking his head in silent laughter, the tall man straightened and started back into the shaded depths of the interior.

Rounding the corner of the counter, his thoughts returned to the red-haired woman that was his wife. So she had returned. And he had not even known. What had he expected? Had he really expected her to come running into his arms? Hell, he was lucky she had even decided to come back at all.

Maybe it would have made him feel less of a heel if she would have screamed or yelled at him instead of that cold cutting voice and icy mask that she had turned on him. That and the very real fear that she showed when he came near her. As she had after he had entered the bedroom yesterday. Those dark-emerald eyes had ripped into his very heart. They had appeared so hurt, so very hopeless; almost lost.

Even the dog, Smoke, had defended her from him. So had both Ted Webster and Chris. Every-one it seemed wanted to protect her.

Taking the rag and rubbing in the last of the condition oil, Randi let her fingers run gently over the leather's smooth surface. Memories crowded in on her then. Memories of the guest ranch, Shawnee and of course, Rod. If he had not come to the guest ranch on summer holiday the mare would still be alive. She would never have had to give the horse up or her job. And she wouldn't have made a complete fool of herself. Oh, she hadn't done it all by herself. Rodger had set his cap for her right off. He could not believe that this little wrangler was his old neighborhood school friend. Not, that she had ever really been a friend of his. She had been one of the younger 'skinny brats' that had followed the older kids around and getting in the way.

She was something of a novelty around that time. She had just won the state championship cow horse reining trials and had also been wrote up in a nationwide magazine for her and Shawnee's ability in trail classes. She had been unaware of the attention that he had received just being in her company. Hadn't realized it until it was too late.

Now look where she was. In love with a wealthy station owner and someone was taking pot shots at her and a bitchy sophisticate was putting false ideas in her husband's head. Besides the point that he did not love her. That was the crux of the problem. She thought that she was made of pretty strong stuff, but she was finding it harder and harder to withstand the hurt that not having his love entailed. Especially when he seemed to believe any and everything that Darla Russell had to say about her. Even to the point of thinking that his trusted friend and accountant would be enticed by his tomboyish wife. She looked upon Ted as a brother. A very nice brother, and good friend.

Besides Ted Webster had a very lovely girl. And one that he wanted to marry. He was always talking about her; when he wasn't talking stations, horses or cattle. A slight smile touched the fine lips. The young man had this thing about being a station owner someday and Randi thoroughly hoped that he obtained his dream.

Sighing sadly she picked up the few dirty rags and turned to the still unopened packages. Just as well get done with it and see what exactly Barb had sent her. But as her fingers came in contact with the old pair of scissors lying on the package closest to her, a trembling started deep down inside and the slender hand was caught back to her side as if it had been burnt. This was silly! But looking at the old, dull scissors, a sick feeling crept up steadily from her stomach to the back of her throat. She could not be ill? That would be too childish.

Taking a steadying breath, she turned away from the packages and the offending scissors only to come face to face with her steely-eyed husband. Trying desperately to calm her features into a similitude of composer, she levelled her green eyes at his frosty gray ones.

She knew her face was pale and if it looked as bad as she felt, it must be a delightful shade of green. Finding it hard to meet his forceful look head on, she turned her face a little to the left and then as he glanced in the same direction, wished she hadn't. The saddle sat there as big as you please for his close inspection. And chancing a look at his hard face she saw that indeed he was staring at the western stock saddle.

The frosty eyes narrowed into mere slits and he stepped closer very slowly. She seemed to be frozen to the floor, completely unable to move even as he turned and approached her like some large, menacing predatory jungle cat. The silver sheen in the gray eyes were mere slits as he narrowed them on her stiff face.

"What's this? It wouldn't be a western stock saddle by any chance, would it, Randi?" snarled Jay almost savagely.

The strong hands were on her slender shoulders; the fingers biting into the tender flesh like steel talons. Forcing her expression to remain calm, she took a shaky breath before answering his questions. "Right the first time. I didn't realize that you were such a good guesser, Jay? Imagine that?"

Startled anger simmered just below the surface as he took himself to task. Was that sarcasm dripping from the soft, husky voice? As he looked into her small face, he realized that the features were strained and hard. His fingers moved to her small stubborn chin, tilting it so that he could see directly into the dark-shadowed green of her eyes. "Where did it come from?"

She could feel the warmth of his breath as it fanned softly across her lips. Her heart was pounding so loud that he had to have heard it. "My sister sent it. It arrived the other day. I guess you could say it was a gift." Pulling her head back, the fingers tightened on her chin almost painfully. The man's lips had a thin white line around them as he tried to assimilate what she had just told him. That he was still angry, she was in no doubt.

Lewis stood close to her, his hand moving now to her jawline and then on to the slender neck. Absently he moved the heavy fall of hair off of her neck and before she could guess what he was about the very male lips descended to a spot behind her ear. Small shooting points of desire rippled over her body. Her breathing became shallow and ragged as his other hand made a steady caressing trail over her midriff and up to her small, firm breast.

The hard white teeth nibbled at her earlobe and then on down the satiny neck; pushing her soft blouse back so that his seeking lips could forage on to the creamy shoulder. A shudder of desire exploded through-out her slight frame. Her skin felt like it was burning up with yearning, yearning for the man that only had to touch her to send her senses reeling.

With a sudden rush of urgency, he jerked her pliant body up against his hard muscled frame. The slender hands went to his chest in a partial protest against the encompassing flame of desire that threatened to consume her, body and soul.

Then as the husky male voice breathed softly against her ear a sudden flash of reality blared ringing through her head. "Randi honey, I want you…..it's been so long and I'm going crazy with wanting yo…"

With the cold blast of his words echoing and re-echoing across her consciousness, the once soft melting body turned stiff and unyielding in his arms. Feeling the sudden change, Jay leaned back and held her at arm's length. The gray eyes were still cloudy with desire and the tanned face unusually soft. Until, that is, he took in the cold, almost expressionless small oval features. Swiftly the handsome face turned stony with not only bewilderment, but also with frustration.

His lips felt stiff and cold as he forced the questioning words past their inflexibility, "What are you trying to do, Randi? Drive me totally crazy? Or are you a tease? Leading a man on and then turning him off….just like that." And he snapped his fingers to stress his point.

Angrily he released her, almost shoving her from him in frustration. Then once again he was pacing back and forth across the narrow stall floor like that predatory cat she had likened him to when he had first appeared at the stables.

Shaking back the silky fall of copper-bright hair almost rebelliously; Randy firmed the trembling lips and glared at the tall, still stalking man that was her husband. "Jay, why don't you go take a cold shower." Then at the sudden stillness of the blonde man at her words, she added harshly, "As far as being able to turn love on and off; you do a pretty fair job of it yourself."

A growl sounded deep in his throat and as he would have advanced toward her; she stiffened the small shape and held her ground. Her husky voice when she spoke dripped ice. "What are you going to do, Jay, cut my hair again in punishment? There is still a little bit left. But I would think twice before trying it again."

For a short moment the tall man stood as if a statue; then his breath came out in a harsh raspy hiss. "You unfeeling little bitch."

With a last cold gray flick of contempt he turned on his heel and stalked out of the stall. For a long moment Randi stood and watched the ramrod stiff back recede into the darkening foliage surrounding the corrals and buildings. Well, that was that. Wasn't it?

CHAPTER TWENTY-SIX

Resting the upper half of her body with the slender, fine boned forearms against the top rail of the corral fence; Randi lifted her face to the cooling breeze that slid around the shadowed corrals. The soft, gentle wind tossed the strawberry wisps of hair about her small, oval face; sounds of commotion, snorting and blowing of horses came faintly across the yards to her. The race day had started in earnest since the very early hours of the morning.

Cars and vans had turned into the area around the far corrals since predawn. All colors and sizes of horse vans had now made like small houses along the tree shaded side of the stables and beside the house. They were everywhere. Little children scampering around in shorts and more western wear like jeans and boots. Teenagers, adults, and senior citizens were all participating in the varied activities.

Just watching them washing and grooming the horses and checking out the saddle gear; brought back the memories of the horse shows at the guest ranch. And with the memories came the realization that it was strictly in the past. Looking at her hands, she was surprised to find that her palms were damp. Even now after all the times of participating in shows and trials, she still became nervous and the butterflies would bunch in her stomach.

Grinning faintly to herself, she let her green gaze rest on the small, lean-muscled red roan. The little gelding was standing not far from her; so close, in fact, that he could touch her arm with his blue-black nose if he would stretch out that slender gleaming neck.

The guests had not been the only ones starting the day out early; Randi had the dainty roan down to the wash rack just as the watery sun was topping the horizon. The horse's coat was a shiny dark-red with silver tips shadowing the smooth hair; the blue-black mane and tall shimmered and rippled in the faint cool breeze. The flowing mane was coal black except for the very tips that were a frosty-white giving the illusion of silver. Watching the small, yet wiry horse; Randi felt pride like she had not felt since Shawnee Fire.

Swiftly she lowered the autumn-colored head to hide the sudden tears that appeared in the misty-green eyes. Determinedly she shook the tears away. Back to the past where they belonged. Fond memories. The sad painful ones were to be forgotten. Feeling a velvet nose touch her cheek, a cool slender hand reached out and rubbed the warm satiny neck of the gelding. "Are you getting excited, fella? Me, too."

Yet, when she thought about it, she found that the old bubbling excitement was now more muted. Subdued. Now she felt more nervous. But not as intense as when she was performing at the rodeos and horseshows. Catching soft laughter coming closer from the direction of the parked horse vans; she shrugged slim shoulders and turned to meet whomever was nearing.

To her relief it was the dark-blonde Chris, tall sandy-haired Ted, and young Ben the Aborigine stable hand. Quickly a false bright smile came to the fine lips as she turned to meet them.

"Hi! Are you about ready for the races to begin?" she asked in a soft, controlled husky voice.

Chris and Ben both nodded and were telling her just when their races would be. While they were expatiating on their assumed wins, Ted stepped back a short way and watched the scene before him. The redhead was dressed in faded denim blue jeans with a shirt of the same color over a body-hugging, thin strapped white tank with aqua pin stripes. The denim shirt was left open with the two ends tied in loose knots, and the sleeves rolled up to the elbows. She looked young and ready to ride the prancing, pawing horse that was standing as close to her as it could get through the wood corral fence that separated them.

Glancing over the two younger men's heads, Randi met the amber gaze of the accountant. A faint smile once again touched her mouth, then she asked curiously, "Ted, where's this girl of yours? Has she arrived yet?"

A dull red crept up the young accountant's tanned neck as he grinned slowly and then answered, "Yes, she just got here. I'm supposed to meet her at the pool with you. Would you come and meet her, Randi?" At her nod, he added quietly, "Randi.......well, uhmm..."

"I'll tell her. It's the Russells. They've arrived. Just a few minutes ago." Interrupted the dark-blonde youth. His young face hard and angry.

Randi sighed and gave a helpless shrug of the slender shoulders before placing an arm around the two young men and heading them toward the crowded pool area. Ben, leaned against the fence and shook his dark, curly head as the little Missy asked if he was coming along.

"No, Missy. I'm supposed to meet Tom here in a few minutes. I have to get Ghost ready for the second race. Also we'll get everything ready for the demonstration." And he chuckled softly.

Chris turned his blue eyes on her face as they walked on toward the house, the warm gaze trying to recognize the meaning behind the cool, pretty features. "Alright, I give up. What was that all about?"

The young woman laughed warmly before saying, "You'll see soon enough, won't he, Ted?"

"He sure will. Randi, remember those magazines that you received from your sister? The ones that you let me take to look over?" The amber eyes were pinned to the delicate face, watching the changing emotions as they tumbled across the expressive features. At her nod, he continued, his voice quiet and gentle. "In one of the magazines there was an article about a sorrel mare and her owner. It had colored pictures and two or three pages of write ups. It was you, Randi, and Shawnee Fire. I just wanted you to know that I knew about it."

The slim figure stopped and the red hair fell forward covering her face. Both young men came to a halt beside her; Ted, his eyes never leaving the small, oval face remained silent. The younger Bellington youth was motionless, not sure what was going on; but too afraid of saying the wrong thing to ask. So he waited.

"What did the article have to say?" her voice was low and muffled.

"It was in tribute to Shawnee Fire." Came the quiet reply.

The woman was silent for a few long moments, then raised the burnished head and looked steadily at the two young men. Finally the dark-green eyes narrowed on the accountant, the small oval face still and quiet as if waiting. "Does Jay know, Ted?"

"Not yet. But he has to know sooner or later. He already knows something is up. The fact is he was going to have me check on your employment records. He said he knew so little about you. Randi? What about the demonstration in a little while? Shouldn't he know before then?"

Looking over at the tense, still silent Chris, Randi grinned softly and remarked, "Wondering what's going on?" at the hesitant nod, she continued with a sigh, "Well, I am from the States. The United States. I used to be a wrangler on a guest ranch and had a very special horse. You might have heard of her. Shawnee Fire. A dark-red sorrel mare that was one of the top cutting and reining horses. Ted can explain the rest to you later." Then glancing at the tall, sandy-haired young man, she answered his question. "Yes, Ted, you can tell Jay. But wait until just before the demonstration starts. Okay, Ted?"

The accountant nodded agreement and at seeing the girl's lips tremble, he placed his arm about her shoulders and they continued on toward the large sun-bathed pool. Chris followed along behind, his thoughts in a jumble.

Letting his blue glance wander over the slight figure of the woman ahead of him, he thought back over the name of the horse she had just told him she had owned. Yes, of course. He remembered now. There had been a television show a few months ago that had featured American Cow horses. She had been flashed on the screen showing the cutting out of calves without the use of a bridle or reins. Was really something to see. But the famous mare had been killed in an accident. A car/horse van accident. A sudden sorrow clouded the brilliance of the dark-blue eyes.

Suddenly a soft feminine voice cut across the humid air surrounding the pool area. Looking up simultaneously, the three caught a glimpse of a slender, dark-haired girl hurrying towards them. Next to her and slightly behind stood the handsome, tall GetAway owner; his very stillness shouting his uneasiness.

At seeing the willowy girl, Ted dropped his comforting arm, a wide friendly smile spread across the handsome features as he stepped to meet the hazel-eyed young woman. "Sara!"

With a simple step he swept in closer and gathered the young woman up into strong arms and twirled her around before placing her gently on the ground and turned to face the redhead and the dark-blonde Chris. His unusual amber colored eyes twinkled with pride as he made the introductions. "Sara, this is Randi Lewis. Isn't she exactly as I told you?"

The tall, willowy girl nodded shyly and the soft, quiet voice answered, "She sure is. I'm pleased to meet you. Finally."

Randi smiled back in return. "You are as pretty as Ted said you were. And as nice. I'm glad that you were able to come. I hate to be a spoil-sport, but I have to get back to the stables and get ready for the races. I'll see you later. Oh, Chris, good luck in your race." And she turned to retrace her steps. Throwing a quick glance in the direction that her husband had been, she saw that he had been joined by the loud and expensively dressed Russells. His tanned features were looking down intently into the cool, sophisticated face of Darla and she had her arm snaked around the side and back of her husband.

Choking back the bile taste of jealousy, she pulled her gaze away and hurried on her way. Let them, who cared? Who was she fooling? She cared like hell. She hurt like nothing she had ever experienced before. Not even when she had to watch Shawnee being put down. No, not even then.

A crowd was gathering around the largest of the yards. There were children hanging on the corral fence near to where their parents were standing. Excitement was heard in the raised voices and hectic murmurings of the different people. Jay was busy talking with Darla and Carl Russell and the elder Bellingtons when Ted Webster stepped up to him and laid a tanned hand on his arm. The young accountant nodded a greeting to the older couple, but ignored the other. Anger formed across the handsome features at the slight of his jack-a-roo. But before he could voice his displeasure, the sandy-haired man said in a quiet, yet somehow urgent voice, "Jay, could I see you a moment, please? It'll only take a moment."

Making his excuses the tall, lean man followed the younger man to a spot back out of the gathering crowd of people. "Alright, Ted, what is it? I hope it warrants the crude manners you displayed toward the Russells."

Ted stared at his boss in disbelief, then he shrugged his broad shoulders and spoke dryly, "I found something out concerning Randi. I thought that you might be interested. In one of the magazines that Randi received from her sister there was an article about her. Do you remember reading or hearing of a reining horse named Shawnee Fire?"

A frown furrowed the tanned brow and then as the narrowed gray eyes widened, the rancher looked closer at the man. "Of course. So, what about it?"

"The mare was killed in an accident and the owner had been….well….well, it was Randi. Jay, she is from America. She is famous in her own right as a top wrangler and as the owner and rider of the famous Shawnee Fire." The young man went on to explain some of the awards she had won on the sorrel mare and also the cowboy races she had rode in.

The ranchers face had hardened, yet had also paled to an awful gray shade. Turning those icy gray eyes on the accountant's face, Jay muttered in a tight rumble. "When did you find this out, Ted?"

Ted's own young face hardened to a stiff mask. "When the magazines first arrived. When you were over to the Burton's out station. I had planned to tell you when you first returned; but, hell, Jay, you acted so….uh…so cruel toward Randi that I decided not say anything at that time. I'm sorry that I didn't tell you sooner, but I more than likely would have done the same thing again. I wanted you to know before this demonstration rodeo started. Randi is in it and she is going to show us the American West technique."

The jaw muscles bunched and the gray eyes were mere slits as he looked not at the young man, but out toward the mountains. He had treated the little redhead shabbily. Had been for quite a while. He hadn't even thought how the rest of GetAway would see his actions. But to find that Randi was indeed from America, even though he had felt that maybe it could be true, was hard to accept now. Turning to the sandy-haired Ted, he asked very softly, "Is Tom in on this….uh….this demonstration?"

Ted nodded in agreement. His amber eyes softened in sympathy for his boss and his friend. Then glancing at the watch on his wrist, he threw a look at the stables. "I've got to go, Jay. I'm supposed to announce the events. Are you going to watch? Your race is right after this. Good luck."

At Ted's first question about whether or not he would watch Randi, the rancher had nodded and now he stood and watched the young man hurry to the makeshift stand with the P.A. system set up for announcing the races and different programs on the agenda. Turning slowly, he walked back toward the two couples he had left just a few minutes before. He would have to tell Jewel and Tad Bellington, but he didn't want to inform the Russells ahead of time.

Standing next to the patient gelding, Randi laid the aqua saddle pad on the gleaming back; then lifted the stock saddle onto the pad. Tightening the front cinch up and then the rear one. She made sure it was snug, but not too tight. She had seen many rear cinches so loose that they hung down, making it too easy for a horse to get a foot caught in them. Laying a gentle hand on the horse's neck, she whispered to him, "You'll do great, my boy." And he turned his refined head and gave her a look as if to say, 'of course.'

Buckling the aqua-colored fleece-lined nylon breast strap to the saddle and underneath to the front cinch, she stepped back and looked him over. Not bad. Then she hurriedly wrapped his front fetlocks with the same color of leg wraps, showing off the clean, straight black legs. Next she put her aqua-colored felt hat on and then the bitless bridle with the same aqua-colored reins. Now horse and rider were color coordinated, which made the flow appear more connected.

After riding into the arena she will remove the bridle and work some cattle. The little roan had taken to cutting with a natural grace and willingness. So taking a deep breath, she swung up into the saddle and smiled at the head stockman, who smiled back and opened the large gate.

CHAPTER TWENTY-SEVEN

As Randi rode through the gate, Tom stepped up close to her and handed a mike up to her. "Here you go. Are you ready for this?"

"As I'll ever be." Nervously grinned the redhead.

The head stockman shook his head and clicked the gate closed, then mounted his horse and rode towards the far corner of the arena where five to six steers were standing with Ben and a couple of other stockmen.

Randi settled herself deeper in the stock saddle, then eased the red roan into a side pass toward the center of the arena. The mike was one of those wireless ones and very light weight. Putting a smile on her small face, she spoke softly into the mike, "Hello, everyone. I am Randi Lewis and this little fella is Sand. We have been working real hard on this special program for all of you. We are going to show you some American Cow Horse techniques. This maneuver is called a 'side pass'. He can do it in either direction and also at an angle like this. You see this in dressage, but the more movement and bending you do with your horses, the better."

Coming to the center, she softly halted the gelding, and while he stood quietly, she continued, "We are going to do some 'cow cutting'; or separating a steer from the herd and keeping it from getting back to it. The bridle I am using is a bitless bridle. I have used them for a number of years and they seem to work extremely well. With this demonstration I will not be using a bridle. I am going to have my friend Tom come over and take the bridle off of Sand."

Chuckling softly, she remarked, "I heard that. Yes, you heard right, I will be doing this without the bridle. Hopefully. You see this is the first time Sand has ever done this with a large audience."

Tom moved his mount up next to the smaller horse and slipped the bridle off the slender head. "There you go, Missy."

Smiling once more, Randi again addressed the crowd. "Because you need to sit quietly, but securely in the saddle, I am going to give this mike to Tom for now. "So here we go."

She deftly handed the mike to the head stockman, then he moved his gray horse back to the gathered bunch of steers. She tugged her hat down on her forehead and then touched the little horse on his side with her leg; he moved off slowly and easily, walking into the milling herd. The cattle moved around and then the gelding singled out a compact, speckled steer and the game began.

It was like watching a dance; his head was lowered and he would move almost head to head. He seemed to know which way the steer was going to go before the steer did. Back and forth, to the left then the right. It would try to run past the gelding, only to be blocked. Finally, Randi sat up and touched the roan's neck and he stopped and let the steer amble back to the herd.

The crowd clapped and shouted. At the sudden noise, the gelding's head shot up and the small black ears flicked forward. Then he turned his head back around to look at his rider, causing the crowd to laugh softly. Then out of nowhere, he looked back at the crowd and lifted his lips in a 'horse laugh'; which in turn caused the laughter to get louder.

Randi leaned forward and rubbed both hands down his neck to his shoulders. As she sat upright, Ben rode up and put the bridle back on, and then handed over the mike once again.

"I think he did pretty well, don't you?" she asked the people, and they answered in agreement.

"Now I'm going to show you a basic reining program. It will contain slides, pivots, rollbacks, flying lead changes and the spin." Again she smiled and handed off the mike, this time to young Ben.

Turning the gelding back to the center, she put him into a lope moving in a left hand circle, moving over half way around the circle, she crossed over and did a flying lead change to the right. At the top of the circle she moved him into a full gallop and then pulled him to sliding stop, with his rear almost in a sitting position. Then she had him pivot and head back the other way; and half way up, she had him do a fantastic rollback then again moved him to the center and put the roan into a spin. As he stopped, she backed him up swiftly. She then halted him in the center again.

Among cheers of awe and admiration, Randi raised a hand to the gathered crowd and expertly backed the agile roan the whole length of the arena; then turned the horse in a flashy pivot that had the crowd once again cheering their pleasure.

Once out of sight of the friendly people the brilliant smile faded and a sadness settled over the delicate features.

She had seen Jay's tall figure leaning against the fence, his frosty-cool gaze narrow and sharp. He hadn't missed a thing. Not one single thing. Thank heaven his race was next. No time for him to jump all over her about being from the States and doing the demonstration without his knowledge. Wait until he finds out she is racing in the endurance race right after his own race.

Chris had won his race against Ben and Ghost. But just barely. The Ghost was only a nose short at the finish line. Darla had placed second to the Rockwood Aborigine stockman on Snowfire in the jumping. Talk about one angry lady. She had let some words fly that even had some of the rougher outback men turning red about the neck.

Sliding off the red roan, she handed the reins to the grinning Ben. "Good show, Missy Randi. Right over there is the best place to watch the Boss ride his race." And the young man pointed to a shaded section of corral fence.

Randi nodded and then said, "Ben, would you put the close-contact endurance saddle on Sand? And don't forget that thinner breast collar? Okay?"

Ben nodded his dark head. "No problem, Missy. I'll have him ready for you."

"Thank you." Randi smiled softly. Then she slowly headed for the fence to watch. If she worked it out just right, she would be on Sand at the starting line before Jay would have a chance to know. Her race was right after Jay's.

Climbing up on the rough-wood fence, Ted's voice came over the P.A. system announcing the Flat Race. The big black, Ebony Warrior, was tossing his dark head, but otherwise was patient. Randi could see the muscles bunch as Jay leaned forward as everyone tensed for the starting gun to go off. And then there was a mass surging of dust and straining horses. Both the black and a cream-colored horse went to the lead, the big stallion slightly ahead. His mile eating gait was swallowing up the track as he increased the distance between himself and the other horses, except the cream who managed to stick to him like glue. It was a short race, almost like that of a quarter mile back in the States. Just a little bit longer in length.

The race would end just about in front of her position on the fence. As the racing bunch came around the curve, Ebony Warrior was in the lead. But still the large cream was right behind him and inching up; but Randi didn't think it would get it done. But it would be close.

Looking towards the stands where Ted was announcing, she caught sight of Darla Russell making her way toward the finish line. As Randi turned back to the racers, she was in time to see the large black streak across the finish line just ahead of the Rockwood Station's cream-colored mount.

Randi had climbed down from the fence and was hurrying to where Jay would bring the winning horse, when she came to a halting stop. Glancing toward the gathering crowd, she had a clear view of the dark-haired Darla as she flung her arms around the tall, blonde-haired man; pulling the handsome face down to meet hers in a deep kiss of triumph.

Quickly Randi bowed her head and checked to see if anyone had seen her move toward her husband. Apparently everyone had kept their eyes on the winner and then on the very revealing scene before them. How could they help but see it, and wonder? Where did that put her?

Reaching the shelter of the trees, the redhead headed swiftly to the stable where Ben would have put Sand. Even before she reached him, the small horse was sending a friendly whinny out to her. The horse could sense her excitement and it showed in his agitated movements.

Running a calming hand down the sleek neck she cooed softly, "It's alright, fella. We'll do fine, you and me. We'll show 'em all."

The red roan snorted his agreement as Randi led him out of the stall, then she tightened the fleece covered cinch and checked all the snaps and buckles. And last, she made sure the leg wraps were smooth and tight. Stepping out into the cloud-dappled sunlight, she swung up into the saddle. Her young face was downcast and the hurt green eyes remained directly in front of the horse's route to the starting line. As she jogged the gelding past the stands, she heard her name called and looked up to see Ray Proctor waving from his position near the top row of the benches. He moved closer to the side, so Randi moved the roan over as near to the lawyer as she could safely get the horse.

"Hello, Ray. Going to wish me luck?" she smiled hesitantly.

The warm brown eyes looked over her carefully before he asked quietly, "Are you alright, Randi?"

A nervous laugh escaped her pale lips as she managed to avoid the concerned brown eyes. "I'm fine, Ray, honest. I'm not worried about this race. Sand will show them all a thing or two. Besides, I've ridden in tougher races than this one." Then looking directly at the kindly man, she added, "Its fine, Ray. I'll be fine."

Ray watched the slim woman on the graceful horse move off to join the other contestants. Worried eyes were still lingering on the pale profile of the girl as she maneuvered the obedient gelding into position. He did not like the tense expression on the delicate features. He had seen her fleeting escape after witnessing the Russell woman's flaunting exhibition. Disgusting. Jay should have told that damn woman to get lost a long before anything as stupid as that display could happen. But even then, his friend had acted as if it had not bothered him. Not one word of censure. Nothing. Ray did not understand Lewis acting so inconsiderately.

A commotion was going on with the endurance race contestants. Quite a bit of milling around of a large chestnut stallion that in turn set the others into a frenzy. The young woman on the small roan was almost swallowed up in the dust and moving horses. But she seemed to have the roan in complete control as the Rockwood stockman, Daniel Robertson, purposely moved the large, rangy palomino in between the chestnut and Randi. Looking up at the accountant, Ray encountered the thin-lipped frown on the sun-bronzed features. Ted did not like what was going on. Glancing down at the lawyer, he muttered under his breath, "Ray, keep your eyes on that chestnut will you? I want to know if you see any rough stuff. That's the Russell entry. It's the racing stallion from Green Plains Stable."

Proctor nodded in silent agreement. What were they doing racing a champion flat track runner in an endurance race? It didn't make good sense.

"Ray, glad to see you made it. Did you see Ebony Warrior win?" called the lean muscled man with the beige-blonde hair. Being careful not to step on anyone he made his way up next to the older man's side on the bench.

"Sure, I saw you just barely get across the finish line ahead of that cream-colored horse. I also saw the greeting that you got from that woman." Frowned Ray disapprovingly.

"By 'that woman' you must mean Darla. What was I supposed to do, throw her off? Besides the winner is supposed to get a kiss from a pretty woman." He responded dryly. His gray eyes narrowed as he faced his long-time friend.

Ray Proctor snorted. "A pretty wife would have looked better. And don't give me any back talk; she was there. I saw her. She was coming to be with you when she ran full tilt into that little revealing scene of yours." Then turning suddenly cold brown eyes on the younger man he demanded harshly, "Why aren't you down there helping your wife with the line-up?"

"What!" He groaned aloud. "I didn't know she was racing in this. Why didn't someone tell me?" He demanded as he threw a discerning look at the accountant above him at the announcing stand.

Calmly Ted looked down at the rancher, his face as expressionless as Jay's could often be. "You have been rather hard to talk too lately. You have been so worried what people would think of Randi, you forgot to listen to those people. None of your neighbors have anything bad to say of your wife. They think she is pretty special." Then glancing at the starting line, he remarked, "Don't look now, but they are off. And from the way that little horse took off, Randi is in the lead."

Standing up suddenly, Jay caught the lightning swift move of the red gelding as he streaked out around the large chestnut. Looking quickly at the lawyer, their eyes met. Sailor Boy and with, not a professional rider, but with Carl Russell up on the broad back. Slowly Lewis sank down on the bench next to the older man. "Oh no. Not Carl…..he'll do almost anything to win." Muttered Jay, his blonde head bent in despair.

Just when he thought that it couldn't get any worse, he looked up to find Tom and Ben walking toward him with very serious faces.

CHAPTER TWENTY-EIGHT

Feeling the roan gather himself to make an effortless jump over a thick stand of brush, Randi leaned closer to the reddish neck. Her gentle fingers barely touching the horse, but sending messages to him just the same. He was running easily, even with over a fourth of the race behind them. She had held him in with the leaders to save his strength for the last half of the rough going race. The race would average out to be a little over a mile in total length and most of it was twists and turns over all kinds of jumps and rough terrain. Included were some man-made brush jumps and of course, natural ones of brush, rocks and fallen limbs from dead trees; anything and everything, whatever got in the way.

Mostly there wasn't any track to follow, just brilliantly colored flag markers.

Throwing a quick look over her shoulder, she could see the large reddish chestnut bearing down on them. Carl was pushing the horse way too early and the stallion was having trouble handling the rough going. She felt rather sorry for the gallant race horse. What with being put in the wrong sort of race for his abilities and then to have that misfit Carl Russell riding him.

Pulling past the half way mark of the solitary stand of straggly trees, they came upon some of the man-made jumps that were set apart with about three strides in between each jump. It made for very good coordination between the horse and rider. The timing had to be perfect or you could end up head over tail.

The roan gelding settled into a mile eating gait that seemed to skim effortlessly over the jumps. The more she asked of him the more he gave. The slender head was still up in the true Arabian running style. A sign that the little horse was still going strong. It was when that head dropped and the neck stretched out that the horse would be about finished.

Without looking she could hear the other horse coming up on her. And not far behind the chestnut, came the rangy palomino, Creeper. Now would be the time for the large chestnut to make up the distance, if he had anything left after being pushed so hard at the first part of the race. If he was going to do anything, he had better do it before the next set of jumps. The much longer stride would tell on the flat stretch. But it would also mean that Russell was still pushing the horse. If that was the case, it would be whether or not the big chestnut could keep up the stiff pace for another half mile and also manage to stay ahead of the increasingly fast moving palomino.

It was then that she felt or sensed something wrong; not with the roan, but a sudden feeling of danger. As the strange sensation rippled through her slender frame, the muscles tensed and transmitted the uncertainty to the galloping roan causing the swiftly moving legs to falter slightly. Just for a brief second, no one but her more than likely could have noticed it.

From behind came a sharp pain. Her back flinched away from the impact as Carl struck once again with the hard, leather-wrapped hand quirt. His face was twisted into a dark menacing grimace and the black eyes were threatening as he raised his arm to strike her yet again!

Just as his arm started to lower, Randi reined the roan out a way to the right of the oncoming horse, causing the man to miss his target. But just barely. With a sudden tightening of the fine lips and clamping the small, even teeth together in stubborn anger she sank her heels into the roan horse and with a sudden surge; the game little gelding lunged ahead and cut in front of the chestnut and his crazed rider.

And then the stallion was coming on, only this time Carl reined the horse into the smaller mount. Again the chestnut's shoulder slammed into Sand's side, this time pinning Randi's leg between their straining bodies. Pain shot up her leg and hip, but she urged the small horse on.

Out of the corner of her eye she saw the arm again raise and silently braced herself for the blow. The pain was so sharp and knifing that she felt sick. Feeling the color drain out of her face, she had to fight to keep from fainting. Anger welled up in her throat, almost choking her. Again the dark-haired man slammed the larger horse into the roan, almost succeeded in knocking him off his feet. The roan stumbled and almost went down to his knees, but at the upward pull of the reins, he gathered himself and surged onward.

Her ribs were burning and with every breath, a sharp pain knifed through her making breathing harder. But she was not going to let that cruel, sadistic example of manhood get to the finish line before her. No way.

Carl, hearing the roan closing in on him again, jabbed the spurs into the already bleeding sides of the stallion. As the girl drew even, he brought the leather bound iron rod up to hit her once again. Just as he was lowering the weapon, a silver streak of fur and bone struck him full in the chest; knocking the evil-looking quirt from nerveless fingers. Together they fell to the ground, the startled stallion running loose across the beige-colored grasses. White, gleaming teeth slashed at his throat and chest. Quickly he rolled, trying to get away from the snarling fury that had every intention of eating him alive.

On his back in the dirt, he looked up into yellow-brown, hate-filled eyes and sharp teeth that clicked together just inches before his face. Afraid to move, he heard a horse pull up and then a cold voice declared. "If I were you, Mister, I wouldn't move a single muscle until that dog decides to let you."

"I won't, I won't! Just get him off me!" Begged the cringing man, his tanned face a sickly gray color.

Daniel Robertson and another of the racers had stopped and now debating on what would be the best action to take. The large palomino jerked his head and pulled at the reins held in the stockman's hands as another horseman appeared on the scene. Looking up he was relieved to recognize Tom, GetAway's head stockman.

Dismounting, Tom glanced first at the two men and then at the cattledog and Carl Russell. "Smoke, release." And as the dog backed away slowly with its slender head lowered, yellow-brown eyes still pinned on the downed man. Glancing first to the two racers, he told them to finish the race; then turned to the Bangon owner. "You can get up now, Russell. Just don't move fast."

About to voice his anger, the dark-haired man caught the angered expression on the man's face and thought better of it. Slowly he dusted off his jeans and as he finished another horseman rode up. Ben eyed Tom and then they motioned Carl to head to the stands. The silver-blue dog still kept a close eye on his every move and stayed within a foot of his leg.

Sweeping past the finish line among the excited cheers, Randi grabbed a hold of the black mane and all but blacked out. Slowly she slid out of the saddle, almost falling to the ground when her legs turned rubbery and bent at the knees. People were milling around trying to see and to give congratulations to the winners. Grimly, she hung to the saddle until her weak feeling legs could support her weight. Her side was still hurting, but she did not think that any ribs were broken, only bruised. Turning slowly, she leaned against the heaving, sweating sides of the horse and came face to face with the dark-blonde haired Chris Bellington.

The boy's face was white with concern and worry. His voice came out low and husky with emotion. "Are you alright, Randi?" At her short nod, he continued, "We saw part of what Russell was trying to do and then Tom sent Smoke after you." Looking at her tense, pale features, he asked quietly, "Are you sure you are okay?"

Straightening up her slender form, the velvety black nose of the roan touched her shoulder and blew softly through the damp red hair. Randi tried to smile and was doing pretty well she thought, until she looked up at Chris and then caught sight of Jay standing with some men and ---- Darla ---- of all people! Didn't he see? Hadn't he been watching?

Even as she watched, the woman reached out a hand and touched Lewis on the cheek and Randi could watch no longer. Her face felt frozen. Even her body felt numb. She knew that she would feel the pain later. But not now. Pulling herself together, she forced a smile of sorts on her lips and not being able to meet the youth's concerned blue eyes, remarked softly, "Chris, I want you to do me a favor. Will you?"

Eagerly the Bellington boy nodded. "Sure, anything, Randi. What do you want me to do?"

With a shaky sigh, she breathed in a steading breath. "First, I want you to take Sand to the stable. To his stall. Don't unsaddle him, but take the bridle off and loosen the cinch. Okay?" at the nod, she continued, "Then I want you to wait there with him until I get there. Will you do that for me?"

Chris looked at the pale face and dark, misty-green eyes. "Sure, I will." And gently he took the rein from her and headed for the stable.

Watching until he and the horse had disappeared around the corner of the stands, she then made sure that no one was about and hurriedly made her way to her bedroom.

With Sand safely with Chris, Randi hurriedly slipped into her room and gathered a few of her clothes and threw them in a cloth bag and some other items into the saddlebags. Stopping off at the kitchen she had found enough food to see her through a few days. Before leaving her bedroom, she had written a short, very much to the point note to Jay and slipping the ring off her finger, she had wrapped the ring in the note. Then putting it in an envelope she returned to the stable and the waiting Chris.

The young man had even rubbed the roan down so he wasn't sweaty any more. As she entered, he jumped to his feet. "I did what you said. He's fine, Randi. You'd never know he just ran a long race."

Randi smiled softly, "That's the Arabian for you. They just keep on going."

She went up next to the roan and tightened the cinch and attached the saddlebags to the rear hooks of the saddle. Then she slipped the bridle on the refined face and led him out of the stall. Just before mounting, she handed Chris the small package, "Give this to Jay. Only to him. But not until I've gone. Promise?"

The young man hesitated, but then nodded the dark-blonde head in silent agreement. And as she swung up on the small horse, Chris asked softly, "You be careful, Randi."

With a sad smile on her lips, she pulled the felt hat down further on the copper-colored curls and absently tugged the jacket closer about her slim shape. Then touching her heels to the roan's sides she headed out toward the darkening mountains with the heavy, gray storm clouds hanging threateningly over them. Just waiting.

CHAPTER TWENTY-NINE

Amber, orange, bright yellow and every now and then a flicker of palest blue would skip across the burning logs in the fireplace. Except for those flickering glowing flames of the fire, the small cabin was in darkness. The dancing glow was reflected in the burnished silky fall of hair as Randi rested her chin on the up-drawn knee and stared unseeingly into the flames. Her thoughts were not on the flames, nor were they on the deepening rumble of the thunder overhead or the steady rat-a-tat-tat of the rain on the windowpane; they were somewhere near GetAway homestead with the tall, lean man that was her husband.

After leaving the station she had headed for the cabin built into the side of a cliff, watching the threatening clouds swirl around overhead. The storm had waited until just before reaching it. Swiftly she had put the roan into the lean-to next to the cabin and made sure the little horse had plenty of water and fresh hay. With the dark, liquid brown eyes, the roan had watched her until she had disappeared inside the cabin.

With the rain came the coolness and the fire gave off a pleasant warmth. Being here, after so long, the memories returned with painful strength. The rain, the flicker of the flames in the fireplace; even the old beat-up tea kettle was starting to boil on the pot-bellied stove.

Her left leg was curled up under her with the other leg drawn up under her chin. The boots were over next to the single cot and her toes wiggled against the fuzzy rug she was sitting on. Her body was sore and stiff from the brutal attack from Carl. The man had to be crazy.

Hearing the kettle start to weakly whistle as the water came to a boil, she knew that she should get up and go turn it off; but just did not want to make the effort.

Gazing once more into the hissing fire, she wondered vaguely what Jay was doing. Did he miss her? What a fool question, of course not. Frowning, she wondered what he had thought when Chris handed him her ring and note. More than likely angry, then it would turn to relief when he realized he was free of her.

Pain rose within her chest like a knife twisting near her heart. Her skin tingled as she remembered when they were here the first time. Would the pain and emptiness ever leave? Or would they remain like memories, always there just waiting for a weak moment to come surging to the surface. What would happen when she finally lost all hope, when the realization hit her square on?

So deep in thought that when the door suddenly burst open, she was unable to move. She had to be hallucinating.......the tall, soaked figure standing in the open doorway could not be......Jay! It couldn't be. He was safe and dry back at the station with his guests....... with Darla. Wasn't he? But if it wasn't him, who was that menacing hunk with the rain pouring off his hat onto the floor?

With the shrill whistle of the kettle blowing somewhere at the back of her consciousness, she slowly rose to her feet as the figure stepped farther into the cabin's one room. At the sound of the door slamming shut, she jerked and backed away. Fear turning the gray-green eyes dark in the pale face.

The wet, rain-darkened hat came off the beige-blonde hair and sailing off in a random direction. The bronzed features were set in a harsh, uncompromising mask. Ooh, dear. It was definitely Jay. A very angry Jay. A chill slithered down her back and an icy pain gripped her wildly beating heart as the man paused briefly and slid the kettle off the fire and then stalked toward her. A thin white line was about the thin-drawn lips and a muscle was jerking in the strong jaw.

With a thump she came up against the cabin's wall next to the cot. Panic rose to the back of her throat, almost choking her with its intensity. Large, strong tanned hands were placed on each side of her head, leaving no escape as the very male body moved in closer to her slim softer one.

His face was next to hers and so close that she could feel the warmth of his breath on her cheek. Faintly she closed her eyes, still hoping that maybe it was really just a dream. But as demanding, possessive lips claimed her trembling ones, she knew that it was no dream. But raw reality. The lips were hard and even cruel as they crushed the inner softness of hers against the small white teeth.

Desperately she tried to move her head out of his punishing grip, but it only made him tighten the now firm hold on the silky hair. Suddenly she was jerked hard up against his solid chest, almost knocking the wind out of her. His shirt was wet and her own knit tee-shirt soaking up its dampness.

The male length was flush against her feminine one and she could feel his male hardness against her skin. Still he had not said a word, but his actions were very clear indeed. With his right hand twisted into the copper mass of hair at the back of her neck, the free one started to make an in depth exploration of her body under the now damp, clinging material of her shirt and camisole. The fingers found their way along her back to the ribcage and slowly reached up and cupped the firm, slight breast. She could feel her body betraying her with its traitorous reaction to his manipulation of her senses with his hands and kisses.

Her breathing was ragged and shallow, her skin tingling where ever his caressing fingers chose to go. The small breast was swelling with desire and as the precise thumb rubbed over the dusky-pink nipple, it hardened with pleasure that was so close to pain that an unconscious sigh escaped through the now bruised lips.

At the faint sound, he drew back and looked down into her small oval face. The gray eyes bleak and hard narrowed as they took in the pale features and desire-drugged green eyes. A faint, slightly cruel smile touched the firm mouth. "Did you really think that you could run out on me, Randi?"

Randi lowered her lashes, hiding the pain that must burn in their shadowed depths. And the deep, longing desire and love that she felt for him. He would most certainly enjoy the power that would give him if he found that out. What was he doing here? Stiffly she moved the stubborn chin and made a pretense of staring at the fireplace.

A hard warm hand firmly gripped the slightly quivering chin and turned her face up so that he could see her features. Flicking a quick glance up at his face through thick, dark lashes she was hoping to find a softening in the bronzed features. But only a stiff hardness met her searching eyes.

Jay's hand was still secured in the coppery mass at the back of her head, and at the slightly mutinous expression on the pale face he tightened his hold and with a lithe, easy movement had lifted her bodily; placing her on the narrow cot. His heavier body moved over her lower body, anchoring it in place.

The bronzed features moved closer and she sucked in a surprised breath as the firm lips caressed the soft skin near her ear. Then hard teeth nipped sharply at her lobe. Desire rippled through her, spiraling from her lower stomach to the very ends of her extremities. The warmth was so hot that she felt as if it was burning her from the inside out.

The moist wet tongue circled slowly around her ear and she tried wiggling away from the tickling, sensuous waves that were assaulting her senses. Softly from far away, it seemed, a husky voice whispered in her ear. "You haven't answered my question, Randi honey."

Her voice came out in a husky whisper. "No, I haven't. How did you know where I would go?"

A deep, sexy chuckle sounded as the lean fingers moved over the sensitive skin of her collarbone around the low edge of the knit shirt. "Didn't really think about it. But where else would you go on horseback? Is that how you solve your problems, Randi, by always running away?"

Anger simmered just below the surface at his taunting. She was running away? What was she supposed to do stay there while he had his fling with Darla? No way. Stiffening her slim body and bringing up the small hands she tried to push the much heavier body away from her.

255

Again he chuckled at her minor attempts to dislodge him. But the laughter only served to ignite the anger to full heat. "Leave me alone, Jay."

"No way my little fireball. Seems to me that this is where we came in the first time. This time I know the score and this delectable little body belongs to me. And I intend to use it ---- thoroughly."

The words rang loudly in her head as she stared blankly up at him. She belonged to him! Her body was his to do with as he wanted! She was not a possession ------ never!

The small hands formed into tight hard little fists. Twisting wildly, she hit out at him, her green eyes spitting fire. Her voice was a harsh whisper, her anger choking her. "No! You don't own me. No one owns me. Definitely not you. Stop it, Jay! You are going to…..to regret this."

He grinned down at her. Her struggles minute against his added strength. "No, I'm not going to regret this. I regretted not finishing something that I started here once before."

She tried bringing up a knee, but at the feeble attempt he moved his own body more solidly over hers. Next his strong tanned hands caught her arms and sliding them down the smooth length of her lightly-tanned skin he pulled the flagging fists close to her sides.

Moving up into an almost sitting position on her midsection, he transferred both her wrists to his one hand and slowly lifted them above her disarrayed fire-colored head. The frosty slate-gray eyes moved carefully over her tense, pale features on down over her creamy neck to the damp, clinging dark-green tee-shirt that emphasized the gentle, firm curve of the swelling breasts. Seemingly irritated at the soft material that covered the bare skin from his probing gaze, he gripped the shirt near the waist band of her slim fitting jeans and tugged it out and lifted it up over her head and off her hands as they were still held tightly within his grip.

Hot color stole over the creamy skin that was now exposed to his icy-gray glance. Anger and a sudden surge of awareness of the desire that her slight body was causing in the masculine figure above her. Desperation that he would realize that she in all truth was in love with him, caused her to fight with renewed strength.

Jerking the held wrists tighter, his other hand went to her chin. With his fingers splayed out over her fine boned cheek and his thumb moving up under her chin; he forced her face up toward him. The ruffled beige-blonde hair fell forward as he lowered his stern mouth to hers. The lips were hard, yet gently persuasive as they moved across the sensitive, bruised lips and then took final possession as the male tongue entered and took all her inner moist self.

Pulling back just fractionally, his desire-filled silver eyes devoured her and then his teeth were nibbling along her jawline and as her head jerked upward, the moist male mouth made voyages down her throat and onto the bared shoulder. With eyes fastened on the small oval face to watch her reaction to the sensuous techniques he was assaulting her senses with.

As the pale lids swept down over the misty-green eyes, his mouth and tongue made an unerring target of the creamy slope of a firm aroused breast. Warm male lips touched the hardened nipple sending shivers radiating throughout her whole body. Unconsciously the young slender body arched itself closer to the male form. Somewhere along the arousal he had arranged his own lean frame alongside hers. As their fevered passion increased, his grip fell away from her once captured hands and urgently traveled over the silky skin of her upper body.

As hands came in contact with the confining material of her faded snug-fitting jeans, he systematically set about removing them. With a soft sigh escaping the masculine lips at the sight of the totally feminine curves and silky smooth shapes, Randi felt a rush of panic engulf her whole being.

Urgent hands caressed and lingered over the flat, smooth belly and around the sensitive skin of her hip. Even as the slightly moist lips made warm trails across her sensitized intimate areas, the clinging shirt came off the sun-brown back and was tossed to the floor. Following closely behind was the belt and boots. With one easy move the jeans followed suit and Randi found the warm, fully masculine body next to hers totally arousing her to a disjointed state of desire and fear.

Throwing out a trembling hand, it encountered the sun-tipped mat of curling hair that covered the well-muscled chest. Without even thinking the fingers traveled down the silky hair to the lower stomach where it disappeared into a slight vee. His hips were slim and the flat stomach firm and warm. She felt him tremble at her hesitating caresses. A sudden feeling of power almost overwhelmed her, but as taking a shaky breath; she unconsciously stiffened her slender body, actually pulling slightly away from him. It was only fractionally, but Jay felt it and hesitated briefly before seemingly renewing his efforts.

As the male lips touched the soft skin of her belly, she became lost in delirious pleasant sensations that took her over entirely. Feeling her apparent enjoyment of his lovemaking he slowly caressed his way up to the slightly parted, very inviting lips. Fiercely he claimed her mouth and twisting slightly he moved over her small shape and forcing his knee between her thighs; entered her on a high note of desire and wanting. A startled cry broke from her throat and she stiffened ever so slightly.

The small oval face was damp and the dark-red tendrils curled tightly about the temples and just before her ears. Carefully and lovingly Jay nestled his mouth in next to her faintly musky-scented neck and nibbled on the exposed lobe.

A soft groan came from the woman still partly under him. He could feel the hard thudding of her heart, or was it his own? As she made almost a whimpering noise, his steel control broke and he pulled her to him as if never to let her go.

Once again Randi stiffened at his fierce handling of her. What did she do now? How long could she live with knowing that he only desired her body; that he would never love her? Tears burned behind her tightly closed lids, but still managed to spill out and down her pale cheeks. Suddenly a tremor ran through the strong male body still so close to her and before she could even guess at the cause; a desperately urgent and brokenly husky voice sounded in her ear, "Oh God, Randi, I love you! I want…..need…..I'm crazy with wanting you."

A stillness settled over her. A numbing and then…..a faint glow spread carefully through her. Still afraid to believe that he could really care for her, she mouthed the words in a hoarse whisper, "What did you say?"

Startled, he pushed up on his forearms to look into the dark, shadowed green of her eyes. Then stammering hesitantly said, "I'm crazy about….."

"No....no, what you said first. Before that." She demanded urgently afraid that she had just imagined that he had said it.

A soft warmth entered the gray eyes as he looked down into her face. "I love you."

Tears flowed anew. Unable to stop them, she mumbled incoherently against his chest. "I didn't think that you could ever love me. I love you so....so very much, you see. Oh, Jay!"

Carefully he wrapped her form in his arms. The strong chin rubbing softly against her red head. She loved him and all the while he had thought that she hadn't. And she had thought that he had not loved her. What fools they had been.

Sitting quietly before the still glowing fireplace, both seemed afraid to let each other go. Afraid that one or the other would somehow disappear. Finally bending closer to her, Jay placed a gentle kiss on the corner of her mouth. "So you were from America. You'll never believe where I thought you had come from. Little spitfire you. You rushed into my life like a small red twister and blew all my preconceived ideas of women right out the window. Randi, if you loved me why did you leave? Why have poor young Chris give me back your ring?"

Frowning sadly, she lowered her head. "Because of your ....uh.... apparent preference for Darla Russell. What about that?"

"I was trying to make you jealous. I figured that if you showed any sign of being put-out it would mean you cared .....some." Then looking down into the warm gray-green eyes, his own took on a very sober covering. "Randi, about Darla.....well.... she was involved in your accident."

Randi looked up into his now hardening features. "Involved, How?"

Sighing softly, he replied, "She shot at you. She is a very sick woman. Also greedy and because of that greed she thought that she had to destroy you." At the confusion apparent on her face, he added, "She had found some mineral deposits and had sent them in to be analyzed. They turned out to be positive, but they were from GetAway property not from hers. And Bangon hasn't been making it for quite some time; though no one knew that. Until today. Tom and Ben had gone back out to where you were ambushed and found some signs. They knew she had done it, but did not have the proof. But her horse, the jumper, had a special brace bar on its shoe and they waited for her to turn up with it at the races. Those men you saw just as you finished the race were law enforcement. Her brother, Carl, was also taken into custody for trying to assault you in the race."

Her eyebrow went up and she snorted softly, "Tried my foot!" then turning her back to him, he sucked in a ragged breath as he saw the dark bruised welts on the narrow back. The handsome face paled and the gray eyes turned steely. "We'll add assault and battery to the charges."

Then smiling softly, he declared, "That was some race. Also some demonstration."

"You liked it, huh?" She asked huskily.

He nodded the sun-streaked blonde head. A grin spreading across his handsome features. Then as he fingered the silky fall of hair, he frowned slightly. "Randi, about my brutal attack on you in the stables. And then cutting your lovely long hair, I…..I…..I'm so sor----"

A small hand came up and fingers pressed to his lips. "No, don't say anything. I've forgotten it; you do the same. Jealousy is dangerous to try and analyze, so let's not."

After a moment, he nodded and smiled softly, "Alright. But it will never happen again."

Twisting around on his lap, she smiled up at him, her eyes shimmering with mischief. "How well did you like my demonstration?"

"Why, it was totally unexpected and brilliant. Why?"

Running a slender finger along his jaw to the strong column of tanned throat and then twisting it into the sun-lightened curly hair on the broad chest, she murmured huskily, "Ooh, I thought that I'd demonstrate some more intricate maneuvers. You know, an exchange of learning between the two countries. Some from mine, some from yours."

Jay smiled and the smile reached the slate-gray eyes and turned them warm with love and desire. Softly he breathed against her ear, "I'm all yours; demonstrate away. We've got a lifetime to learn about each other."

Randi snuggled closer and a soft smile touched the fine lips. "You know, Jay, I was just looking to GetAway. And I believe I did."

"Yes, my love, welcome home. Oh and, Randi, Happy Birthday." And he kissed her deeply and gently.